BOOKMARKED FOR
MURDER

BOOKMARKED FOR MURDER

V. M. BURNS

WHEELER PUBLISHING
A part of Gale, a Cengage Company

LIBRARY OF CONGRESS CIP DATA ON FILE.
CATALOGUING IN PUBLICATION FOR THIS BOOK
IS AVAILABLE FROM THE LIBRARY OF CONGRESS.

ISBN-13: 978-1-4328-8556-4 (softcover alk. paper)

Published in 2021 by arrangement with Kensington Books, an imprint
of Kensington Publishing Corp.

Printed in Mexico
Print Number: 01   Print Year: 2021

ACKNOWLEDGMENTS

As always, I want to thank my agent Dawn Dowdle at Blue Ridge Literary and the wonderful people at Kensington who help make my dreams a reality, John, Paula, Michelle, Lauren, and all the folks who do so much behind the scenes.

I am blessed to have a broad network of friends who support me in so many ways, including Patricia Lillie and my fellow Seton Hill University tribe. Thanks to the Barnyardians, Tim, Chuck, Lindsey, Jill, and our fearless leader, Sandy, for all the support and shameless promotional plugs. Thanks to my official team, Amber, Derrick, Eric, Jennifer, Jonathan, and Robin. I also have to thank my unofficial team, Deborah, Grace, Jamie, and Tena. Once a trainer . . .

Thanks to Trooper Tony for the technical assistance with police and TBI policy and Abby Vandiver for the legal insights. Thanks to Alexia Gordon for assistance with medical questions and for the unicorn support from both you and Kellye Garrett and the Crime Writers of Color. I appreciate the Cozy Mystery Crew, SinC, and Guppies. Thanks to Dru Ann Love, Karen Owen, Colleen Finn, Jerri Cachero, Lisa A. Kelley, Karen Kenyon, and Lori Caswell for the support, encouragement, and for all you do to help authors.

Thanks to my family, Ben Burns, Jackie Rucker, Christopher (Carson) and Crosby Rucker, Jillian (Drew) and Marcella Merkel. Special thanks to my friends Sophia and Shelitha for always having my back.

Lastly, thanks to Linda Herold for coming up with the title.

CHAPTER 1

"Samantha Marie Washington!"

It was never good when my grandmother included my middle name. Mid-thirties and I still cringed as much as I did as a kid. I snapped the book I was perusing closed and looked up. "What?"

"You *own* a mystery bookshop where you spend 99 percent of your life. It's our last day in the Windy City, and you want to spend the time we have left before our bus leaves in a mystery bookshop?" She straightened her nearly five-foot-ten frame to its fullest extent and looked down her nose at me.

"It's research." I glanced around the room to make sure the owner who greeted us when we came in wasn't within hearing distance. Thankfully, the owner, Linda Herold, was occupied with another customer. Linda was a stunning woman with a statuesque frame and immaculate hair, nails, and clothes. She looked as though she'd just stepped off the cover of *Vogue* rather than out of the back of a storage room. I stared down at my blue jeans and tried not to slump at the realization I looked more like a country hick than an aspiring author and mystery bookshop owner. I leaned closer to Nana Jo and whispered, "Keep your voice down."

"If you don't put that book back on the shelf and get your hiney out of this store at once, so help me God, I'm going to take you over my knee." She turned to march out of the store, but something caught her attention and she stopped. "Isn't that the man Irma picked up at the bar the other night?"

"Are you joking? Irma Starczewski picks up at least two men every day of the week. I don't even try to keep track." I followed Nana Jo's gaze.

She was looking at a secluded area in the back of Murder Between the Pages. The bookstore wasn't large, but it took advantage of the vertical space. There were tall bookshelves along the walls and narrow rows with five-foot bookshelves. In the back corner, there was a spiral staircase that led to a loft area that was dark and filled with books. An older man wearing a hat and heavy coat was upstairs arguing with someone I thought to be a woman.

"I can't see his face."

"Stand over here." She stepped aside and pulled me closer. "His face looks familiar, but, for the life of me, I can't remember where I've seen him before." Nana Jo stared.

"I know what you mean, but maybe he just has one of those faces . . . Maybe he just seems familiar because he was wrapped around Irma at the House of Blues." I laughed.

"Shhhh." Nana Jo inclined her head toward a big man wearing tight jeans, a tight leather jacket, a baseball cap, and sunglasses standing nearby. "Check out Mr. Big."

Nana Jo leaned close to me and whispered, "Even if he wasn't wearing sunglasses inside a store, he'd stand out like a stripper at a Baptist camp meeting."

Nana Jo's metaphor might not have been politically correct, but I couldn't argue with her logic. "Mr. Big" definitely stood out. Wearing mirrored sunglasses inside was only part of his disguise fail. Add to that, the extra tight leather jacket, which rode up in the back and exposed part of the butt of a gun in the back waistband of his jeans, and he might have had a neon sign over his head that read "Security."

"Yeah. He's holding that book upside down," I joked.

Nana Jo stared at me. I smirked and she flashed a brief smile and then narrowed her eyes. "Don't try to get on my good side, Samantha Marie. I want you outside in two minutes." She turned and walked out.

More than the use of my middle name, I recognized the tone. I sighed and returned the book to the shelf. I took one last look at "Mr. Big" and then hurried outside. I could always come back to Chicago another time and check out the store, preferably without my pushy grandmother in tow.

Outside, Nana Jo impatiently tapped her foot, one hand on her hip, and had a look I knew could silence a classroom of rambunctious teens from her days as a high school math teacher.

I slunk up to my Nana Jo and gave her a kiss on the cheek. "I'm sorry."

The corners of her lips twitched. All was forgiven.

"Where are the girls?"

Nana Jo pointed to a line of people that wrapped around the corner. "They refused to leave the city without popcorn."

When we agreed to take the Shady Acres four-day shopping excursion to Chicago, we knew time was limited. The trip fee was

10

extremely reasonable and had included four days and three nights at a four-star hotel in the theatre district, tickets to a play, and one meal in the hotel dining room. The theatre district was close to the large Macy's and a short cab or elevated train ride from Michigan Avenue shopping. There was so much to do in the limited time we were there, each of the five of us identified one thing we wanted to do while in the city. Dorothy Clark wanted to shop, so we spent several enjoyable hours walking the Magnificent Mile and admiring the lights and seasonal atmosphere. The week between Christmas and New Year's wasn't the best time for outdoor excursions in Chicago. The wind from Lake Michigan could be bitterly cold, even in warmer months. However, we all dressed warmly and the wind was bearable. Excursions into Water Tower Place, Nordstrom, and Bloomingdale's provided warmth and major hits to a few credit cards but was well worth the journey. Nana Jo chose a matinee performance of the *Nutcracker* ballet with live music by the Chicago Philharmonic as her one must-see event, and the performance was spectacular. Irma Starczewski, true to her nature, wanted to dance and pick up men, so she chose a night at the Chicago House of Blues. I chose tea

11

at one of the fancy hotels downtown. We'd all managed to fit in everything, except Ruby Mae Stevenson's wish. All Ruby Mae wanted was to get popcorn from a well-known Chicago attraction, Garrett's Popcorn.

The tiny popcorn shop wasn't much bigger than a telephone booth, but each time we walked by, the line of people was outside and wrapped around the building. We promised to try again every day in hopes of finding a time when the line wasn't so bad, but here it was our last day and we still hadn't found that moment.

"I'm glad Ruby Mae is getting her popcorn. Maybe I should go and take her place in the line." I started to walk toward the line.

Nana Jo nudged my arm. "No need. Here they come."

I looked up and Ruby Mae, Irma, Dorothy, and a tall good-looking gentleman followed with two large shopping bags in each hand.

The group approached and Ruby Mae broke into a big grin. "Sam, I want you to meet my cousin Arnold's boy, Terrence."

Terrence was a dark-skinned young man with a bright smile. He nodded politely.

"We better hurry if we're going to get back

12

to the hotel in time to catch our
Jo glanced down the street, lift
and let out a whistle that would
those produced by most trains.

A yellow taxi skidded to a stop
and the five of us piled inside
rence and the taxi driver cra
shopping bags in the trunk.

Not surprisingly, the traffic
was bumper to bumper. The tr
relatively short, was an adve
driver jammed on his brakes
times on the short five-block jo
hotel, which would have sen
the front windshield if we
crammed inside like sardines.
what I could only assume wer
in a foreign language at leas
fellow motorists. When he pul
curb in front of our hotel, we p
out of the car, and I overca
desire to drop to my knees
ground.

"That was certainly an adv
Jo fanned herself as she st
slowly. "I think he just took
my life."

Ruby Mae patted Nana Jo
der. "He certainly has impr
life. I don't think I've prayed

13

quite some time."

orothy staggered out of the front seat.
r purse was clutched to her chest. "I
ught the taxi drivers in New York were
d, but they're tame compared to Mario
dretti back there." She pointed at our
ver.

'e stared as the taxi sped away from the
b so quickly he left skid marks in the
et and a barrage of horn blasts in his
e.

Come on, Josephine. Don't just stand
e gawking, get a move on." Irma prod-
Nana Jo in the back. "I see Max getting
he bus and I need to get up there and
re my seat before that hussy Velma Lev-
on gets it."

na's back was to Nana Jo, so she missed
ng her raise her purse like a bat. Fortu-
ly, I grabbed her arm and stopped her
re she could club Irma.

m going to brain that dingbat one of
days," Nana Jo said through clenched
1.

na ran to the bus in the six-inch heels
a Jo called hooker heels, and I marveled
r balance.

na Starczewski was a petite woman,
y reaching five feet, even in her hooker
. In her mid-eighties, she was the old-

est of Nana Jo's friends. Years of heavy chain-smoking had left their marks and she spoke with a raspy voice and had a persistent cough, which was either a result of the smoking or the alcohol she kept in a flask in her purse. She swore like a sailor and flirted with every man she met. Irma also had a big heart, and I knew Nana Jo loved her like a sister.

We'd checked out of our rooms earlier and left our luggage with the bellmen, so there wasn't much for us to do except get onboard the charter bus and sit for the two-hour drive back to North Harbor, Michigan.

The bus driver, a tall man who looked to be in his thirties, stood at the door and offered a hand to each of us as we loaded onto the bus.

Nana Jo was in front of me. "You're new. What happened to Earl?"

From the angle where she stood, Nana Jo probably wasn't able to see the man's face, but a bright red patch spread from his neck. However, it was quickly gone.

The man smiled. "Earl had an emergency and had to leave. However, I promise to take real good care of you." He smiled again, but there was something behind his eyes that sent a shiver up my spine.

I forced myself not to wrench my hand

away as the driver assisted me into the bus, but I couldn't help wiping my hand on my jeans once I was inside and safely out of sight.

Nana Jo scooted over so I could sit next to her. "Something clammy about that one, isn't there?" She inclined her head in the direction of the driver. "I wonder what really happened to Earl."

"I'm sure it's just like he said. Earl probably had something come up and had to go home."

"Hmm . . ." She tilted her head to the side and stared at me.

"What?"

"You look like my granddaughter, but she's smart enough to recognize cow dung when someone shovels it out."

"She's also smart enough to know when something is none of her business, and she knows how to keep her nose out of trouble."

She raised an eyebrow but said nothing.

Irma had outrun Velma Levington. She cozied up next to Max Franck, a short, bald man with glasses and an air of something European. Irma met Max at the House of Blues a couple of nights ago. Apart from being able to hold his own with Irma when it came to shots, Max was also an enthusiastic dancer. He and Irma hit it off and spent the entire night drinking, dancing, drinking, and then drinking. Not unlike many residents of large cities like Chicago, Max didn't drive and was surprisingly enthusiastic when Irma told him about the bus trip to North Harbor. At the time, I wondered why anyone from Chicago would want to go to North Harbor, Michigan. However, the look in Max's eyes led me to believe his interest had less to do with the location and more to do with Irma.

They were so close at the House of Blues, I felt sure Irma would take him back to her hotel room. However, she was disappointed when he begged off, saying he had business he had to take care of but promised to join her today. Irma had been looking forward to his visit to Shady Acres and barely spoke of anything else. The bus wasn't full, and the activities manager permitted Max to join the trip for the ride home for free since he hadn't stayed at the hotel, eaten any meals, or taken part in any of the other activities. Besides, two residents had paid for seats on the trip but had been unable to attend at the last minute due to medical reasons. Max wasn't the only new addition to the bus. There was another woman I hadn't recognized from the first trip. She stood out because she didn't seem like one of the seniors, although it was hard to tell. She had on a large hat, which hid part of her face. She walked down the aisle. As she passed by Max and Irma, I thought I noticed a glint of recognition in Max's eyes.

Nana Jo leaned close. "I wonder who that is."

I shrugged. "Probably someone's daughter or granddaughter getting a free ride to North Harbor."

Nana Jo nudged me. "Look, it's Mr. Big."

I stared after the man in question. He was the big, stocky man from the bookstore we'd seen earlier, with tight jeans and mirrored sunglasses.

"I wonder if he still has that gun in his pants?"

Nana Jo patted her purse. "Well, if he does, I've got my peacemaker with me and I'll drop him like a Thanksgiving turkey if he so much as reaches a finger toward his waistband."

He sidled down the aisle with a duffle bag. He took a seat directly across from Irma and Max. I could have sworn a look of recognition passed across Max's face, but with sunglasses, it was hard to tell if Mr. Big had the same reaction and the recognition was mutual.

When Velma boarded, she glanced toward

Max and Irma. For a brief second, she hesitated. That momentary hesitation brought a look in Irma's face which could only be described as gloating. Velma glared. However, she quickly plastered on a fake smile and glanced around for a seat. Velma was about the same height and weight as Irma, but she lacked Irma's outgoing personality. She had long white hair, which she usually wore in a tight bun. Velma's most distinct feature was her eyes. They were blue, a cold, steely blue like Lake Michigan in the winter when the ice covered the water. Velma turned toward the seat next to Mr. Big but was thwarted when the stranger picked up his duffle bag from the floor and placed it in the empty seat.

"Well, I never." Velma stomped down the aisle in search of another seat.

If Mr. Big took note of Velma's ire, it was well hidden behind his sunglasses. He slouched in his seat and pulled his cap down so most of his face was hidden. Arms folded across his chest, he presented a stony barrier that screamed, "Do Not Disturb," louder than any placard on a hotel room.

If the smile on Irma's face and her body language were any indication, Irma reveled in her victory over Velma, whom Irma viewed as competition. Velma hadn't been at Shady Acres long, but, in just a few short months, she and Irma had become bitter rivals in practically every area. This round was definitely scored in Irma's favor.

Max, on the other hand, seemed agitated and distracted. He was definitely not as attentive to Irma as he'd been in the bar. Whether due to the light of day, lack of alcohol, or improved judgment, which often occurred outside of bars, Max wasn't nearly as flirtatious and enamored with Irma as he'd been in the House of Blues.

The bus filled up and, once the new activities director made sure everyone was present and accounted for, we were off. At the House of Blues, Max was jovial and charming. However, on this return trip, his disposition appeared to be quiet and taciturn. However, I grew tired of people-watching and pulled out a book I'd picked up at Murder Between the Pages by Ellery Adams, *The Secret, Book & Scone Society,* and buried my head in murder, mystery, and intrigue set in a bookshop.

I went to college in the Chicago suburbs many moons ago. However, after more than a decade, the one thing that hadn't changed much was the traffic. Traffic in Chicago was a nightmare, especially on weekdays. I knew many natives who owned cars but left them at home and used public transportation, especially the elevated trains, known locally as "the EL," to avoid the rush hour. There was even a commuter train that ran between River Bend, Indiana, and Chicago, which was popular with commuters and anyone who wanted to take advantage of the theatre, shopping, or sports events without the hassle of sitting on the interstate for what felt like eons. Charter bus trips, like the one Shady Acres provided, were very popular as a way to enjoy the sites of the city without the hassle of driving or dealing with parking.

Normally, the interstates were less busy on weekends. However, the holidays were on the weekend this year, which would have meant several of the places we wanted to visit would be unavailable. So, this trip was Monday through Thursday. I had hoped the holidays would mean less people on the interstate and, hopefully, less traffic congestion. However, road construction on the toll road had diverted a lot of traffic onto the expressway, and we spent several hours inching our way eastward. What should have been two hours and twenty minutes turned into four hours and we'd barely crossed over into the state of Indiana.

Once we finally began to move, I noticed a rumble coming from the crowd. I lifted my head when I heard Nana Jo shout. "Hey, driver. We're going to need to stop at a rest area."

I looked up and saw the driver glance in the mirror, but he neither slowed his pace nor acknowledged the request as he sped past several exits.

"There's a toilet in the back." Our driver glanced into the rearview mirror and gave a halfhearted smile to soften the words.

"It's broken," someone yelled from the back. I didn't recognize the voice, but I definitely recognized the tone.

Our driver passed two more exits with no signs of slowing down. That was when the buzz got louder and less polite.

"We've been on this missile for four hours. You've got old people with small bladders," Nana Jo yelled. "Listen, Bub, I suggest you pull this tank over or you're going to have a lot of clean up."

Whether it was Nana Jo's tone or the look in the eyes of some of the other prisoners, her message finally came through.

The activities director, Caroline Fenton, leaned forward and whispered something to the driver, who then pulled off the interstate into a rest area.

Nana Jo was one of the first people at the door. When the driver assisted her down, I heard him whisper, "My name is Bob, not Bub."

Nana Jo hurried off, but I could tell by the set of her shoulders and her ramrod straight back, she'd heard him.

There was a mass exodus to get off the bus. I was half the age of most of the people on the bus, so I stayed in my seat to allow the others to leave first.

"Come on, Max. Let's take a walk." Irma stood up.

"No. I think I'll just wait here." Max looked around. "You go on." He smiled and stood up to allow Irma to slide past him into the aisle before he returned to his seat.

If the call of nature hadn't been so strong, I suspect Irma might have spent more time cajoling Max to join her. Instead, she hurried down the aisle and off the bus.

I stood and stretched. Velma looked to be asleep in the back of the bus. Mr. Big with the mirrored glasses remained in his seat. Max and the activities director were the only other ones left as I got off the bus.

Public restrooms, especially at rest stops, are often a place I avoided whenever possible. However, while I was fine while sitting, gravity wasn't my friend. Once I stood, the urge to go increased. So, I took a few deep breaths and did what I had to do.

Nana Jo waited for me near the vending machines. She juggled chips, bottled water, candy bars, and donuts.

"You can't possibly be planning to eat all of that."

She never took her gaze from the vending machine. "You got any ones?"

"I'm not hungry."

"You will be before we get home."

I stared at her. "We're through the worst of the traffic now. We should be home in less than an hour."

She smirked. "What do you think the likelihood is our prison guard is going to stop for food?"

I stared at her for several seconds and then reached in my purse and pulled out my wallet. "Good point. Maybe you should get some of those beef jerky things and cheese crackers."

Once our bags were full of snacks, we headed back to the bus. The driver was nowhere to be found and the doors of the bus were locked. Several of the others stood outside waiting.

Caroline Fenton, the activities director, hurried to the front of the line. "What's wrong? We should get back on the road."

"The door's locked." I pointed to the door.

She smiled. "That's impossible." She shook the door and realized what we already knew, and the smile left her face. She looked around like a frantic rabbit. "Where's Bob?"

We shrugged and looked around.

"I assume he went to the bathroom," Nana Jo said what we all thought must have been obvious.

At that point, Bob hurried to the front.

"Sorry." He pulled keys out of his pocket and unlocked the doors and climbed into the bus.

He helped each of us onto the bus, same as before. Sarah Howard was the first person on the bus. The only person onboard was Max, who hadn't left his seat. We each returned to our seats. Irma was one of the last to board. When she got to her seat, she waited for Max to stand and allow her to return to her seat. However, he didn't move.

She gave him a playful shake. "Maxie, wake up. I need to get by." When Max didn't respond, she shook him harder. "Max, come on."

People huffed with impatience, as did the bus driver.

Miss Fenton stood and looked back. "If everyone would take their seats, we'll be able to leave."

Irma shook Max harder. This time, Max slumped over in his seat and slowly slid to the floor. Irma stood in shock for what felt like a full minute. Then she let out a blood-curdling scream and fainted.

CHAPTER 2

The rest stop on the Indiana toll road wasn't exactly the most restful place I'd ever been. I'd been to rest areas with restaurants, gas stations, and even showers for truckers. This wasn't one of those. The building was a basic concrete block. There were restrooms for men and women, vending machines, and a display stand with brochures and maps. Outside, there were picnic tables and an area for dogs to play and relieve themselves, complete with trash receptacles and plastic bags for the waste. It was much too cold outside to sit at the picnic tables, and the public restrooms didn't lend themselves to long stays. The state police wouldn't allow us back onto the bus until the forensics team finished. So, a busload of seniors and about four people who had yet to make it to the half-century mark were all huddled inside the concrete building. The vending machine looked as though it had been raided by locusts. The only things left in the machine were a pack of chewing gum and a Milky Way that had gotten twisted and was impaled on the spiral coil used to push it forward.

"Hand me a piece of that shoe leather." Nana Jo reached out her hand.

I gave her one of the pieces of beef jerky I had left.

"My teeth aren't what they used to be, but I'm starving."

Dorothy stared at the flat stick. "Josephine, you must be pretty desperate to even consider eating that." She frowned. "I don't think my teeth could take it."

"I'm desperate. It's either the shoe leather or I'm going to pass out." She bit into the jerky and tugged. Unfortunately, it had been in the machine quite a while and was tougher than rubber.

Ruby Mae scowled. "If we could get to our luggage, I could get my popcorn."

The police had taped off the area around the bus and, unfortunately, our luggage was within the boundary and therefore, off-limits.

"Well, I can't eat this." Nana Jo tossed the beef jerky stick into a nearby trash can. "Where are we?"

Dorothy pulled out her cell phone. "Hey, Siri."

"How can I serve you today, my queen," Siri responded.

Dorothy didn't bat an eyelash. "Where am I?"

After a few moments, the phone responded with an address.

"Ask her to order ten large pepperoni pizzas and have them delivered." Nana Jo turned around to face the majority of the crowd. "We're ordering pizza. Who wants in?"

Every hand raised and Nana Jo took a quick count. "Better add five cheese to the order."

Dorothy promptly updated her request to her cellular servant.

"I wonder how Irma's doing?" Ruby Mae craned her neck to look around the crowd toward a small maintenance closet where Irma had been carried after she fainted.

"No idea, but she's surrounded by men, so I'd say she's in hog heaven," Nana Jo said.

It took less than thirty minutes for a Volkswagen Beetle that was probably older than me, with a black roof, baby-blue body, one green door, and one orange door to arrive at our rest area. The myriad of police cars had cordoned off the area by the bus, but the car chugged its way to the front. The driver pulled up front. He left the car running, hopped out, and looked around. Nana Jo and I went outside.

"You ordered fifteen pizzas?" A freckle-faced kid, who looked about twelve, with curly red hair, ripped jeans, a red hoodie with a *Star Trek* insignia, and red Converse All-Stars, held up a smartphone that looked as though it cost more than the car.

"Nice shoes." Nana Jo scribbled her name with her finger.

"Thanks. All the old ladies usually like them." He reached inside his car and handed out the pizzas. "What happened over there?" He inclined his head toward the bus.

The coroner was removing the body from the bus.

"That's what's left of the last person who called me an old lady. Remember, on *Star Trek*, the red shirts always die first." Nana Jo handed me half of the pizzas, turned, and walked toward the building.

The driver stood there staring for a half minute and then laughed.

I hurried to catch up to my grandmother. "What's that mean, 'the red shirts always die first'?"

Nana Jo smirked. "And I thought you were a trekkie."

I thought about her comment and that was when the lightbulb went on and I chuckled.

As we were about to enter the building, everyone started to come outside.

"What's going on?" I juggled my pizza boxes to alleviate some of the heat and grease coming through the boxes.

Caroline Fenton pointed to the back. "The replacement charter bus finally arrived." She reached for some of the boxes. "Let me help you."

"Great. Maybe we can get home soon," Nana Jo said.

"Unfortunately, we can't leave until the police finish questioning everyone, but at least we can sit down." She followed the herd of seniors heading to the bus.

Like lemmings, we marched to the bus. Once onboard, everyone dug into the pizza and found seats. The new bus driver had come prepared with a cooler full of bottled water and everyone was grateful.

Everyone wanted to give Nana Jo something for the pizza, but she declined. Caroline Fenton said Shady Acres would reimburse her for the costs.

Fed and finally able to sit, I hoped we

would be able to leave soon. My brother-in-law, Tony Rutherford, had been looking after my dogs, Snickers and Oreo, so I knew they were in good hands. However, my sister, Jenna, wasn't a big fan and the medicine Snickers had to take for her heart disease was causing her kidneys to fail. Combined with the fact she was fourteen, she had the occasional accident. Too many accidents and Jenna would blow a gasket. I'd called earlier to let them know what happened, but they weren't home.

"Boy, that hit the spot." Nana Jo wiped her mouth with a napkin. "I was so hungry I was getting hangry."

"How can you tell the difference?" Dorothy leaned over the seat.

Nana Jo swiped at her friend. "Very funny."

"I wonder what happened to the cop."

I looked back at her. "What cop?"

Ruby Mae Stevenson sat next to Dorothy in the seat behind Nana Jo and me. She pulled out her knitting from a bag, which she always carried with her, and started knitting what appeared to be a baby hat. She knitted a few more stitches. "The one that was sitting across from Irma and Max."

"How do you know he was a cop?" I asked the question but something in my mind

32

knew she was right.

She looked up over her glasses. "The mirrored sunglasses, the gun he had in the back of his pants, the policeman-military haircut under the baseball cap." She shrugged. "It all adds up. He's either a cop or he's a former policeman. Plus, there's just something about police." She stopped for a moment. After a few seconds, she shook her head and continued knitting. "They always have an air of authority about them." She shrugged again. "Besides, he and Irma are the only ones allowed to walk around."

I thought about what she said and realized I hadn't seen Mr. Big since we were ushered off the bus and told to wait. I should have recognized that, but, seeing him at the mystery bookstore, I suspected something sinister from him. "I wonder why he was following Max."

We shared what we'd seen at the bookstore, but no one had answers.

Nana Jo stretched. "I'm tired. I think I'll take a nap."

She pulled her coat close and snuggled down in her seat.

Dorothy pulled a book out of her purse and Ruby Mae continued knitting.

I sighed. I wasn't in the mood for my book. Suddenly, my reality was much more interesting than my book. I pulled a note-book out of my purse that I had taken to keeping with me all the time. I flipped to a blank page.

"I'm shattered." Lady Penelope flopped onto a chair in an unladylike manner.

Lady Elizabeth Marsh looked intently at her niece. "I hope you haven't overdone it. Boxing Day shopping at Harrods is a lot, especially for someone in your condition should —"

"Don't you start too." Lady Penelope stared at her aunt, but, after a few seconds, her eyes and voice softened. "I'm sorry. I know you mean well, but I've had enough babying from Victor." She reached across the table and pat-ted her aunt's hand. "I don't mean to be cross, but I'm fine. Dr. Haygood says I'm as strong as an ox and the baby is doing just fine." She patted her stomach. "Besides, we've got a long way to go."

"How's the morning sickness?"

"I'm much better. Mrs. McDuffie suggested tea and soda crackers first thing and amaz-ingly, it's done the trick." She smiled. "Victor brings them religiously every morning and won't let me move until I've eaten them."

"Good." Lady Elizabeth relaxed and smiled at her niece. "I suppose hitting the Boxing Day sales is enough to wear anyone out." She sighed. "I'm fairly shattered myself."

A very prim and proper waitress placed a pot of tea on the table in the department store dining room along with a triple-tiered plate stand, which was piled high with scones, sandwiches, and tarts.

"That looks scrumptious." Lady Penelope helped herself to a scone and slathered a generous helping of clotted cream and strawberry preserves over the top. She took a bite.

Lady Elizabeth's niece closed her eyes and moaned. When Lady Penelope opened her eyes, her aunt was staring at her and both ladies laughed.

"I just needed a little nourishment and then I intend to get back into the fray. There are some sheets I want to get for the nursery." Lady Penelope washed her scone down with tea and then tackled a cucumber sandwich.

Lady Elizabeth sipped her tea and listened as her niece talked about her plans for decorating the nursery and the preparations she and her husband, Victor Carlston, were making for their first child. She smiled as she listened to her niece's enthusiastic plans. Lady Elizabeth shared her excitement at finding the perfect fabric for curtains for the bedroom at Wickfield Lodge, which was being shared by Josiah and Johan, the two Jewish boys the Marshes were keeping from the

35

Kindertransport. Lady Elizabeth feared the nursery where the young boys stayed, along with their younger sister, Rivka, was too frilly for two rambunctious boys. Not having any children of their own, Lady Elizabeth and Lord William Marsh had only experienced girls, having raised their nieces, Lady Daphne and Lady Penelope, after their parents were killed in an automobile accident. Lady Elizabeth knew the children wouldn't be staying with them long, but she was determined to make what time the children did stay as pleasant as possible. It was clear these Polish refugees had witnessed not only the death of their parents but had seen atrocities that could scar them for life. Lady Elizabeth knew curtains, a few toys, and warm clothes couldn't wipe away the horror, but she hoped she could help to create an environment of safety and love where they would now see there were people who cared.

"Penny for your thoughts," Lady Penelope joked.

"I'm sorry, dear. I was woolgathering." Lady Elizabeth smiled. She reached into one of her bags and pulled out a lovely Chinese silk pillowcase. "I found these wonderful silk pillowcases for the boys' rooms. I have no idea what these markings mean, but the color was perfect. What do you think?"

Lady Penelope admired the pillowcases and nodded her agreement about the color.

Lady Elizabeth glanced up and noticed an elderly woman staring at her. When the woman made eye contact, she smiled broadly and hurried to the table.

"Hello, I thought that was you. It's been such a long time." She glanced around nervously.

"Hello," Lady Elizabeth said hesitantly. She put the pillowcases back into the bag.

"I saw your lovely Chinese pillowcases." She reached out a hand. "May I?"

Lady Elizabeth passed the woman the pillowcases.

She examined them and smiled. "Beautiful embroidery." She glanced at Lady Elizabeth. "Do you know what it says?"

Lady Elizabeth shook her head.

"It's the English equivalent to Sweet Dreams." She smiled. "My husband and I lived in China for many years. It's not easy learning the language, but I was determined to master it and I found an excellent teacher." She sighed and reluctantly passed the items back.

"That's wonderful. Thank you. They were the perfect color and I got an excellent price, so I bought them, but then I wondered if I should have. I had just asked my niece about the markings."

The woman looked as though she was

remembering something extremely pleasant. "I loved China. My husband and I were missionaries." She sighed. "I love puzzles and China and all things Chinese, especially my Chinese puzzle boxes." She looked at Lady Elizabeth. "You don't remember me, but then why should you. It's been such a long time since we've seen each other. It's me, Eleanor . . . Eleanor Forsythe." She looked around nervously, then turned back to Lady Elizabeth. "Do you mind if I sit for a moment? I'm a bit tired."

Lady Elizabeth clearly didn't remember, but good breeding took over. "Of course. Forgive my manners. Please, won't you join us?"

The lady eagerly sat down.

The waitress had been hovering nearby and hurried over to the table with an extra cup and plate setting for the new arrival. She'd barely finished filling the woman's cup, before the woman whisked it to her mouth and drank as though she was parched.

Lady Elizabeth requested more sandwiches and the waitress hurried to fulfill the order.

Eleanor Forsythe was a thin woman with wispy white hair, which was a bit wild. Her hat and coat were of a good quality, but they were old and outdated. Her hat was slightly askew and sat at a rakish angle. She hungrily ate the sandwiches and scones that the waitress

brought and drank several cups of tea, all the while maintaining a steady stream of conversation. "How is his lordship?"

"He's well. He's been plagued by gout. I think he outdid it at the wedding."

"Wedding? Don't tell me I missed a wedding?" She turned to Lady Penelope.

"Not Penelope. No, it was my other niece, Lady Daphne, who married Lord Browning, the Duke of Kingfordshire."

Eleanor smiled. "How wonderful. I positively love weddings. I love puzzles and I love weddings. I'm sorry to have missed it." She looked around nervously. "I don't get out much anymore. My cousin Desmond, and his wife, Constance, have moved into my home at Battersley Manor." Eleanor leaned forward as she spoke and stared into Lady Elizabeth's eyes and reached out and clutched her hand. "They are so careful about me getting out . . . afraid I'll catch a cold or take a fall. They do worry so."

Lady Elizabeth stared back. "Yes, one can never be too careful."

Eleanor Forsythe's eyes darted around. "No, indeed, especially as I've aged. I have gotten so forgetful. Only last week when my nephew was out of town, I slipped on a bar of soap. I would have broken an arm or a leg if my maid, Dora, hadn't come to fill my hot water bottle."

She gazed at Lady Elizabeth. "I don't even remember taking a bath, but Constance, that's Desmond's wife, says I did. I'm so forgetful these days."

"Gracious. You are so fortunate to have Dora," Lady Penelope said slowly.

Eleanor nodded. "Yes, it was fortunate, indeed. Although, my cousin says the taxes are so bad and my investments aren't doing well. He doesn't know how much longer I will be able to afford to keep her, but Dora is wonderful. She appreciates my treasures. She's the only one who does."

"I see." Lady Elizabeth's gaze never wavered from Eleanor. After a moment, she looked around. "How did you manage to get out today?"

"Constance and Desmond went out of town for Christmas. They left the new housekeeper, Mrs. Sanderson, in charge. Actually, Muriel is a distant cousin of my late husband, but I managed to get out." She looked around. "I don't have much time."

A large, barrel-shaped woman rushed into the dining room like a blustery wind. She looked around the room with a frantic gaze.

"Is Mrs. Sanderson a large woman with a rather equine-shaped face and a no-nonsense way about her?" Lady Penelope cast a sidewise glance toward the front of the dining room.

Mrs. Forsythe nodded.

"I think she may be looking for you." Lady Penelope inclined her head toward the front of the dining room.

Mrs. Forsythe glanced over her shoulder and her eyes took on a frightened expression, like a deer caught in the headlamps of a car. She turned toward Lady Elizabeth and clasped her hand tighter. "I don't have much time. Please, they're trying to kill me and take my treasures. Please, I —"

"There you are. I've been looking all over for you. I just called your cousin Desmond. I was so frightened." Mrs. Sanderson rushed to the table.

She looked quickly at Lady Elizabeth, and something in her manner changed. Lady Elizabeth was accustomed to the change. She'd experienced it many times before. In the woman's voice and in her bearing, something changed. She'd assessed Lady Elizabeth Marsh and knew she was a well-bred woman of status. Whether due to the cut of her simple, but well-made clothing, her expensive coat with its luxurious fur collar, or perhaps due to the intelligent expression on her face, Lady Elizabeth Marsh was a woman of prominence and Mrs. Sanderson's attitude and mannerisms adjusted accordingly.

"I'm so sorry if she's been bothering you. I'm afraid the poor dear is easily confused." She smiled.

"Not in the least. Eleanor and I are old friends." Lady Elizabeth smiled and patted the older woman's hand. "We were just enjoying a chat."

The waitress returned. "Would your ladyship care for anything else?"

"Your ladyship?" Mrs. Sanderson muttered.

Lady Elizabeth turned to the gaping woman. "Would you care to join us for tea?"

Mrs. Sanderson's face grew red and she shook her head. "No . . . no thank you."

Lady Elizabeth turned to the waitress and indicated she was done and would like her bill.

The young girl bobbed a curtsey and then hurried away.

"Excuse me, but . . . your ladyship?" Mrs. Sanderson said.

Lady Elizabeth smiled. "I'm sorry. I didn't introduce myself. I'm Lady Elizabeth Marsh and this is my niece, Lady Penelope Carlston."

The housekeeper's already red face grew redder. "Your ladyship." She made a slight curtsy. She nervously glanced from her charge to Lady Elizabeth. "Did you say, you and Mrs.

Forsythe are friends?"

Lady Elizabeth waved her hand. "Yes. Eleanor and I go way back. It's shameful how people lose touch these days, but I intend to rectify that." She turned to Mrs. Forsythe. "I was just saying, we'll have to come by Battersley Manor soon, and, of course, Eleanor has an open invitation to visit us at Wickfield Lodge. I know Lord William will love to see you."

Mrs. Sanderson's face registered surprise, but she quickly tried to hide it. "Well, of course, your ladyship is welcome any time, but Mrs. Forsythe isn't well and can't get out like she used to." She collected the woman's purse and helped her up from her chair. "In fact, I'm afraid this excursion may have been too much. She's looking rather flushed." She glanced from Mrs. Forsythe to Lady Elizabeth. "I'd better get the old dear home before . . . well, before she gets worse. Plus, I need to call Mrs. Tarkington and let her know you're safe. She was so concerned about you. She was actually going to come and help me look for you."

Mrs. Forsythe, who moments earlier was alert and talkative, was suddenly quiet and withdrawn.

The housekeeper hustled the older woman away, leaving Lady Elizabeth and Lady Penelope staring at their hasty retreat.

"Now, that was odd," Lady Penelope said. "Do you believe her? Do you really believe her family is trying to kill her?"

Lady Elizabeth stared after the retreating ladies. "I don't know. There's definitely something suspicious going on, and it's clear Eleanor believes it."

"What are you going to do?"

Lady Elizabeth was silent for a moment. "There's not much I can do about it today." She smiled at her niece. "Now that I've regained my energy, I'm going to fight my way through the crowd and get the rest of the things on my list. I'll tackle the problem of Eleanor Forsythe tomorrow."

Lady Elizabeth achieved success and acquired everything on her list. Laden down with packages, she and Lady Penelope hurried to the Knightsbridge station to catch the train which would take them home. The ladies were jostled along by the crowds who'd packed the station. The station bustled with activity as people anxiously awaited the approaching train.

Just as the ladies left the ticket hall with their first-class tickets and hurried to catch their train, they heard the rumble of the train as it pulled into the station. The ground vibrated and the engines roared.

They queued up to get on the escalator to descend to the platform. The impatient crowds pushed, shoved, and jostled their way onto the metal stairs of the escalators and were carried underground.

Lady Elizabeth felt a tug on her sleeve and turned as a woman screamed and then fell headlong down the metal stairs onto the concrete platform below.

Lady Elizabeth gasped but then quickly collected herself and hurried down to the platform.

Sprawled on the ground lay the body of Eleanor Forsythe. Her eyes glanced up at Lady Elizabeth, who quickly knelt down and attempted to assess the lady's injuries. "Someone get a doctor," Lady Elizabeth ordered. However, it was obvious from the unnatural angle in which she lay, that her injuries were severe. She felt a tug on her arm.

Mrs. Forsythe's lips moved, but she was unable to speak loudly. Lady Elizabeth bent close to the woman's face and Mrs. Forsythe whispered into her ear.

After a few moments, Mrs. Forsythe's lips stopped and she lay very still.

Mrs. Sanderson suddenly appeared and stared at Lady Elizabeth. "Gracious me. The poor woman must have lost her footing. What did she say?"

Lady Elizabeth stood. " 'Murder.' She said, 'I was murdered.' "

CHAPTER 3

"Sam, pay attention." Nana Jo followed up the request with a sharp jab to my side.

I looked up from my writing. "What?"

She pointed toward the front of the bus, where a large man with a potbelly that overflowed the top of his pants and a head full of thick, curly hair stood.

"Ladies and gentlemen, my name is Sergeant Dominic Davis. I'm sorry for the long wait, but we'll get to all of you as quickly as possible."

"Too late," Nana Jo yelled.

"Shhush." This time it was my turn to nudge her, but my elbows weren't as pointy and she simply ignored me.

"We've been on this bus for hours. We're cold and ready to go home," Nana Jo said.

There were a lot of shouts of agreement from everyone on the bus.

Sergeant Davis held up his hands to quiet the rowdy crowd. "I'm sure you're all very anxious to get home. However, we need to get statements from everyone. As soon as we finish, you'll be on your way." He stared at Nana Jo. "Why don't we start with you?"

Nana Jo climbed over me to get out of her seat. "Gladly. I'll do anything to get this over with. I need a shower, a stiff drink, and the comfort of my own bed, and not necessarily in that order."

The process for taking statements was slow and methodical. There were four policemen assigned to take statements, of which Sergeant Davis was one. It took two hours to get all the statements. I felt like a youngster compared to some of the other people on the bus, and I was exhausted. Even though most of the residents of Shady Acres Retirement Village were more active than me and enjoyed activities like surfing, martial arts, and their newest obsession, Hip Hop Dancing, I felt guilty about going in front of people who were my elders, at least in years, so I waited until most of the others had gone before I left to give my statement.

When it was my turn, I was directed by a rather good-looking policeman to a make-shift office area with a folding chair in the utility closet of the rest area. Sergeant Luis Alvarez was young, probably late twenties, with a clean-cut face, olive complexion, and

dark hair, which was shorter on the sides and curly on top. He had blue eyes the color of Lake Michigan in the summer and the whitest teeth I'd ever seen. When he smiled, I was dazzled and found myself staring at him and giggling like a teenager.

"May I see your driver's license?"

I stared for a few seconds. He had a very nice accent, which took several seconds for my brain to decipher. I watched his lips moving but wasn't exactly focused on the words coming out of his mouth. When I finally realized he was waiting for a response, heat rushed up my neck and I fumbled in my purse for my wallet. "Sorry."

He smiled again and I giggled. I needed to pull myself together. This was embarrassing. I took a bottle of water from my purse and concentrated way too much effort into opening the top.

"Mrs. Washington, did you know the deceased?" He had a deep voice that was soft and smooth and very sexy. "Mrs. Washington?"

Unfortunately, I squeezed the bottle too tightly and when the top came off, water overflowed all over my lap. "I'm sorry."

He handed me a few napkins he found nearby.

"What was the question?"

"I asked if you knew the victim?"

I took a deep breath and tried to focus on the dead body and ignore the water seeping down my pants or Sergeant Alvarez's super white teeth, smooth voice, or . . . darn it. This wasn't working. I dug my fingernails into my palm and looked straight at Sergeant Handsome. "I met him for the first time about two nights ago at the Chicago House of Blues. He was . . . interested in my grandmother's friend, Irma Starczewski."

"You'd never seen him before?" He asked the question as though he found the fact hard to believe.

I shook my head. "Noooo. I'm pretty sure I haven't."

He looked at his notes. "Your grandmother, Josephine Thomas, says you own a mystery bookshop in . . . North Harbor, Michigan."

I eased up on the nails in my palm. "I do. I used to be an English teacher but after my husband, Leon, died, I retired and opened Market Street Mysteries." I was rambling, but I didn't know what owning a mystery bookshop had to do with Irma's dead boyfriend.

"You read a lot of mysteries?"

"I used to, although I don't have as much

50

time to read now."

He leaned back and tapped his pen on his thigh. I tried not to look, but I knew my gaze kept going to his thighs. He had very nice thighs.

"Umm, excuse me. Did you say something?" I went back to the nails in my palm. Darn. This was a lot harder than talking to Detective Stinky Pitt in North Harbor.

"I asked about the type of books you read."

"I read a lot of cozy mysteries mostly."

He scowled. "What's a cozy mystery?"

Now I was on comfortable footing. I could talk about cozy mysteries for hours. "Cozy mysteries are mysteries with an amateur sleuth, usually female. There's no sex, violence, or bad language in cozies. Have you ever seen *Murder, She Wrote*?"

He nodded.

"That's a cozy mystery. The point is to find the clues and figure out whodunit."

He nodded and something in his eyes told me he knew exactly what a cozy mystery was. The thought crossed my mind that I needed to be on my guard, but I had no idea why. So, I sat quietly and waited.

"Do you read any other types of mysteries?"

"Sometimes, but I don't like books with

51

lots of violence, so I usually stick to cozies."

"Are cozy mysteries the only types of books you sell in your store?"

"Of course not. Just because I read cozies doesn't mean everyone does. I sell all types of mysteries."

He extended a hand to indicate I should elaborate.

"I sell cozies, police procedurals, soft- and hard-boiled private detective books, true crime . . . pretty much anything mystery or crime related."

Apparently, I'd said what he wanted to hear.

Sergeant Sparkling Teeth smiled and leaned forward. "So, you sell true crime books."

Considering I'd just said that, I became instantly suspicious. My left eyebrow lifted on its own. "Why is it important what types of mysteries I sell in my *mystery bookshop*? I sell pretty much all types of mysteries and true crime books."

He tapped his pen on his thigh, but I was no longer focused on his thighs . . . well, not much anyway. "Would you consider yourself an expert?"

"On what? Mysteries?"

"Your grandmother said you not only read mysteries and sell mysteries, but you write them too."

My grandmother had a big mouth. "I write cozy mysteries, but I'm not published yet."

"You must do a lot of research for your books."

"That's true. I write cozy mysteries that are set in England in 1938. I do a lot of research, especially on the time period. You have to make sure the details are as accurate as possible."

"What type of research do you do? I mean do you look up weapons?"

"I research weapons, but not a lot. Cozy mysteries don't have a lot of violence, so I don't spend much time on weapons."

He chuckled. "You write murder mysteries. Unless you're an expert on weapons, wouldn't you have to research different types of weapons and wounds?"

"In cozies, typically the murder isn't graphic. These books aren't really about the act of murder. Like I said before, it's about the clues and figuring out whodunit."

He looked puzzled.

"It's like story problems when you were in school. It's a story. The author is writing a story and hopefully, the reader is enjoying the story. The author drops clues in the story. Does the fact that the butler had mud on his shoes mean something? Or is it a red herring, a false clue. The author's job is to weave the clues into the story and hope the reader figures out whodunit at the same time as the detective. That's the best case." I shook my head. "The actual weapon used to murder the victim isn't really that important, unless it's some specialized weapon that only one or two people knew how to use." I paused and thought. "Like a bow and arrow or some rare poison only found in the rain forests of South America."

He nodded and tapped his pen. However, now the pen tapping didn't interest me in the least. "I just wonder how you read true crime books and you sell true crime books, and yet you say you didn't know Max Franck."

"Who is Max Franck? Was he an author?" Sergeant Alvarez spread his hands wide.

"What did he write?"

He grinned. "You've never heard of him?"

"Sergeant, mystery is one of the most popular genres of fiction, surpassed only by romance. There are millions of mystery and suspense novels published every year. I'm guessing by your response that Max Franck must have been some type of writer." I was frustrated and Sergeant Alvarez's appeal had diminished considerably.

"Are you saying you've never heard of him?"

"I'm saying, I've heard of and read a lot of books. If I have read anything he wrote, I don't remember it at this moment."

He stared.

However, my days as a high school English teacher had taught me the value of silence and given me the patience of Job. I waited patiently and quietly, volunteering nothing. We sat in silence for nearly a minute.

If this was a game of chicken, he blinked first and I could tell by his body language, he wasn't happy about it. "Max Franck was a writer, like yourself. He wrote true crime."

"Then he was not like me. I don't write true crime."

He waved away the differences. "He was a Pulitzer Prize-winning journalist."

Despite my resolve to remain disinterested, I was very interested in the fact that Irma had picked up such a distinguished date. "What did he win the Pulitzer Prize for?"

"You really have no idea?"

I shook my head. "I really have no idea."

He sighed and looked at his notes. "He earned the Pulitzer Prize for an exposé on government corruption, but he was best known for his work on the Kennedy assassination."

That was when the lightbulb went off. I sat up straighter in my seat. "I remember him now. He's supposed to be writing another book." I snapped my fingers, trying to remember. "There was something in the paper recently, wasn't there?"

He nodded. "Yeah. He was writing another book."

"That's it. He wrote books about JFK's assassination and was about to publish a new book about the assassination of Robert Kennedy. That's Max Franck? That's the man who picked up Irma at the House of Blues?"

He nodded. "And you didn't know any of this?"

"Well, obviously I knew it. It must have been buried in my head, but I didn't remember until you brought it up. He certainly didn't talk about it . . . Well, he didn't really talk to me much, anyway."

"He never mentioned his books?"

I shook my head. "He barely said anything to me. He spent his time drinking, dancing, and, as my grandmother would say, 'feeling up' Irma."

He chuckled. "Yeah, I think those were your grandmother's exact words."

I nodded. "Wow. So, Max Franck was a

writer." I sighed. "I wish I'd known that. I would have liked to have talked to him about it. His life must have been fascinating."

Something about Sergeant Alvarez's demeanor shifted. His shoulders relaxed and his face muscles were much smoother. He was back to being the charming policeman I'd first thought him. "Tell me all you know about Max Franck, even if it seems irrelevant."

I took a moment to collect my thoughts and told him everything I knew, which really wasn't much. "He and Irma met at the House of Blues. They flirted and danced and drank and flirted and well, when they were done flirting, they flirted more." I told him how he and Irma planned a romantic tryst at Shady Acres and how he ended up on the bus.

He scribbled in his notebook. When I stopped, he looked up. "Is that all?"

"Well, I don't think it means anything, but we saw him earlier today." I described what we saw at Murder Between the Pages.

He asked quite a few questions about the lady we saw arguing with Max Franck, but, unfortunately, I couldn't provide a lot of information. I described her, but the angle of the loft meant that I couldn't see her face. Surprisingly, he didn't seem nearly as excited about Mr. Big with the mirrored sunglasses and the gun in his waistband as I would have expected. In fact, he didn't seem to be taking notes.

"Aren't you going to write this down?"

He shook his head. "We've already cleared Mr. Sherman."

"Sherman? Is that his name?"

He nodded. "Sidney Sherman isn't a person of interest in this investigation."

"I don't know why not? He was obviously following Max Franck. Plus, he had a gun."

Sergeant Alvarez sighed. "If you don't have any other useful information, I think we're done. I have your address and telephone number. If we have any more questions, we'll get in touch." He handed me his business card.

He stood and ushered me out of the utility closet. Outside, I glanced around the corner and noticed Mr. Big, aka Sidney Sherman, standing around with some of the other policemen, drinking coffee. They looked pretty chummy.

I was one of the last people interviewed, so when I got on the bus, I heard Nana Jo say, "Thank God. I thought they'd never finish. Maybe we can leave now."

Sergeant Davis had accompanied me onto

the bus. "Ladies and gentlemen, we appreciate your cooperation. We have all your contact information. If you think of anything else, please feel free to call us."

Irma was the last person to board. Irma was the oldest of Nana Jo's friends. She was also the vainest. She dressed and acted years younger and took pride in still being able to attract men of all ages. However, the woman who climbed aboard the bus looked and acted decades older. She looked tired and, while she was already a petite woman, she seemed to have shrunk in the past few hours.

Irma walked toward the same seat she'd had previously. Even though this was a different bus, she stopped just short of her seat, and the color left her face.

I stood up and moved into the aisle, using my body to block the seat that mirrored the one Max had died in earlier.

"Irma, come over here." Nana Jo stood and placed an arm around her shoulders.

Irma allowed herself to be led into the seat I'd just abandoned next to Nana Jo, and I took the seat across the aisle.

I settled into my seat, but I zoned out on the last bits of Sergeant Davis's spiel. Mr. Big had followed me onto the bus. He sat in his seat, mirrored glasses and aloof attitude both securely in place. The glance I had of him with the other policemen told me he wasn't one of us. The question I wanted answered was, who was he?

CHAPTER 4

The remainder of the ride home was, thankfully, uneventful. Less than one hour after we pulled out of the rest area, the driver pulled up through the gates of Shady Acres Retirement Village.

The passengers left the bus quickly, stretching and complaining.

Nana Jo stood her nearly six-foot frame and stretched. "Now I know what Gilligan must have felt like."

I grabbed my book and other belongings. "What do you mean? You feel like a castaway?"

"No. What was supposed to have been a three-hour tour turned into three years on that blasted island. The drive from Chicago should have taken two hours. It's been twelve since we left."

Ruby Mae followed. "I'm going to bed. What time are we meeting?"

I stared at her. "Meeting for what?"

Nana Jo, Dorothy, and Ruby Mae all stared at me as if I'd suddenly lost my mind.

"What time are we meeting to figure out who killed Max?" Irma said softly. "You have to figure out who killed Max." She swallowed hard. "We owe him that much."

"The police are going to find his killer. That Sergeant Alvarez is a lot smarter than Detective Pitt. I'm sure he'll be able to catch Max's killer without our intervention. Besides, do we even know he was killed?" I looked at their faces. "Maybe it was natural causes?"

Nana Jo scoffed. "You've got to be joking. Of course he was murdered."

"Maybe he was. Regardless, it doesn't have anything to do with us."

Irma's eyes filled with tears. "Please, Sam. You don't understand."

I stared from her to Nana Jo and the others, looking for help. However, their faces clearly said they were aligned with Irma on this one.

"Nana Jo?" I looked at my grandmother.

She looked at me. "I'm sorry, Sam. I know you don't like getting involved, but we need you, this time more than ever."

"I don't understand. Why is this time more important?" I was tired and my voice sounded more whiney than ever. "I don't think any of those detectives believe you killed Max," I pleaded with Irma. "There's no need for us to get involved this time."

Ruby Mae supplied the answer. "Because this time, it's one of us."

"What?" I stared at her.

Nana Jo shook me by the shoulders. "Sam, I know you're tired, but you have to see this. Max Franck was alive when he boarded that bus. Someone on that bus killed him."

Ruby Mae nodded. "It had to be one of us."

"There's a murderer at Shady Acres, and we need to find out who it is," Dorothy said.

"This time the murder is too close for comfort. We need you to help us catch a murderer, Sam."

CHAPTER 5

It was the early hours of the morning and I was exhausted. I wanted nothing more than to sleep through the remaining three days and into the new year. My loft over my bookshop would be quiet, especially without my dogs, Snickers and Oreo, to help welcome me home. Nana Jo stayed in my guest bedroom most weekdays, but then went to her villa at Shady Acres on the weekends and spent time with her boyfriend. She offered to come back with me, but I knew she was concerned about Irma, so I declined.

When my husband, Leon, died, I sold the home we shared and took the proceeds and the insurance money and followed our dream and opened a mystery bookshop. That was over a year ago, and I had no regrets. The building we'd walked by for years and dreamed about "one day," "when our ship comes in," was now the home of Market Street Mysteries and the upstairs was my new home.

I pulled into my garage and noticed the apartment above my garage was dark and uninviting. Not only were my grandmother and my poodles gone, but my tenant, Dawson Alexander, was gone too. Dawson left earlier today with the Michigan Southwest University Tigers, MISU to the locals, football team. MISU had gone undefeated this season and were going to be playing in their first bowl game in over a decade. Dawson was the quarterback as well as my part-time assistant and master baker.

As I climbed the stairs to my loft, the dark, empty space weighed on me more than ever before. Normally, I relished being alone and wasn't one of those people who needed to be surrounded by people to feel comfortable. However, tonight was different. Tonight, I felt not only alone, but lonely.

The hours on the bus left me exhausted. It took everything in me to drag my body up the flight of stairs to my loft. I didn't have the energy to drag my suitcase too, so I left it at the bottom of the stairs. I'd get one of my nephews or Frank to help me haul it up the stairs later. Frank Patterson was my not-quite-a-boyfriend-but-more-than-a-friend and I smiled at the thought of him. He was a good man, and I was fortunate to have him in my life. I marveled at the fact I was feeling more comfortable with him. Initially, I'd felt like I was cheating on my husband, even though he was dead. However, I knew in my heart Leon wouldn't want me to be alone and that helped.

Upstairs, I showered and prepared for bed. However, the events of the past few hours had my mind racing in a hundred different directions. My body was fatigued, but my mind refused to shut down. I tossed and turned but couldn't stop thinking about Max Franck. After an hour of restlessness, I gave up and flipped on the lights. Maybe the physical action of flipping on the lamp in my bedroom flipped on the lightbulb in my head. I tossed the covers off, grabbed my robe and slippers, and hurried downstairs.

"You're right, Sergeant Alvarez. I own a freakin' mystery bookshop."

Once downstairs, I disengaged the alarm system and hurried to fire up my point-of-sale system. It didn't take long to find Max Franck. As luck would have it, I owned one of his books and went in search of it. When I opened the bookstore, I debated how to shelve the books. Should I shelve them by genre and subgenre or by author? In the early hours of the morning, I was extremely thankful I had shelved the books alphabetical by author. The only exceptions were a cozy section that showcased my personal favorites and a newly added children's section.

I hurried to the *Fs* and grabbed Max Franck's book, *The Kennedy Conspiracy.* According to the medallion on the cover, the book was a New York Times Best Seller, an Edgar Award winner, and a Booker Prize finalist. Normally, a true crime book with the word "conspiracy" in the title, wasn't anything that would grab my attention. However, award-winning books sold well.

I grabbed my book, reset the alarm, and hurried back upstairs. I debated whether I should have coffee while I read. The last thing I wanted in the wee hours of the morning was anything that would keep me awake, but there was something about drinking a warm beverage when I read that always made me feel warm and cozy. I was more than a little curious about Max Franck, but the last thing I wanted was to be awake all night. I compromised. Instead of coffee, I made a cup of Earl Grey, grabbed a blanket, and curled up on my sofa. Best-case scenario, I would learn who wanted to kill Max without leaving my living room. Worst-case scenario, *The Kennedy*

Conspiracy would put me to sleep. Either way, I won.

Several hours later I heard the alarm being disengaged. I looked at the time on my cell phone. I had been reading all night or rather, all morning. As was often the case, neither the best-case, nor the worst-case scenario had occurred. Reality had been somewhere in the middle. I hadn't fallen asleep reading nor did I know who killed Max Franck. However, I had spent the night reading a well-written, thoughtful, and extremely well-researched book about the murder of President John F. Kennedy.

I heard the eager clicking of nails on hardwood floors, which let me know Snickers and Oreo were on their way. Knowing they would smell my presence before they saw me, I braced myself.

At twelve, Oreo was the younger of my two chocolate toy poodles. Despite his age, he was more like a rambunctious toddler than the old dog the charts at my vet's office stated he was. He flew at me like a torpedo, tail wagging and body in constant motion. Snickers, on the other hand, was a distinguished female of advanced years. Nevertheless, she too leapt onto my lap. Oreo's constant movement and eagerness always made me laugh. He had such a zest for life. However, laughing was a mistake I should have been prepared for. Snickers stood on my lap on her hind legs and the moment my mouth opened, she licked.

"Blaagh. Ack!" I turned my head and used the blanket to wipe my mouth.

"Hey, Aunt Sammy. Welcome back."

My nephew Zaq followed the dogs upstairs. He was a twin and I heard footsteps that indicated his brother, Christopher, was on his way. "Hey."

Christopher followed and placed my suitcase in the living room. "Welcome home."

"Thank you."

My nephews were juniors at Jesus and Mary University (JAMU) and were much more literate than their dialogue demonstrated.

"Good morning. Thank you both for taking care of the store and please thank your dad for taking care of Snickers and Oreo."

Snickers was lying on her back, using her paw to guide my hand while I scratched her tummy with one hand. My other hand was occupied scratching the spot behind Oreo's ear, which made his eyes roll back in his head and always caused his leg to twitch.

The twins laughed. They were both tall and thin, just like their dad. Even though they were identical twins, their personalities made it very easy to tell them apart.

"Hey, you're paying us." Christopher shrugged. He was the more serious of the two. He liked to dress in what would have been described as "preppy" in my day but which he called "snappy casual." Christopher was a marketing major and was great at helping with my displays and promotional campaigns.

Zaq punched his brother in the arm. "He's joking. We'd help even if you weren't paying us." Zaq was the technology geek. He loved computers and was a whiz at managing my point-of-sale system and had created an amazing website for the bookstore and was just about done with one for my author platform as well.

They grinned. I knew their playful banter well after more than twenty years.

"Dad said someone died." Zaq sat on the sofa and Oreo moved from my lap to his.

I told them what I knew, which really wasn't much.

"You going to solve another murder, Aunt Sammy?" Christopher asked.

"Of course she is."

I was so engrossed in recounting the story to my nephews, I hadn't heard Nana Jo come in.

The boys got up and gave their great-grandmother a kiss.

"Now, it's almost time to open up. You two better get downstairs." She went to the kitchen and made a cup of coffee in my single-cup coffee maker. "You planning to lounge around all day or are you planning to do any sleuthing?"

I wanted to go to sleep, but that ship had sailed. Instead, I took a long, hot shower and got dressed. I got a whiff of two of my favorite things, bacon and coffee, and followed my nose into the kitchen.

"I knew that would get your attention." Nana Jo slid a cup of coffee to me and then handed me the bottle of sweet creamer from the refrigerator.

I climbed onto a barstool and Nana Jo handed me a plate with bacon, eggs, and toast.

Nana Jo allowed me to eat and drink my coffee in peace until the moment the last bite of toast and eggs hit my lips. "I told the girls to meet us at Frank's place for lunch."

I didn't respond.

"Sam, I know you don't want to get involved solving a murder, but we need you. You've got a knack for this stuff." She paused. "I'm not a young woman, and most of the time I'm doing good to remember

71

where I left my keys."

"Don't give me that old, pathetic, woe-is-me song and dance. There's nothing wrong with your little gray cells. You're physically fit and mentally sharp as a knife."

She chuckled. "True, but everyone has their strengths. I excel as the sidekick. I'm great at coordinating the team, doing the legwork, and acting as a sounding board for you to bounce ideas off. Plus, I'm your muscle." She stretched, tilted her head from side to side, and cracked her knuckles like a prize fighter getting prepared to go into the ring.

I laughed and nearly spit out my coffee.

She smiled. "Seriously, I'm not the master sleuth. Putting all of the clues together and figuring out how everything fits together, that's what you're good at."

I sighed. "I didn't say I wouldn't help. I was just hoping to relax a bit. We just got through the entire nightmare with Mom's wedding and Lydia Lighthouse." I sighed again.

"Two sighs in less than a minute means there's more going on here. What's wrong?" She leaned against the counter and waited.

I sat for a few moments and tried to gather my thoughts. "I miss Lexi and Angelo."

Nana Jo reached across and drew me into

a hug. I placed my head on my grand-mother's shoulder and cried.

"I know you thought the bus trip would help me get my mind off the fact they were leaving, and I know I only had them here for a short time, but . . ."

"It's okay to miss them. I miss them too."

I looked up. "You do?"

"Of course I do. The twins are grown men now, and it's been a long time since there have been any children around."

Lexi and Angelo were two orphans Frank found asleep in the back of his restaurant a few weeks ago. They had run away from their foster family in Chicago and made their way to North Harbor. The bruises on their bodies told a tale that I shuddered to think about. However, Lexi and Angelo had family in Italy who had been looking for them. When Frank Patterson found their family, they rushed to the United States for a reunion.

"It's only been a few days and they need time with their family."

I sniffed. "I know."

"Besides, their grandparents promised to bring them back to say goodbye before they left the country."

"I know."

She held me at arm's length and looked

into my eyes. "Then, what's the real problem?"

I shook my head. "I don't know. I just feel in a bit of a funk. Maybe it's the holidays or maybe it's another senseless murder." I took several deep breaths. "I mean, what is wrong with people? Why do people think it's okay to kill each other?" I shrugged. "I feel like, what's the point. There's no value for human life anymore."

Nana Jo looked at me. "That's why we need you."

I looked up at her. "What do you mean?"

"Someone has to care. Look, someone killed that poor man. Too many people don't want to get involved. They go about their lives and try to stay out of trouble. They work and go home. The reason people abuse children, rape, steal, and kill is because they *think* they'll get away with it. There used to be a time when people looked out for each other." She shook her head. "Now, it's mind your own business or I'm not my brother's keeper. Your fellow man is your business. It's all of our business and, unless more people get involved and become their 'brother's keeper,' nothing changes." She paused, taking several deep breaths. "I'm sorry, honey. I don't mean to preach. It just burns my butt to think about Irma crying her eyes out and this . . . Max Franck getting killed on that bus." She shivered. "The same bus we were on."

I stared at her. "You think the murder was random? That the killer meant to kill someone else?"

She paced. "I don't know what I mean." She stopped, turned, and looked at me. "No, I don't think it was random or that the killer meant to kill someone else." She shook her head. "The killer took a big chance. I find it hard to believe anyone would take that kind of risk unless they were very angry or . . ."

"Or very desperate."

She nodded. "Look, if you really don't want to get involved, then I'll understand. You've got a lot on your plate with the bookstore and your book, and you're entitled to a little romance." Nana Jo forced a smile that didn't reach her eyes. "I'll call the girls and let them know we're leaving this one up to the police. That Sergeant Alvarez was a hottie, but I think he has brains too, at least a lot more than Stinky Pitt. Maybe he'll nab the killer before the new year." She reached into her bag and pulled out her cell phone.

"Wait."

She looked up.

I took a deep breath. "You're right. More people do need to get involved." I sighed. "I'll help."

"Are you sure?" She stared into my eyes.

"Yes. I'm sure." I nodded.

She smacked her hand on the breakfast bar. "Hot diggity!"

Showered, dressed, fed, and caffeinated, I still couldn't sleep. I finished Max Franck's book and spent a little time on Google, trying to find out as much as I could about him. The Internet was an amazing source of information, even though everything on the Internet wasn't true. Nevertheless, there were links to books and articles at the library and other sources I knew were trustworthy. I marveled at all the information available online. No wonder people were paranoid about "Big Brother." It wasn't long after I started surfing for information about Max Franck that I started getting items in my news feed about the Kennedys and conspiracy theories. Following the threads led me from one rabbit hole to another, with tons of information. I found a lot of fascinating information about some of the lesser-known Kennedys. A couple of hours later, I emerged from the last rabbit hole I'd tumbled down. Since sleep remained elusive and I still had time before lunch, I might as well be productive and write.

Lady Elizabeth Marsh sat in the first-class compartment of the train that would take her from the lights and the bustling streets of London home to the peace and quiet of Wickfield Lodge in the English countryside. In spite of the darkness, she gazed out of the window as the train raced through the night. Despite the lateness of the hour and the traumatic events she'd witnessed, she sat straight with her back and head held high. The casual observer would never guess the path her thoughts had taken. Like cream rising to the top, breeding and manners always showed through. Only those on the most intimate terms would notice the lines between her normally smooth brow and the firm set of her mouth, usually quick to smile and welcome, but now with a distinct downward curve.

"Aunt Elizabeth," Lady Penelope spoke loudly.

Lady Elizabeth shook herself and forced a smile. "I'm so sorry, dear. I'm afraid I was distracted." She turned her gaze toward her niece and waited expectantly.

Lady Penelope smiled. "I shouldn't have roused you, but I suddenly felt in need of conversation." She shook herself. "I don't know. I just felt cold. I can't seem to get that poor woman out of my mind."

Lady Elizabeth reached across and patted her niece's hand. "I've been thinking about Mrs. Forsythe too."

Despite the fact that they were alone, Lady Penelope looked around as though to make certain they wouldn't be overheard. Then she leaned forward to her aunt, who sat across from her in the compartment, and whispered, "You don't really believe she was murdered, do you?" Her eyes searched her aunt's face for the truth. "You don't honestly believe someone pushed her."

Lady Elizabeth thought for a moment. "Actually, I very much believe she was pushed."

Lady Penelope shivered. "I suppose it was rather an odd coincidence that not only was Mrs. Sanderson there, but her cousin Desmond, and his wife, Constance, just happened to be in the tube station at the exact time Eleanor tumbled down those stairs."

"That's too many coincidences for me to accept."

"What are you going to do?" Lady Penelope stared at her aunt.

Lady Elizabeth was silent for a long moment. "I didn't know Eleanor Forsythe. She might just be a balmy old dear." She sighed.

"I will admit, for a moment, I was tempted to do nothing. It's none of my business if an old woman I just met falls down an escalator. If there was something sinister going on, then it's up to the police to find the truth."

"I sense a 'but' coming." Lady Penelope smiled kindly at her aunt.

"But, she was a human being. I think our world has far too many people who don't value lives." She bowed her head for a moment. "I keep thinking about Johan, Josiah, and poor little Rivka." She swallowed hard. "Someone needs to care. Bad things are happening to human beings, and it's our duty to do something." She paused. "Besides, I had tea with her." She shook herself. "I think she chose to come to my table because she thought she could trust me, and I'm determined to see that her trust wasn't misplaced." She sighed. "Whatever the situation, she deserved better. I'm going to find out the truth. If she was murdered, then I intend to find the person who murdered her and see that justice is served." She looked out the window into the darkness and spoke quietly. "It's the least I can do."

"Samantha!" Nana Jo yelled.

"I'm sorry. I was lost in my writing."

"I could tell that. It's time we leave to meet the girls."

I looked at my watch. "It's noon already?" My stomach growled. I'd been surfing the Internet and writing for close to four hours. "Let me grab my coat and I'll meet you downstairs."

The poodles had curled up together in the dog bed I kept under my desk. Nana Jo's entrance had roused them from their slumbers. They stretched several times as though they had been the ones who were awake for more than twenty-four hours instead of me.

"Come on." Nana Jo patted her leg. "Let's go get a treat."

Nana Jo knew the magic word that was capable of rousing the poodles from a dead sleep, "treat." I'd always heard that poodles were smart, which was why they were often used in circuses, because they were easy to train. However, it wasn't until I discovered exactly how smart they were that I was able to truly appreciate them. When I looked into their eyes and saw the lightbulb of recognition at the word "treat," that's when I realized these creatures were intelligent beings.

The poodles followed Nana Jo downstairs, fully aware that a biscuit awaited them if they simply went potty outside rather than inside. It was definitely a cushy life.

Once the poodles were tended to, Nana

Jo and I bundled up and walked down the street to North Harbor Café, the restaurant owned by my friend, Frank Patterson. We promised to bring lunch back for my nephews too.

When we walked in the door, I immediately looked toward the bar. Frank was behind the counter. He smiled. He was tall with salt-and-pepper hair, which he wore cut short. Even though he was wearing jeans and a polo shirt, there was something about him that screamed I used to be in the military. I thought it was the haircut that former military and policemen often continued long after they left the service. However, as I stared at him, I wondered if it was something in his bearing. He was lean and fit with a straight posture and confident stride.

"You gonna stand there gawking all day?" Nana Jo jostled me, and I realized I was standing in the middle of the floor staring.

I hurried to the tables the staff had pushed together for our group. Ruby Mae, Dorothy, and Irma were already there.

Nana Jo and I sat at the two empty seats and removed our coats and hats.

Frank brought a large pitcher of water with lemons in it to the table and placed it in front of me. He greeted everyone and leaned down and whispered in my ear, "Welcome home. I missed you."

The warmth of his breath tickled my neck and my breathing increased as his lips lightly touched my ear.

"I missed you too." I'd kept him in the loop through a series of texts and phone messages over the past day. Had it really only been one day since Max Franck was killed? It certainly felt like a lot more time had passed.

"I'm looking forward to hearing all about it tonight. Are we still on for dinner?"

I'd forgotten we'd arranged to have dinner tonight. "Definitely." I worked to avoid a yawn.

He stared. "You look tired."

I smiled. "Thanks. That's just what every woman wants to hear."

He placed a hand over his heart. "My apologies. Please forgive me."

I smiled. "You're going to need to do better than that."

"Maybe I can make it up to you," he whispered, and his lips brushed my ear and sent a shiver up my spine.

"Ahemm." Nana Jo cleared her throat. "Normally, I would never dream of interrupting my granddaughter's flirtations, but we have a mystery to solve."

Frank bowed to Nana Jo, turned, and winked at me.

Nana Jo yelled, "And you're looking rather tired yourself, Frank. You need to hire an assistant."

Frank raised an eyebrow and smiled and then hurried back to work.

I could still feel the effects of the gentle caress of his lips and the heat rose up my neck. I took a sip of water and tried to focus my attention on something other than Frank Patterson. My husband, Leon, and I had been married for a long time and after his death, I was out of practice when it came to flirting. However, practice made perfect, so I was just practicing. At least that was what I told myself.

"Earth to Sam."

Nana Jo's prompting, and the laughter I heard from the others, forced me to drag my mind back to the task at hand.

"Sorry."

We gave our orders to the waitress, and I watched my grandmother, determined not to allow my thoughts to drift into danger-ous waters.

"Now, who wants to go first." Nana Jo pulled her iPad out of her large purse and prepared to take notes.

Irma raised a hand. "I think I should go

first since I knew him better than the rest of you."

We all nodded.

Irma coughed. "I didn't know Max long, and, to be completely honest, we didn't spend much time talking." She cast her gaze downward and took a deep breath. "I knew he used to be married. Although, he's been divorced for decades and his ex-wife is deceased. They had one child, a daughter." She paused and looked up as though trying to remember. "I think he said her name is . . . Rosemary." Irma paused.

"Is she married?" Nana Jo asked. "Is her last name Franck?"

"I don't . . . wait, yes. I think he said she's married and has a daughter." Irma paused again. "I don't think they had a very good relationship. He was a journalist and traveled a lot. I think he and his daughter were estranged, but . . ."

"What? Anything he said might prove important," Dorothy encouraged her friend and reached across the table and squeezed her hand.

Irma nodded. "I got the impression that he had seen her recently and wanted to make things right between them, but . . . I don't think it was going well." She looked up. "At least, I got that impression."

Nana Jo looked at her friend with more compassion than usual. "That's great, Irma. You've given us a lot to go on."

Irma smiled.

"Now, who's next?"

I raised my hand. "Something Sergeant Alvarez said made me think Max Franck was an author, so when —"

Nana Jo smacked her hand against her forehead. "That's where I knew him." She glanced around the table. "I read in one of those publishing newsletters you subscribe to about a new book deal he had." She looked at me. "I'm sorry, dear. I didn't mean to interrupt."

I shook my head. "It's okay." I pulled the book I'd shoved in my bag onto the table. "Apparently, Max Franck was an investigative journalist." I read the back cover of his book, which listed the many awards he'd won. Then I told them about his book about the conspiracy he believed surrounded the assassination of Robert Kennedy.

The others listened silently. The waitress brought our food and we paused for a few moments to allow her to distribute it.

"That's fascinating, and I'd love to read the book." Dorothy wiped her mouth. "I just don't see what that could possibly have to do with his murder?"

85

"I don't know that it does. It's just background information more than anything." I chewed my BLT, minus the T. "I think it speaks to the type of person he was . . . his character, more than anything."

"Anything else?" Nana Jo's voice held a nervous excitement that told me she was eager to share.

I shook my head. "Not really."

"If no one minds, I'll go next." She gave a courtesy glance around the table, but no one objected.

"I was a little bummed because I didn't have much to talk about, but after hearing Sam's information, I remembered something important. In fact, I may know why Max Franck was killed."

After dropping that bombshell, Nana Jo, the ultimate performer, waited until surprise showed on everyone's face. "Like I said, I read one of those publishing newsletters Sam has and I remembered reading about Max Franck." She looked around. "I knew his name sounded familiar, but I couldn't figure out why. There was no picture in the newsletter, so I think I buried the information in the back of my head."

Dorothy Clark leaned forward. "Josephine, if you don't hurry up and get to the point, I'm going to brain you. You're starting to

86

sound like Irma." She leaned toward Irma. "No offense."

Irma waved away any offense.

"Well, Max Franck's agent announced that, after years of hiding, Max Franck had written a new book, which would blow the lid off all other books dealing with the assassination of Robert Kennedy." She glanced around. "According to this agent, the book that would name names, answer questions, and forever close the door on all speculation about the assassination of Robert Kennedy had been sold for a six-figure amount."

We gasped and demonstrated the appropriate amount of surprise to satisfy my grandmother, who sat looking as pleased as a cat who'd caught a mouse.

I pondered that information. "You think he was murdered because he was about to release a book that would identify a murderer?"

Nana Jo shrugged. "I don't know, but I do know I don't believe in coincidences. I think the moment that announcement about the book was posted, Max Franck was a marked man. That book marked him for murder."

CHAPTER 6

Neither Ruby Mae nor Dorothy had anything to contribute, although Ruby Mae had a third cousin who used to work for the *Chicago Sun-Times.* She contacted him and was waiting for information about Max Franck.

"I'm not sure where to start with this one." Dorothy gave Irma a sympathetic look.

All faces turned toward me.

I struggled to find the right words, which must have been evident on my face.

"Spit it out, Sam. No point in trying to sugarcoat anything," Nana Jo said.

"I think we need to look at everyone on the bus." I looked around the table. "Present company excluded."

Irma reached into her purse, which wasn't unusual. However, when she pulled out a sheet of paper rather than her flask, that shocked all of us. "I thought you might want something like that." She unfolded the sheet. "I wrote down the names of everyone on the bus. Counting the five of us, there were twenty-five." She looked up. "If we divide the names, we could each take four." She looked at me. "If that's okay with you, Sam."

"Of course. It's perfect." I was shocked and tried to shake it off. Normally, Irma was much more interested in flirting and having a good time. This murder must have really left her rattled.

The girls divided the names on the list, and I noticed my names included Mr. Big, whom Irma described as the large hunk with the mirrored sunglasses. I took a pen and wrote Sidney Sherman next to his name so I wouldn't forget.

The meeting ended with Nana Jo promising to get what she could from her boyfriend, Freddie, who was a retired policeman and whose son was a state policeman.

Nana Jo and I walked back to my building after the meeting. I was tired but still not sleepy. I helped out in the bookstore for a couple of hours to allow the twins to eat their lunches, but the traffic after Christmas wasn't nearly as much as it had been prior to the holiday. I puttered around for a while but eventually gave up and went upstairs.

"Are you still stressing about this murder?" Nana Jo asked.

"I don't know." I paced. "I just realized I won't have Stinky Pitt to help with this one."

Nana Jo snorted. "I never thought I'd hear the day when you'd be missing Stinky Pitt."

Detective Pitt, Stinky Pitt, as he'd been labeled as a child, was a detective with the North Harbor Police and we'd crossed paths several times in the past. Normally, he wasn't a fan of what he referred to as "nosy amateurs" meddling in police investigations. However, Detective Pitt, as Nana Jo often said, wasn't the sharpest knife in the drawer and we'd helped him out several times. Our help hadn't exactly endeared us, but it had forced him to tolerate us.

"It's not that I miss *him,* exactly. It's more that I'm missing the access to the police and coroner's report."

"Hmmm. You might have a point." Nana Jo poured herself a cup of tea. "Maybe that sexy Sergeant Alvarez will share his . . ."

I was shaking my head before the words left her mouth. "Sergeant Alvarez isn't a small-town policeman who doesn't know how to investigate a murder." I followed Nana Jo into the kitchen and poured a cup of tea for myself. "He doesn't need our help and he's not likely to share any information with us." I took a sip. "In fact, he probably still suspects us of the murder."

"You're probably right." She smiled. "However, you have to admit, he was definitely a hunk." She started to walk away but stopped abruptly. "Are you done with that book?"

I gave Nana Jo Max Franck's book from my purse.

She settled onto the sofa with the book and her tea and, within a few moments, was engrossed.

I paced around my bedroom for a few moments, trying to decide what to do. I felt anxious, probably from my lack of sleep. After a few moments, I grabbed my coat and headed out. "I'll be back."

Nana Jo grunted an acknowledgment.

I got in my car and drove, something I often did to clear my mind. Despite the cold weather and the snow on the ground, the streets were clear. North Harbor was an economically depressed city situated on prime real estate alongside the Lake Michigan shoreline. The city was separated from its twin city of South Harbor by the St. Thomas River, which flowed out into the Great Lake. In contrast, South Harbor was a prosperous, quaint town of cobblestoned streets, lighthouses, and thriving shops.

Practically on autopilot, I pulled into the lot for the North Harbor Police Department, which was attached to the county courthouse. Memories of an unpleasant experience where an overzealous police officer mistook Nana Jo's iPad for a weapon reminded me to double-check my purse before I got out of the car.

Inside, I walked through the metal detectors without incident and breathed a sigh of relief.

I recognized the policeman behind the desk, although I didn't know his name. Apparently, he recognized me too because when he looked up from his computer, he said, "You here for Detective Pitt?"

I nodded and he picked up the phone and dialed.

It didn't take long for Detective Pitt to come up for me. The scowl on his face told me he was as happy to see me as I knew he would be.

"Whaddaya want?"

I smiled. "I'm glad to see you too, Detective Pitt. I'd like a word with you in private, if you can spare the time."

He narrowed his eyes and stared for several seconds. Eventually, he sighed. "Might as well come on." He turned and walked down the hall to the closet he had transformed into an office.

I followed Detective Pitt down the hall, but after many trips to the North Harbor Police Department, I knew my way by heart.

The office had, indeed, once been a closet, and he had to suck in his stomach and turn sideways to get through the doorway if anyone was sitting in the guest chair. Once inside, he flopped down onto his chair and turned to face me. "No one's died in the past week, so what brings you out."

Detective Pitt was short, fat, and balding. He chose to take the few remaining hairs that still clung to the edges of his head and comb them over the rather large dome on top. The task of covering his egg-shaped skull was too much for the strands that remained and many of them refused to lie quietly and instead stood at various angles as though looking for an escape route. His fondness for polyester was evident from the too-tight polyester pants and shirt he wore to the polyester jacket that he had draped over the back of his chair. His office reeked from the cheap cologne he wore and the half-consumed liverwurst sandwich that lay on his desk.

"Did I interrupt your lunch?"

"Never mind that. Whaddaya want? No one's died. No reason for you and those batty old broads to interfere."

I took a deep breath and reminded myself I was asking for a favor and would need to stay on the detective's good side. I forced myself to remain serious and not think of how Nana Jo would react if she heard him refer to her as a "batty old broad." "Actually, that's not entirely true." I took a deep breath.

"What's not entirely true?"

"That one part."

He leaned forward. "What part?"

"The part about no one having died in the past week . . . That's not exactly, ah . . . true."

Now I had his complete attention. He smacked his hand on the desk. "What? Who's dead? Nobody told me!"

The flash of anger he'd exhibited moments earlier instantly vanished. Instead, the spark was replaced with a wariness that caused his gaze to dart around the small room. He leaned across and whispered, "Who was assigned the case?" He leaned forward. "It's Wilson, that brownnoser, isn't it?" He muttered. "Backstabbing traitor."

"No. It's not Wilson. It's not a local murder."

He stared. "Whaddaya mean?"

The English teacher in me cringed every

time he mushed his words together and slurred them into some mutation that barely resembled the English language, but I screwed my smile on tighter. "The murder happened on a bus trip from Chicago."

I could tell by the way he relaxed and leaned back he was about to dismiss me. "Not my jurisdiction." He picked up his sandwich and took a bite. "Amateurs don't know how these things work." He forced the words around his food as he chewed, giving me a good glance of his teeth in action.

"I understand the murder took place in another state, but the victim was on a Michigan bus, in fact Shady Acres chartered the bus. So, nearly all the passengers were locals. Plus, the bus was en route to Shady Acres. So, it really gives you a better chance of solving the murder since you're already more familiar with the people involved than some out-of-town Chicago policeman coming on your turf and trying to make a name for himself by solving a high-profile murder."

He sat up in his chair. "High profile?"

My bait had worked. I'd hooked my fish. Now, if I could just reel him in. I nodded, took a deep breath, leaned close, and whispered, "Yes. The victim was a well-known author — a Pulitzer Prize–winning, bestselling author."

"You don't say." He rubbed his chin.

I wiped the tears from my eyes. His cologne, combined with the liverwurst, which was obviously covered in onions, and the closeness of the space was overwhelming.

He reached in a pocket and pulled out a lime-green polyester handkerchief. "Did you know the victim well?"

I shook my head. "Not at all. It's just the thought that Detective Alvarez will come over here and solve a murder and will probably make a name for himself and end up in the newspaper and on television when . . . well, it could be someone local." I gave him a pointed stare and blinked to get the tears out of my eyes.

He leaned back. "You say the victim won awards?"

I nodded. "A Pulitzer. Plus, he was about to publish another book, some big exposé about the murder of Robert Kennedy. You know something like that always generates tons of media attention."

He sat up. "*The* Robert Kennedy? As in brother to the late president of the United States?"

I nodded.

Detective Pitt looked up and smiled. After a few minutes he looked at me. "I'll bet you have some angle on this case."

"Same deal as last time. If you help me get the forensic information and police reports, then when we solve the case, you get all of the credit."

He was silent for a moment. "It may not be easy to get the forensic information on this one. The Chicago Police Department isn't just going to turn that stuff over to me."

"I was thinking maybe you could ask to be added to the case as a local consultant or something. I mean, I can't believe the Chicago Police Department has the money or the resources to stay in North Harbor. Couldn't you do some of the local . . . legwork or whatever it's called?"

"Maybe . . . it's the holidays and most police departments are short staffed around this time of year, including us."

"I'm sure they'd be happy to have your help." I hesitated. "That is, unless you're super busy."

Detective Pitt's desk always looked as though a tornado had passed over the papers. However, the magazines he'd tried to conceal under the files told a different story.

"We're at rather a slow time right now. Most of the college students from MISU are gone for Christmas break, and we don't get many tourists during the winter. So, things are slower than normal at the moment. Just a few domestic disputes and bar fights, but nothing to really sink your teeth into." He leaned back. "I might be able to manage a few hours. You better give me the specifics and I'll see what I can do."

"Great." I smiled.

It took thirty minutes to fill Detective Pitt in on what I'd learned about Max Franck. He surprised me by asking quite a few questions about Sergeants Alvarez and Davis. However, I felt the more information he had, the better, so I told him all I knew.

I drove home and went back upstairs. Nana Jo was in the exact same spot where I'd left her with her nose glued to the book. I smiled and headed to my bedroom. I still wasn't sleepy, so I decided to take a trip to the British countryside.

Lord William Marsh sat in the library of Wickfield Lodge and watched. He was accustomed to his wife, Lady Elizabeth, sitting quietly while she knitted. However, there was something different about her silence tonight. He puffed on his pipe and watched through the haze of smoke. Eventually, the silence grew too much for him. "All right, let's have it."

Lady Elizabeth looked up. "What do you mean?"

He puffed. "What's wrong?"

Lady Elizabeth opened her mouth to speak, but Lord William interceded. "And, don't tell me there's nothing wrong." He tapped the ashes from his pipe onto an ashtray the butler, Thompkins, had placed nearby. "I know when something's wrong. Now, you just tell me. It has to do with that woman . . . Forsythe or some such name. Something about that has you bothered."

Lord William was a kind, portly older man, a blustery English gentleman who enjoyed his pipe, rich foods, wine, and family. His fondness for rich food and wine had led to a bit of overindulgence during his niece's wedding and the holiday meal that followed and the kindly man was paying for his intemperance with an attack of gout. He sat with one leg wrapped heavily and propped on a cushioned footstool.

Lady Elizabeth finished the row she was knitting. "I don't know what's wrong. I just know something isn't right."

Lord William took several puffs on his pipe. "People do fall." He tilted his head and stared at his wife. "You said it was crowded. Isn't it possible she lost her footing and fell?"

Lady Elizabeth knitted. After a few moments, she stopped and looked up. "It's possible. In fact, it's highly probable." She stared at her husband. "That's what's so darned difficult. It's the type of accident that happens every day. An elderly lady loses her footing on the escalator of a busy tube station and falls to her death." She knitted. "It's on the back page of the paper and no one thinks twice about it."

"Then what's the problem?"

She knitted. "If I hadn't met her earlier. If I hadn't talked to her . . . shared tea and scones with her, I would write her off as some batty old dear who wasn't quite right in the head, but . . ."

Lord William waited. "But?"

"I don't know. She wasn't batty. She was intelligent and she made complete sense. She was scared and she honestly believed some-one was trying to kill her."

Lord William leaned forward and winced. He took a deep breath and patted his leg. "Isn't that what batty old dears do? They may be normal in every other respect, but they get some bit of nonsense fixed in their heads and they can't let go." He sat back. "Like that chap over in Kent who believed he was a Chinese emperor or that fellow in . . . where was it . . . Torquay who believed he was Napoleon." He shook his head. "Normal in every other respect, except no one could convince him he wasn't Napoleon Bonaparte." He shook his head.

Lady Elizabeth smiled. "I understand what you're saying and, in my head, I know you're absolutely right. After all, I'd only known the woman a short time and she may very well have been exactly as you say."

"But, you don't believe it."

She shook her head. "No. I don't."

Lord William nodded. "Well, what are you going to do about it?"

"I thought I'd call our friend Detective Inspector Covington at Scotland Yard and invite him down for a few days."

Lord William smiled. "Ah . . . I see."

Lady Elizabeth glanced over at her husband. "What do you see? He's always been so helpful before when we've had problems. I just wondered if he could find out some information about Mrs. Forsythe and a few of the people in her household."

"Hmmm." Lord William smiled and puffed on his pipe.

"I hope you're not implying there's more to my desire to invite the detective inspector down than my desire to get his help."

The corners of his lips twitched as he tried to conceal a smile. "Of course, dear." He took several puffs on his pipe. There was a long pause. "I'm sure your invitation has nothing at all to do with the fact you've received a request from your cousin Mildred to put up her daughter, Clara, for a few weeks." His lips twitched with the effort to keep from smiling. "Clara just happens to be about the same age as Detective Inspector Covington, isn't she?"

Lady Elizabeth glanced at her husband for several seconds and then smiled. "She is indeed."

Before Lord William could respond, Thompkins, the Marsh family butler, quietly entered the room. He stood tall and erect and gave a discrete cough. "I beg your pardon, but there's a phone call for your ladyship."

Despite the fact that the Marshes' prim and proper servant rarely displayed emotions, he was able to convey his displeasure quite well.

"Who the dickens would be calling at this time?" Lord William pulled out his pocket watch and frowned when he saw the lateness of the hour.

Lady Elizabeth looked concerned as she glanced at the clock over the mantle. "I hope everything is okay with Daphne and James." She clutched at the pearls around her neck.

"I'm sorry, m'lady. I didn't mean to distress you. It's a person named Desmond Tarkington." Thompkins hurried on. "I asked if there was a message I could convey and have your ladyship return the call tomorrow, but he was insistent."

Lady Elizabeth breathed a sigh of relief. "Thank goodness." She stood. "It's . . . okay, Thompkins. I'll take the call."

The butler bowed stiffly.

"Who in the blazes is Desmond Tarkington?" Lord William asked.

"That's the cousin of Mrs. Eleanor Forsythe, the woman who died today."

Lord William was momentarily stunned. "What could he possibly want at this hour?"

Lady Elizabeth shook her head. "I have no idea." She turned to walk out of the door. "However, I intend to find out."

"Snickers. Oreo. Wanna treat?" My nephew Zaq called from the living room and my two companions, who were just, moments earlier, sound asleep in a dog bed, hopped up and ran barking into the living room.

I glanced at the clock on my computer and realized it was later than I thought. Frank and I had a date and I needed to get dressed.

I stretched and tried to figure out the answer to Lord William's question. What could Desmond Tarkington possibly want?

Nothing came to mind, so I tucked the question back into the recesses of my brain and focused on a more important question. What was I going to wear for my date?

Despite a warm, invigorating shower, the best my brain, and my limited closet selection, could come up with was a black dress and black boots. I stared at my reflection in the mirror and knew this wasn't my best effort. My dark hair was curly and today was one of the days it decided to rebel. Instead of laying down when I combed it, the static electricity gave it a life of its own and it stuck out like Albert Einstein's. I grabbed a can of what I thought was hair spray but, after a few spritzes, I realized was starch, which made my hair stiff and sticky. The comb was barely able to make it through the strands. As the starch dried, it acted like glue. My comb was now glued to my hair. I gave it a yank and it broke off. I'd need to go get scissors and cut it out. This wasn't going well. I took another look at my drab reflection in the mirror and grabbed a colorful scarf Lexie and Angelo gave me for Christmas, to keep from looking as though I was going to a funeral. The lack of sleep had finally caught up with me and, as much as I wanted to see Frank and spend time with him, I couldn't muster up the energy to make a greater effort at looking date worthy. Tonight, I was a dating fail. My boots weren't even the high-heeled fashion boots I'd bought in Chicago. One glance at the snow outside confirmed if I tried to walk in those boots, I'd end up flat on my backside before I made it to his car. Besides, those boots cost a small fortune and as a native Michigander, I knew very well the effect snow and salt had on leather boots. My feet would be wet and the boots would be ruined from the white salt residue, and I'd have a broken ankle from the attempt. Nope, those babies would get worn indoors or only when the weather was dry and boots were a fashion accessory rather than a mobility requirement.

I went to the main living area to wait. Nana Jo was still reading on the sofa. She looked up from her book at my entrance and I gleaned her appraisal of my ensemble in her silence and a single raised eyebrow.

"Don't start." I flopped down on the sofa next to her.

"I didn't say a word."

"No, but your eyebrow spoke volumes."

She flipped the page of her book. "Going to a funeral?"

"I haven't slept in twenty-four hours and I'm dead on my feet. It's going to take all the energy I can muster to eat, make polite conversation, and keep from dozing off during the soup course."

She patted my leg. "I'm sure Frank will understand if you postpone your date. You're beat."

I picked up one of the magazines on my coffee table and flipped to a survey. "Are you pushing your man into the arms of another woman?" I waved the magazine at her. "According to this magazine, I'm a pathetic excuse for a date. I fail in practically every category *except* keeping date night."

Nana Jo took the magazine and glanced at the survey. "This is rubbish and if you weren't so tired, you'd realize it too. Any man would be lucky to have you and if Frank Patterson doesn't recognize what a prize you are, then he doesn't deserve you."

I smiled and leaned over and kissed my grandmother. "Thank you. You're sweet, although you may be slightly biased."

"I'm more than slightly biased. However, it's true, regardless. Frank Patterson, or any man, will be lucky to have you . . . although."

I waited for the other shoe to drop. "Although?"

"You should probably take the comb out

106

of the back of your hair."

I felt the back of my hair and realized that I'd forgotten the comb glued and tangled in my hair. I forgot the scissors. I fiddled with it but only got it more entangled.

Nana Jo reached over. "Here, let me help you." She grabbed at the plastic comb and gave it a hard yank. "What's in your hair, glue?" She pulled the plastic out and handed it to me.

I wiped the tears from my face and tried not to notice the strands of hair fused to the comb. "I mistook the starch for hair spray."

Nana Jo stuck her head behind her book to hide her face, but the laughter rang out anyway. She gave up trying to conceal the fact she was laughing at me and put down her book and laughed heartily until she had to wipe tears from her eyes.

"I'm glad one of us is able to enjoy themselves at my expense."

"Sam, I'm sorry, but you're exhausted. I don't care what that magazine says. Canceling a date when you haven't slept in over twenty-four hours isn't a dating fail. It's common sense and Frank will understand."

"Understand what?" Frank walked up the stairs.

I hopped up and grabbed my coat. "Nothing. I didn't hear you come in."

"One of the twins let me in." He came up and gave me a kiss. "You look . . . nice." He lied and I appreciated him for that. Although, his eyes kept staring at my hair.

"What's wrong? Don't tell me there's more of that blasted comb in there?"

He shook his head. "No, but your hair just looks different tonight."

"She's trying a new product . . . sizing." Nana Jo laughed.

Frank frowned. "Starch?"

I handed him my coat so he could focus on something other than the fact that my grandmother was intent on sharing my humiliation. "Yeah, well, we'll see you later."

I hurried downstairs before Nana Jo could respond and felt Frank's presence behind me. He was a gentleman who liked to open doors and I knew he wouldn't linger once I started. Thankfully, I was right. At the bottom of the stairs, he turned me toward him and looked into my eyes. "You okay?"

I stifled a yawn. "Of course."

He hesitated but gave up and opened the door for me.

The bookstore was a brownstone in downtown North Harbor. The front of the building was on Market Street. Like most of the buildings on Market, the building backed up to an alley. Unlike the other buildings, this building wasn't as deep as the others and occupied a corner lot. The previous owner had built a garage at the back of the property and enclosed the lot with a fence, which created a courtyard. So, I was able to drive through the alley and enter the garage. There was a door that led to the back courtyard from the building and a side door that led out to a parking lot, which separated my building from the others on the street on one side. Technically, I owned the parking lot, but when I purchased the building, I continued the "gentlemen's agreement" the previous owner had and shared the parking lot with the church, which worked out well since the church mostly used the lot on Sundays.

Frank had parked his Porsche Cayenne in the parking lot near the side door. He went out and pulled the car as close as possible to the side door and kept the engine running so I only had a few steps on concrete before getting into the warm interior.

I slid onto the soft, supple leather seat and ran my hand across the leather, always amazed at the softness.

Frank came around the back of the car and got in. "Any place in particular you want to go?"

I shook my head. "No, I'm game for what-ever."

"Great. There's a great little Greek restaurant in South Haven I've been dying to try." He glanced at me. "Are you up for the ride?"

I nodded. "Sounds great."

He pulled out of the parking lot and I prepared to enjoy the ride.

Frank's car was luxurious in every respect, and the smooth ride felt like you were floating on clouds. The seats were warm, and I adjusted the thermostat so I was warm and toasty. He had satellite radio and smooth jazz played through the speakers as we drove through the dark.

I leaned my head back onto the headrest and thought about Max Franck. There were no easily identifiable signs to indicate the method of his death. As far as I could tell, there were no gunshots, at least not visible. There hadn't been a lot of blood that would indicate a stab wound. He could have been poisoned, but I didn't recall seeing him eat or drink anything on the bus. Although, it could have been administered while we were at the rest area. Someone could have come back onboard and given him something laced with poison and then removed the evidence afterward. It was clear the timeline would be critical. We'd need to find out where everyone was and verify.

"Sam." Frank shook my shoulder.

I opened my eyes. For a split second, I had no idea where I was. I looked around and saw Frank staring at me.

"I'm sorry. I must have dozed off." I reached down to remove my seat belt.

Frank reached his hand over and clasped my hand. "We don't have to do this —"

"I want to . . . I'm sorry about falling asleep, but your car is so comfortable and —"

"And you haven't slept in more than twenty-four hours." He smiled. "I should have realized you were exhausted." He leaned over and kissed me. "I'm sorry. Let's do this another time."

I started to protest but realized opening my eyes had been a huge struggle. I glanced over at Frank, who had backed the car out of the restaurant parking lot and was turning around. "I'm sorry. I didn't want to disappoint you."

"You could never disappoint me."

I could tell by his voice he was smiling, even though it was dark in the car and I couldn't see his face. "Are you sure?"

"Of course. We can go another night."

"I'll make it up to you."

He stopped at a stoplight, leaned over,

and kissed me. "Now that sounds promising."

I managed to stay awake for the ride home, but I was grateful when we arrived. He pulled up to the side door and hurried around the car to open my door. I unlocked the building and turned off the security system. I turned to Frank and we made our good night brief.

Inside, I rearmed the security system, called on the last dregs of energy, and climbed the stairs. Nana Jo must have finished the book because she had vacated the sofa and her bedroom door was closed.

Snickers and Oreo were asleep in my bedroom. I should have taken them downstairs to take care of their business, but I knew there was no way I'd be able to tackle those stairs again. I didn't even have the energy to undress. Instead, I flopped down on the bed, boots and all, and fell fast asleep.

I woke up once during the night with a ten-pound weight of a poodle on my chest. I opened my eyes and Snickers was staring into my eyes. I rolled over onto my side, forcing her off. "You're just going to have to go potty in the house. I'll clean it up later."

She marched around for a few more moments but eventually must have decided she could hold it. She walked in circles a couple of times and then curled into a ball near my chest. Within moments, I heard a gentle snore coming from her.

Oreo was in his crate near the foot of my bed. The only sound from him was a soft, "woof."

I wasn't sure if he was dreaming about chasing squirrels or ripping the stuffing out of his stuffed toys. Whatever the source of his dreams, he was a happy dog. My last thought was of Oreo running free in a field with his ears flapping in the wind and it made me smile. I snuggled close to Snickers and fell back asleep.

The next time Snickers woke me up, she not only walked on my chest, but this time, she followed it up with a lick to my nose.

"All right. I'm getting up." I stretched.

Snickers jumped off the bed and ran to the door. Oreo was sitting up in his crate.

I was still wearing the clothes I'd worn last night, boots and all. So, I opened the bedroom door and hurried the poodles downstairs to take care of their business.

Both dogs were anxious to go and barely made it over the threshold.

I appreciated the fact that they hadn't gone in the house and planned to reward them with extra treats when we got back upstairs.

It snowed overnight and the ground was covered by another blanket of snow. Snickers wasn't a fan of the cold Michigan winters. She hurriedly took care of the call of nature and was back inside before her paws got too cold. Oreo, on the other hand, liked to run and play in the new snow and was halfway across the small yard before his under belly registered the cold. Then he quickly ran to the door, expecting *entré*. However, I'd learned from experience to watch and make sure he had not just peed but had also pooped before letting him back inside.

He stood at the door and looked at me with sad eyes that seemed to ask, *aren't you going to let me inside too?*

I steeled my heart and kept the door closed and waited. Eventually, he wandered to the side and pooped. This time, I had the door open wide to welcome him.

He shook, and snow flew everywhere. I grabbed the towel I kept at the back door and wiped as much of the excess snow from his underbelly and paws as possible for both of our comfort and well-being. Snow beaded up on his belly, which I was sure was cold. When the snow melted, it left trails across the floor, which I stepped in whenever I walked around without shoes. Snickers rarely ventured too far away from the shoveled path and rarely needed the towel. Instead, she stood by and watched while I dried off Oreo, and looked at me with an expression that said, *he's not the brightest dog in this pack, is he?*

I ignored her.

Upstairs, I stripped off the clothes I'd slept in, showered, and allowed the warm water to pelt my skin. I washed the starch out of my hair, which took longer than I'd expected. However, perseverance and a lot of shampoo did the trick. When I finally emerged, dressed and thoroughly refreshed, I sniffed the air. Coffee, sausage, and something cinnamony drew me to the kitchen.

"Hmmm. What is that wonderful smell?"

Nana Jo smiled. "Dawson left us a gift." She placed a bubbling cheesy dish on the counter beside a plate of warm cinnamon rolls.

"How? He's in Florida getting ready for his bowl game."

She took two plates from a cabinet and placed them on the counter. "He called when you were in the shower and said he made us a breakfast casserole and put it in the back of the refrigerator. He also made homemade cinnamon rolls."

115

I breathed in the delicious aroma and my stomach growled in response.

"It's supposed to sit for ten minutes, but I can't wait." Nana Jo grabbed a spatula and cut into the casserole, which sizzled and bubbled. She scooped out servings for each of us. I burned my fingers grabbing a cinnamon roll with hot icing, but it was well worth it.

We both tucked into our breakfast and didn't speak for several moments.

"That's so good." I sloshed down some hot coffee.

"How was your date last night? You were back pretty early."

I was tempted to fib and tell her the restaurant was closed and we decided to make an early night of it, but I was a horrible liar. When I finished explaining that I fell asleep in the car and Frank brought me home, she laughed, making me wish I were better at lying. At least she refrained from saying, "I told you so." However, the smug look she cast over her coffee cup said what her mouth didn't.

We sat in blessed silence for several moments.

"What are your plans today?" she asked.

"I think I'll go to Shady Acres and tackle the people on my list."

"Great idea. I'll go with you and work on mine." She walked over to her purse and pulled her iPad out and brought it back to the kitchen. She swiped a few times and then asked, "Who do you have?"

I unfolded the paper I'd stuck into my pocket before coming out for breakfast. I glanced over the list. "I've got the activities director, Caroline Fenton, Sidney Sherman —"

Nana Jo frowned. "Who on earth is Sidney Sherman?"

"Mr. Big."

She nodded. "Aww. Okay."

"Lady in the big floppy hat, Bob the bus driver, and Sara Jane Howard." I paused. "Why does that name sound familiar?"

Nana Jo smiled. "Because Sara Jane Howard is the nosiest woman in Michigan."

I tilted my head back and smacked my leg. "I remember now. When we were investigating the murder of Maria —"

"Yeah, that's her." Nana Jo had a lot of bad memories about Maria Romanov's murder, especially since the police thought she'd had a good reason for wanting her dead. Sara Jane Howard hadn't helped matters. "Looks like Irma gave you the people she doesn't know well and the ones she doesn't like."

117

"I was thinking the same thing, although, maybe that's good. If it's someone she knows, it'll be easier for her to talk to them. Plus, if she leaves the ones she doesn't like to someone else, then it should help eliminate any biases."

"Good point."

"Who do you have?"

Nana Jo read off her list of bus patrons. Most were names I'd heard mentioned but weren't people Nana Jo or the girls had mentioned a lot. The only person who would prove interesting was Velma Levington.

We finished eating just as my nephews arrived. They finished off the rest of the cinnamon rolls and began working on the breakfast casserole like locusts.

The drive to Shady Acres was short and uneventful. I made a detour on the way and stopped at one of my favorite bakeries and picked up a few pastries. There was nothing like fruit tarts from A Taste of Switzerland Bakery to help put people in the mood to chat.

We pulled through the gates into the parking lot of Shady Acres Retirement Village. The development sat on the Lake Michigan shoreline and contained single-family detached homes, referred to as villas, that were painted pastel colors and sat with views of the lake. There was also a large building that housed condos that could be purchased or rented. Nana Jo bought into the village in the early stages and had a great villa with lake views. Dorothy, Irma, and Ruby Mae all lived in condos. Dorothy owned her unit, while Irma and Ruby Mae rented. Although, now that Ruby Mae had moved into one of the larger apartments, she was contemplating purchasing too. The village was restricted to people sixty and over and the wait list was always very long.

I let Nana Jo out at the main building. She took the large boxes of pastries inside while I found a parking space.

Once inside, I looked around. There was a guard at the front desk, Larry Barlow, who was a friend of Nana Jo's boyfriend, Freddie. They'd been on the police force together. He was eating a pecan roll and talking to Nana Jo. I decided not to disturb them.

I walked into the main public living space, which was comfortable with a large fireplace and comfortable chairs and sofas placed to provide conversational areas. Ruby Mae sat on the sofa with her knitting and was talking to another woman. She nodded when she saw me, but I could tell she was engrossed in conversation and didn't want to stem the flow of information.

Back in the lobby, Nana Jo had finished talking to Larry and motioned for me to join her. "I've got good news and bad news. Which one do you want?"

"I need some good news."

"You're in luck. Larry said Earl is still here."

I scoured my brain, but eventually gave up. "Who's Earl?"

"Earl was our original bus driver. I was afraid he'd have hightailed it back to Chicago."

"So was I." I pondered for a moment. "I wonder why he's still here."

"According to Larry, he's staying for a few days." She raised an eyebrow and gave me a look that suggested she questioned Earl's intentions for staying on.

I ignored her look. "What's the bad news?"

"Mr. Big went back to Chicago last night."

"Darn it."

"No need crying over spilled whiskey. Let's just be thankful for what we have and we'll figure out the rest later." Nana Jo looked at her watch. "Jujitsu starts in ten minutes. If I hurry, I can get changed and join in."

"Aren't you supposed to be investigating, not practicing your martial arts?"

"Velma Levington has a green belt in jujitsu. I'll bet my vintage Colt .45 she's in that class."

"I'm sure cornering Velma Levington is your only motivation for getting to jujitsu class and has nothing to do with the fact you're hoping to go for your brown belt next month?"

She winked. "Two birds, one stone. Don't knock it."

Nana Jo hurried to the jujitsu class and I followed the signs that directed me to the office of the activities director.

Caroline Fenton's office door was open. She was pacing in her office. She was a husky woman with dark hair, which she wore cropped at her shoulders, brown eyes, and bushy eyebrows.

I rapped on the door.

She turned around. "Come in."

I extended my box of goodies. "Hello, I hate to bother you, but I was hoping you had time for a coffee break."

She craned her neck. "Are those from A Taste of Switzerland?"

I nodded.

She closed her eyes momentarily and her

face took on a look I'd seen many times from people who thought they could resist the pastries. However, resistance was futile and she opened her eyes and nodded vigorously.

I should have felt bad for tempting her, but all was fair in love, war, and coercing people to talk and give up information when you had no legal authority. So, I did what I had to do.

In her office, she had a small personal coffeemaker. She grabbed two individual coffee pods and two coffee cups and made coffee for both of us. Once the coffee was made, she settled behind her desk and stretched her neck to look over the options in my glorious white box. Her eyes lit up when she saw the lemon tarts. She reached for one and stopped and looked up at me.

"Go ahead. It's all yours."

She reached over and grabbed the tart. She bit into it and moaned as the gooey yellow filling squirted out the sides of her mouth.

I was tempted to hand her a napkin, but experience had told me she'd rather use her tongue than waste any of the lemony goodness.

I knew I was right when I saw her lick the powdered sugar and lemon filling from the sides of her mouth and her fingers.

She glanced at me once, but, at the time, I was having a spiritual moment of my own with a caramel apple tart.

We sat and ate in silence for several moments. When we finished, we both sat back and drank our coffees. I suspected she was doing the same thing as me, swishing the liquid around in her mouth to get the crumbs, but I couldn't be sure.

"Okay, you've tamed the savage beast." She smiled. "What can I do for you?"

I'd thought a lot about how to approach her on my drive to Shady Acres. "Irma was really upset about the sudden death of her friend the other night. I know he wasn't a resident at Shady Acres, but I wondered if anyone was planning a memorial or any type of funeral services?"

She sighed. "I hadn't really thought about a memorial since he didn't live here." Her gaze darted around the room and she reluctantly put down her cup and picked up a pen and started to make notes.

"I really want to help. I know you're busy and I'm sure there have to be a hundred things on your to-do list. Would it be okay if I helped? I'm more than willing to organize it."

"That would be great. There *are* a lot of

things to do and I'm a bit short staffed at the moment with . . . well, you know, they haven't replaced Denise Bennett, the administrator." She blushed. "You know what happened to her."

"Yes, I definitely remember her."

She cleared her throat. "Anyway, I'm doing both jobs at the moment."

I scooted to the edge of my seat. "I'd love to help."

She smiled. "Great."

"Would we be able to have the memorial observance here?"

She nodded and pulled a calendar up on her computer. "I'm sure we can arrange that. The only events we've got planned for the next week are the New Year's Eve Dance and a tailgate party to watch the MISU bowl game and cheer the Tigers on to victory." She smiled at me.

"I don't think we'll need much. Do you think Gaston could provide a few . . . snacks?"

She nodded. "I'm sure that won't be a problem."

"Then the only other thing I need would be a few names."

She tilted her head. "Names?"

"For the invitations."

"I have a mailing list for the residents, I can —"

"I'm not concerned about the residents, actually. I'm sure between my grandmother and her friends, they can get the word out to those who live here. I was thinking about some of the people who were on the bus who don't live here."

She leaned back. "Most of those people probably didn't really know Mr. Franck. I can't believe they'd want to come back to Shady Acres to attend a memorial service for a complete stranger."

"You may be right, but well . . . we spent several long hours together at that rest area and developed a bit of a bond. Plus, being on the bus when someone dies is a traumatic event. It might actually provide closure for some of them . . . us." I didn't want to lay it on too thick, but I needed to make it personal.

She reached across the desk and patted my hand. "I'm very sorry. I didn't really think about it from that angle."

I sniffed and bit the inside of my cheek to bring a tear to my eyes. It worked.

She opened a drawer and pulled out a box of tissue and slid the box toward me.

I pulled two tissues from the box and dabbed at my eyes. "Thank you."

"I guess there's no harm in giving you the names and contact information for the people who were on the bus." She tapped the keys of her computer.

After a few seconds, the printer on the file cabinet behind her came alive and spit out several sheets of paper.

When it finished, she reached around and collected the sheets. She glanced at them and then folded them and handed them to me.

"Thank you."

"No, thank you for thinking of this. I'm afraid I've only been thinking about the paperwork from our corporate office and filling out the insurance paperwork. I hadn't really thought about it from the people side." She shook her head. "I'm sure Mrs. Starczewski must be really upset."

"She is. Irma really liked Max Franck a lot."

She scooted her chair back in preparation of rising. "I wish I'd gotten to know him better."

"Did you?"

She looked puzzled.

"Did you know him?"

She shook her head. "No, not really. I only met him that day on the bus for the first time."

126

Something about the way she avoided eye contact made me think there might be more to it than Caroline Fenton was letting on. I waited, allowing the silence to work its magic. Eventually, she gave in to the pressure of silence.

"Well, I wouldn't say I *knew* him. I knew *of* him, of course. I was born and raised in Chicago." She picked at an invisible piece of lint on her sleeve. "You couldn't grow up in Chicago without hearing of the great, renowned Max Franck." Her tone implied she thought Max Franck anything but great.

I waited silently and worked to make my face appear as sympathetic as possible, but the inside of my cheek was pretty sore and I wasn't sure the expression was working. What I hoped was a sympathetic smile felt like a lopsided grimace. Nevertheless, she must have felt some type of compassion because she caved in.

"I don't know why I'm hesitating." She sighed. "It'll probably come out anyway." She looked at me. "I didn't know Max Franck, not personally, but I knew who he was." She swiveled around in her chair so she could look out of the window, which had a view of Lake Michigan. "Max Franck was a mean, vicious, cruel man — a crusader."

"That's different from what I've read about him." I tried to hide the shock on my face. "Everything I've read indicated he was a highly thought of journalist who dedicated his life to exposing government corruption."

She snorted. "That's what the newspapers said. The great Max Franck, investigative journalist intent on uncovering corruption at all costs." She took a deep breath. "Even if it cost a man's life."

"What man?"

"My father. Max Franck killed him. He killed my father."

CHAPTER 7

I was dazed by her response and sat gaping for several seconds. I pulled myself together and asked, "How? What?"

She sat still for so long, I thought she wouldn't answer the question. However, eventually, she took a deep breath and gazed out the window as though watching a movie. "My father was a good man. He was kind and gentle and loved his family." She swallowed hard and paused. "He worked hard . . . so hard. He was a cop. He worked the southside of town. He was loyal and he never took a bribe. He believed in doing everything by the book." Tears streamed down her face.

"So, what happened?" I asked softly.

She swiveled her chair around and pulled tissues from the box she'd offered me earlier. "Twenty-two years on the force and he never had one black mark against him. His one fault was his loyalty. His boss, Chief

Roland Waters . . . Uncle Rolly, I called him." She scoffed. "Chief Waters was on the take. When Max Franck's story first broke, my dad wouldn't believe it . . . he couldn't believe it. He'd known Roland Waters for years. They started on the force together." She returned her gaze to the window. "Uncle Rolly's career skyrocketed and he was promoted rapidly. My dad wasn't jealous." She looked earnestly at me. "He was glad, happy for his friend. He believed him to be a good man and Chief Waters promised to always take care of my dad." She snorted. "He looked out for him all right."

"What happened?"

"Max Franck went undercover. He found the information he needed and he approached my dad for corroboration, but my dad refused." She turned and held her hands out. "How could he corroborate? He hadn't known. He believed his friend was honorable, but Max Franck wouldn't believe him. When the story broke, he painted my dad and anyone who supported the chief with the same brush of corruption." She bowed her head. "It crushed my dad. He was investigated by internal affairs and cleared of any wrongdoing, but the court of public opinion wasn't so forgiving. People who had been his friend and looked up to him, treated him like dirt and it broke my dad." She cried in silence for several moments. Eventually, she wiped her eyes and pulled herself together. "Something died in him after that. So, when the doctors diagnosed him with cancer, he just gave up. He refused treatment and refused to fight. He died within six months of the diagnosis. My mom died a month later." She sniffed. "So, Max Franck took both of my parents from me."

"Your father died of cancer," I said softly. "Surely, you can't —"

"I can't what? Blame Max Franck? But I do. I do blame him. My dad used to be strong. He was a fighter. The cancer wasn't advanced. It hadn't spread. With surgery and chemo, he could have beaten it, but he didn't have the will to fight after Max Franck destroyed his life. I had to move to this two-bit town to escape the scandal while the mighty Max Franck was exalted as a champion of justice . . . a man of the people." She pushed her chair back, hopped up, and paced around her small office like a tiger in a cage.

"Did you confront him?"

She took several short trips back and forth across the room before she stopped and folded her arms across her chest. "I waited

for everyone to leave the bus. Velma Levington was asleep in the back, as was that
woman . . . Rosemary."

"Rosemary?"

She waved her hand. "The woman in the
floppy hat."

I nodded and made a mental note to write
Rosemary beside the floppy-hatted woman
on my list. "Were those the only two people
who stayed on the bus?"

She paused in her pacing. Then she
shrugged. "I think so. Those two and his
bodyguard."

"Bodyguard?"

She sighed. "The big guy with the sunglasses. You couldn't miss him."

I nodded. So, Sidney Sherman was Max
Franck's bodyguard. Another mental note
to see what I could find out about him.

Caroline Fenton seemed anxious to finish
her tale now that she'd started. "He finally
got off the bus to smoke a cigarette." She
laughed. "A cigarette, can you believe it?
My dad died of lung cancer and this idiot
was smoking a cigarette with no ill-effects."
She shook her head at the irony. "Anyway,
he got off and lit his cigarette. That's when
I confronted him. I told him exactly what I
thought of him and how I held him personally responsible for the death of my parents."

"What did he say?"

She huffed. "Nothing. The cretin just stood there puffing on his cigarette. When I was done, he flicked his cigarette away and turned and got back on the bus." She was breathing heavily with anger. "Can you believe it? He just turned his back on me as though none of it mattered." She paced, her steps filled with anger. "I was furious."

"What did you do?"

"Do? I didn't do anything. I was too angry to do anything." She looked away. "I walked around the parking lot to give myself time to cool off." Her eyes blazed and she snarled. "But I wish I'd been the one to kill him. I wish I'd had a gun and could have shot him dead right there." She stopped and turned away toward the window. "I'd have slept well knowing I'd performed that community service."

I left Caroline Fenton steaming in her office and went in search of my grandmother. One glance at my watch told me Nana Jo's jujitsu class was over. I found her, Ruby Mae, Dorothy, and Irma waiting for me in the living room.

"There you are, Sam. We were just talking about whether we should stay here for lunch or go out." Nana Jo tilted her head. "Are you okay?"

133

"Sure. I'm thinking maybe we should stay here for lunch and talk to a few more people." I looked around at the girls. "Unless you're all finished?"

"Lawd, no. I still have a few more people on my list," Ruby Mae said.

The others nodded.

"Good. I need to talk to Gaston about catering the memorial too, so maybe we should eat here and push our meeting back to dinner."

Everyone agreed.

"Great." Nana Jo fanned herself. "I, for one, need a shower. That jujitsu class wore me out."

"I know a better way to work up a sweat." Irma glanced at a white-haired gentleman who walked down the hall. "I'm going to track down Melvin Cooper. That man has buns of steel. You could bounce a penny off his a—"

"Irma!" we all shouted.

Irma burst into a coughing fit. "Sorry." She fumbled in her purse for her flask and took a swig and returned the flask to her bag. She made a few adjustments to her blouse, patted her beehive hairpiece into place, plastered a smile on her face, and then waved. "Melvin." She stood up and pushed her chest out and glided in the direction of her prey, like a lioness about to pounce on a gazelle.

"Looks like Irma's back to normal." Dorothy smiled.

"Heaven help us," Nana Jo said.

Nana Jo went to her villa to shower. Dorothy and Ruby Mae spotted others on their lists to question and managed a seemingly random encounter.

I headed in the direction of the dining room in search of Gaston Renoir, Shady Acres' chef. A graduate of France's Le Cordon Bleu, he relocated to Michigan and found his way to the kitchens of Shady Acres. His love of cooking prevented him from merely sitting back and enjoying retirement. Instead, he had negotiated a reduced rate for staying at the retirement village in exchange for the opportunity to do what he enjoyed most, sharing his love of food and cooking skills with the residents. Prior to Gaston's arrival, the meals provided at Shady Acres were okay, but they were certainly nothing to write home about. Since his arrival, his wonderful meals were the subject of conversations not only with Shady Acres but in the surrounding community. He'd won an award in a local competition, and I knew, from my connections with Frank, he'd been approached by local restaurants seeking to coerce him out of retirement.

Finding the chef proved relatively easy. I merely followed my nose to the kitchen where the smell of a lemon garlic roasted chicken was making my stomach growl and my mouth salivate.

The kitchen at Shady Acres was an industrial space with lots of stainless steel. It was busy but exceptionally clean. Several young people manned various workstations and Gaston moved effortlessly from one station to the other, tasting, stirring, chopping, and throwing out instructions.

"Ah . . . the beautiful Samantha." Gaston hurried to my side and kissed both of my cheeks. "What an honor it is to see you. What can I do for you?" He smiled broadly.

Gaston Renoir was a man who was happy, confident, and flirtatious. "Aw . . . where is that nice man of yours? If I were a couple of years younger, I might try to steal you away from him."

I giggled. "You're a terrible flirt, you know that."

"What is the fun in life if a man cannot eat what he wants, drink wine, and flirt with a beautiful woman." He shook his head. "He might as well be dead." He laughed.

"You have a lot more people working back

here now." I looked at the younger people who rushed around the kitchen.

"*Oui.* I am now an instructor." He puffed out his chest. "You must call me Professor Gaston now." He laughed. "The Hospitality Program at MISU, they contact me. They ask if I will consider teaching at the school."

"Wow. That's impressive."

He smiled. "I say, NO. I can't possibly leave my kitchen here. But, if you want to send your students to me, then I will teach them here." He spread his arms out wide. "And, what do you think? They say yes. So, now I have students who come here to learn from me." He proudly patted himself on the chest. Then he turned to me. "But you did not come here to listen to me talk. No, you come here to eat, yes?"

I laughed. "No. I came to ask a favor."

He hurried to the stove and dipped a spoon into a sauce one of the students was stirring. He rushed over to me and held it out. "You taste and give me your opinion."

I tasted the sauce, which was creamy and delicious. "Hmm that's yummy. What is it?"

"Ah . . . that I cannot tell. It is a secret. I don't even tell my students all of my secrets." He laughed. "However, you will have it tonight if you dine here."

"I'm definitely planning to dine here."

He clapped his hands. *"Magnifique."* He leaned close and smiled. "Now, what favor do you need? If it is at all in my power, you will have."

I smiled. "I think this will be an easy one." I explained about the memorial service for Max Franck.

"Ah. I heard of the death. Although I did not go on the trip to Chicago, I heard of this. I will be honored to cook."

We discussed a few simple foods, which he assured me he would be happy to provide. I promised to confirm once I'd checked with Caroline Fenton and left.

As luck would have it, when I left the kitchen, I spotted another one of my assignments sitting in the dining room looking out of the window, Sarah Jane Howard.

Sarah Jane Howard was a big woman. She wasn't fat but was what my mom called, "big boned." Her features were big and whenever I saw her, I was reminded of the lines from *Little Red Riding Hood* when Red says, "Oh, Grandmother, what big ears . . . eyes . . . hands . . . and teeth you have." Sarah Jane Howard was big and when she smiled, I knew what poor little Red must have felt when faced by the talking wolf dressed up to look like her grandmother. Nevertheless, there was a murder to solve, so I took a deep breath, stood tall, and prepared myself.

"Samantha, what a pleasure to see you." She smiled big and flashed her large teeth at me.

"Hello, Mrs. Howard."

"Why don't you call me Sarah Jane. Everyone else does." She smiled again. I tried to focus on some part of her face that wasn't big and didn't remind me of a wolf ready to pounce, but her nose was also big and rather bulbous on the end. I focused instead on the mole on her chin. It was big too but didn't seem the least bit threatening.

"How are you today?" I sat down across from her and smiled.

"I'm doing rather poorly today, I'm afraid." She preceded to tell me about her racing pulse, blood pressure, heart fluctuations, and bowel disorder that completely turned my stomach.

"I'm sorry to hear you're unwell."

"Thank you, dear, but I suppose every day above ground is a blessing."

I nodded to the mole. "You're right. Things could always be worse, like that poor man who died on the bus."

That intro was all it took to divert her attention away from her personal maladies so she could talk about Max Franck.

"Dear me. I was so shocked to have something like that happen and see that poor man dead on the bus. It practically rattled my insides and, I tell you, my digestion hasn't been the same since."

Clearly, I was wrong about diverting Sarah Jane Howard away from her digestive issues and was forced to listen to several more minutes of the complaints that occurred because of the death. When she slowed talking long enough for me to interject, I tried again. "The death was definitely a distressing ordeal. Did you by any chance know Max Franck?"

She reluctantly shook her head. "No. I'd never met him before. But I had heard he was famous."

"He was a famous journalist and author."

She shook her head. "I wish I'd had time to talk to him."

"I don't suppose you noticed anyone who did talk to him?"

"Well, funny you should mention that." She leaned closer and smiled her big smile. "I returned to the bus a little early because I'd forgotten my gloves and it was bitterly cold outside and those winds are terrible for my rheumatism."

I prayed silently the story of her rheumatism was a short one. Thankfully, she merely spent two minutes describing the pain.

"Now, where was I?"

"You returned early to the bus."

"Yes, that's right. As I got there, I saw that man . . . Max . . . arguing with a woman."

My heart sank and I tried not to let my disappointment show. "That must have been Caroline Fenton. She had words with —"

"No, dear, not Caroline. I know her. It was another woman."

I stared. "Do you remember who?"

"I didn't recognize the woman. She had a large floppy hat on, and I couldn't see her face." She shook her head in disappointment. "I don't think I knew her anyway. She wasn't from the Harbor." She sniffed.

I sat up eagerly. "I don't suppose you remember what they were arguing about?"

Sarah Jane Howard smiled slyly. "Well, I'm not one to eavesdrop on conversations that don't concern me, mind you." She looked at me with the most serious expression.

I stifled a desire to laugh. "No, of course not."

"However, they were arguing and I just thought it was unseemly and perhaps I should stand nearby in case the gentleman

141

got rough and the lady might need assistance." She opened her big eyes even larger.

"What a wonderful idea." I made a mental note to add lying through my teeth to the list of things I needed to seek forgiveness for when I said my nightly prayers. "You never can tell these days."

"My thoughts exactly." She leaned even closer. "That woman called him a good many names that nearly curled my hair, I can tell you."

I'll bet they did. "Shocking."

"It was indeed. I'm a woman of a delicate constitution, and I wasn't raised to use such language." She fanned herself. "Then she said she'd never asked him for anything in her whole life and wouldn't be asking now if it wasn't a matter of life and death, but there was nothing she wouldn't do for Isabelle."

"Really?"

She nodded vigorously.

"What happened next?"

Her expression changed to one of disappointment. "That's when the man, Max, noticed me standing near the bus and called me a busy old broad and accused me of deliberately listening in on his conversation."

"The nerve of the man." I managed to avoid laughing by digging my nails into my palms.

She nodded. "My thoughts exactly. Why, I was just minding my own business and they were the ones fighting in the streets like common hooligans."

I nodded my agreement.

"Did you tell the police about this?"

Sarah Jane Howard looked as though I had slapped her. "Of course not. I'm not one to gossip and I certainly was never raised to have *dealings* with the police, especially after the last time when that man was murdered here. Why, I had people call me a nosy busybody." She bristled. "I can tell you, I made up my mind then and there, that I would never get involved with the police again."

Apparently, Max had waved her off and she hadn't even been able to get on the bus and get her gloves, which she attributed to her current arthritic distress. She didn't have anything else of value to add and I managed to slip away with the excuse I needed to find my grandmother.

I walked away to find a quiet place to think. All the time, I wondered who the lady in the floppy hat really was and who was Isabelle? Could the floppy hat lady have actually threatened to kill Max Franck? Was it his death she was talking about? Or, was someone else in danger?

CHAPTER 8

My mind was reeling with all of the information I'd found and I needed to think. I sent Nana Jo a text message and learned she had just tracked down Velma Levington and would "corner her," her words, not mine, to get what she could out of her.

I walked the short distance to Nana Jo's villa and let myself inside. As much as I enjoyed Gaston's food, I needed a little quiet to sift through everything I'd heard.

At Nana Jo's, I found a can of vegetable soup in the cabinet. I heated it and made myself a peanut butter and jelly sandwich. Nana Jo's beverage selection was limited to alcohol, coffee, and Coke, but I found a shriveled-up lemon and made a glass of lemon ice water. One of the best features of Nana Jo's house was the unobstructed view she had of Lake Michigan. I put my food on a tray and sat in the sunroom at the back of the house where I could curl up on the window seat and eat and enjoy the view and think.

Before I could take my first spoonful of soup, my phone rang. When I glanced at the picture that popped up, I smiled. Lexi and Angelo stared back at me.

I quietly swiped the phone and smiled. "Hello, how are you doing?"

Lexi and Angelo were both excited and talked quickly and simultaneously, so it was hard to distinguish what they were saying, but it didn't really matter. The sound of their voices was far more important to me than the actual words being spoken. Both were happy and that was the important thing.

"You've met your cousins, already?"

Lexi and Angelo were orphaned when their parents were killed several years ago in a car accident while on a trip from New York to Chicago. Unfortunately, their relatives in Italy had no idea where the children were. Both were too young to remember their family roots extended to Italy, although they both spoke Italian. When the pair landed in Frank's restaurant, he'd used his connections to discover the history none of the governmental agencies had been able to find. The grandparents had been so excited when they learned the children were alive and well. They had immediately flown to the States. The plan was the grandparents would spend the week in the States getting reacquainted with them before taking them back to Italy after the new year. However, it appeared, the grandparents weren't the only ones who'd traveled to the United States. If Angelo was to be believed, he had lots of cousins who had flown over, and he was enjoying playing with them and teaching them English.

"That's great. I'm so excited for you both." I tried to keep the sadness out of my voice. It really was a wonderful thing that the pair would be reunited with family. Their foster family in Chicago had been horrible and I didn't relish the idea that they would ever have to see that couple again.

Our call was short. Both children merely wanted to say hello and it warmed my heart to hear their voices.

When we disconnected, I cried a bit and then pulled myself together and reheated my soup in the microwave.

After I ate, I sat on the window seat, looking out the window, and pulled my notepad out of my purse. I jotted down notes from my conversations with Caroline Fenton and Sarah Jane Howard, while they were still fresh in my mind. I tried to make sense of what I'd learned, but, after about twenty minutes of doodling, I gave up and decided to do something else to help organize my thoughts.

Writing British historic cozy mysteries had been a dream of mine for a long time. After my husband's death, I realized life was too short to keep dreams bottled up and had pursued not only our shared dream of opening a mystery bookstore but my dream of being a published author. Nana Jo was the one who first helped me realize that writing allowed my subconscious mind to sort through the details of what I was dealing with in real life. So, I decided a little writing might help me make sense of things.

Lady Elizabeth Marsh picked up the receiver of the telephone and had barely finished with her greeting before Desmond Tarkington interrupted.

"Lady Elizabeth, I hate to bother you at this late hour, but as you can imagine, the tragic accident that has led to the death of my beloved cousin has left me bereft."

Lady Elizabeth struggled to keep the irritation out of her voice. "I'm very sorry to hear that, but I hardly see how I —"

"I've heard from Mrs. Sanderson, how incredibly helpful your ladyship was during the last hours of her life. I was hoping you might be able to provide some comfort during our time of mourning and would consider a trip to Battersley Manor." He paused briefly before hurrying on. "Or I would be more than happy to make a trip to Wickfield Lodge, if that would be more convenient."

She was silent for several moments. "Actually, I promised Eleanor I'd stop by Battersley, and I like to keep my word. So, if it's convenient, I'd prefer to come there."

Desmond Tarkington was ecstatic to entertain her ladyship and spent several minutes thanking her for her kindness, generosity, and compassion to condescend to visit his humble abode.

Lady Elizabeth confirmed the plan to visit Battersley Manor the next day and hung up the phone. She paused for a brief moment before entering the library. She searched for a few moments until she found the book she wanted and then pulled it down from the shelf. It was a favorite by Jane Austen, *Pride and Prejudice.* Lady Elizabeth flipped through the pages of the much-read novel until she found the passage she wanted. She smiled to herself while she read.

Lord William watched his wife in silence. When she was done, he asked, "What could that Desmond Tarkington fellow possibly want at this time of night that would draw you to Jane Austen?"

Lady Elizabeth returned to her seat and picked up her knitting. "He called to invite me to Battersley Manor."

Lord William stared at his wife in shocked silence for a moment before blustering. "You can't be serious. What nerve. I hope you sent him away with a flea in his ear."

Lady Elizabeth smiled. "Actually, I accepted his invitation."

Shocked speechless, Lord William stared at his wife in disbelief. "You can't go . . . why . . . this is ridiculous. I won't stand for it." He slapped his leg, which was propped on the footstool, causing the duke to clench his jaw in pain.

"I'll be fine, dear. No need to worry. I shan't go alone, and I certainly won't be staying in that house. I looked up Battersley Manor, and it's very close to Dinsmore." She stared at her husband. "You remember Dinsmore is where Lady Alistair goes to take the waters. I think I'll ask her to accompany me." She stopped knitting and thought for a moment. "Maybe I'll even take Clara with me."

"Disgusting odor." He frowned.

"I know the mineral baths do have a rather potent odor, but many people swear by them."

Lord William was familiar enough with his

wife to realize when she'd made up her mind. "Well, it's clear you can't go unaccompanied. I'll just have to go with you."

Lady Elizabeth smiled fondly at her husband. "Don't be ridiculous, dear. You can't possibly travel with your gout."

"Maybe I'll take the waters," he blustered.

"Excellent idea. We can ask Thompkins to come and bring a chair to wheel you to the baths." She smiled at her husband.

Lord William muttered and folded his arms.

Lady Elizabeth smiled fondly at her husband. She knew her husband would rather have his leg amputated before he would allow himself to be wheeled around.

Lord William started to protest but was stopped when Lady Elizabeth said, "However, I may ask Detective Inspector Covington to join us. I'm sure even policemen must be able to take a holiday sometimes." She knitted while smiling.

"If you're going to do this, maybe you can at least humor me and tell me what that young man could possibly have said to you that caused you to consult *Pride and Prejudice*?"

Lady Elizabeth smiled. "Nothing, really. I just thought I recognized some of the flowery language used by Desmond Tarkington as belonging to Mr. Collins."

Lord William gaped at his wife. "Mr. Collins?"

151

Lady Elizabeth nodded. "Yes, I think Mr. Desmond Tarkington must be, like Mr. Collins, one of the stupidest men in England."

CHAPTER 9

"Sam," Nana Jo yelled in my ear.

I nearly jumped out of my skin. "My God." I placed my hand over my heart in an attempt to slow its rapid pace. "I didn't hear you come in."

"I gathered as much." Nana Jo smiled. "Especially since I've been calling you for a good five minutes."

I felt confident Nana Jo was exaggerating, but I was still unnerved from the scare she'd given me, so I didn't take the time to argue.

"We're picking up the girls in front of the main building in fifteen minutes." She stood over me. "You better shake a leg."

I took my dirty dishes into the kitchen and prepared to wash them when Nana Jo stood over my shoulder. "What're you doing?"

I wondered if this was a trick question. "I'm washing my dishes."

"I know that." She swatted my arm. "Why are you washing dishes when I have a

153

machine built for that exact task." She waved a Vanna White hand in front of the dishwasher and then opened the door.

"It's just a couple of things. It hardly seems worth it to run a full load and waste water for these few items."

Nana Jo grabbed the items and loaded them into the dishwasher. "I don't have to waste water. I just load the dishes and when the dishwasher is full, I turn it on."

There were already a few items in the dishwasher, so I shrugged and packed up my notebook.

I walked to the car and drove to the front and picked up the others, who were waiting in the lobby.

"Where to?" I glanced in the rearview mirror as I pulled away from the building and headed toward the gate.

"I've got a taste for seafood. Let's go to The Catch," Nana Jo said.

There were no disagreements, so I headed toward downtown. The Daily Catch was the restaurant's real name, but locals always shortened it to "The Catch." It had good food and a 1970s-themed décor, which was somewhat off-putting to tourists until they tasted the food. It was located on the inlet where the St. Thomas River met Lake Michigan. Inside, if you looked in one direction, you saw the boats docked on the river. If you looked in the other direction, you had an excellent view of the beach and the Lake Michigan shoreline. The restaurant needed an update. However, every time I went, I was glad it hadn't been done. I loved the retro style.

I let my passengers out at the door and parked. Timing was everything, and I lucked into a parking space near the door. Inside, I saw Nana Jo and the girls seated near the window that faced the river. The booths were large, with high-backed wooden seats that resembled church pews. The seat backs were so tall, it was impossible to see people behind you, but conversations could easily be overheard if you weren't careful. During my last visit, I left with bruises from banging my head and elbow on the wood benches while trying to eavesdrop on someone I suspected might have been a murderer.

One of The Catch's signature attractions was their handmade onion rings, which they brought out on a large spindle. Nana Jo usually ordered two spindles whenever we came. So, when the waiter came, I just ordered an ice water with lemon.

Once I was settled, Nana Jo pulled out her iPad. "Now, I know we all collected a lot of information so we better get started."

I raised my hand and relayed the information I learned from Caroline Fenton, along with the information from Sarah Jane Howard.

Nana Jo took notes. "Do you think the woman Sarah Jane saw arguing with Max was the same woman we saw him arguing with in the bookstore?"

I shrugged. "I have no idea. Part of me thinks it has to be the same woman. How many different women could he have ticked off in one day?"

Nana Jo smiled. "At this rate, that list could be fairly long."

Ruby Mae raised her hand to go next. "I didn't learn much from any of the people from Shady Acres who were on my list." She pulled out the knitting she was rarely without. Tonight, she was knitting a pink baby blanket for one of her countless relatives. Ruby Mae Stevenson was my favorite of all of Nana Jo's friends. In her mid-sixties, she was also one of the youngest. Ruby Mae was an African American woman with dark skin that reminded me of coffee with a touch of cream. She had salt-and-pepper hair that she wore pulled back at the nape of her neck in a bun. Nana Jo said when she let her hair down, it reached down so far, she could sit on it, but I'd never seen it down. Ruby Mae was born in Alabama and had a soft Southern accent. Her story was an interesting one. She moved to Chicago in the early sixties to live with her older sister when both of her parents were killed in one of the civil rights marches. She had just graduated from high school. She met and married a plumber who walked out and left her to raise their nine children single-handed. Ruby Mae cleaned houses to feed, clothe, and educate her children. She was proud of the fact that all nine of them had graduated from college and were very successful. While I knew she was proud of all of them, I suspected her youngest daughter held a special place in her heart as she had started her own cleaning business. Ruby Mae was retired, but she had a host of grandchildren, nieces, nephews, and friends who always stopped to talk to her wherever we went. Tonight was no different. One of the cooks came over to the table and gave Ruby Mae a big hug. They chatted for a few minutes and Ruby Mae introduced him as her cousin's boy Carl. Carl greeted us and quickly hurried off to continue working. However, when several plates of appetizers showed up, which we didn't order, we knew Carl had been busy.

There were so many appetizers that we didn't bother to order entrees. Instead, we munched on seafood tacos, onion rings, crab cakes, crab stuffed mushrooms, calamari, and a few other items that looked and smelled delicious, but I was too full to try.

Ruby Mae put away her knitting while she ate, but when she was full, she wiped her hands and pulled out her knitting, which I suspected helped her think. She picked up the conversation right where she left off. "Like I said, I didn't get much out of the people on my list from Shady Acres. None of them saw or heard anything. But remember I told you my third cousin Darius worked at the *Chicago Sun-Times*." She knitted a row and updated the row counter on the end of her needles. "Darius knew exactly who Max Franck was. Apparently, the man was a legend around Chicago. We've already found out most of what Darius told me. He won a lot of awards and had written several books. But Darius found someone who knew Max personally and he found out he had a tumultuous relationship with his ex-wife and his daughter, Rosemary."

"Great. I sure hope he gave you a description of the girl."

She shook her head. "No, but he's going

to email me some articles from the newspaper, so if there's a description or picture of her in any of them, I'll send them to everyone."

We nodded.

"Apparently, Max Franck was so obsessed with his career, he neglected his family. His wife divorced him and moved out with their daughter." She looked over her glasses at us. "According to Darius, it took Max about six months before he even noticed."

"That's horrible," Irma said. "That dirty piece of sh—"

"Irma!" we all said.

Irma coughed.

When the commotion died down, Ruby Mae continued, "Well, recently, Rosemary reached out to someone at the newspaper, asking if they knew where her father was."

"How sad she had to ask someone," Dorothy said.

Ruby Mae nodded. "They didn't know but, apparently, she said her daughter has some rare disease and needs a bone marrow donation. Neither she nor her husband are matches."

"The poor little girl. Where's the mother, Max's ex-wife?" Nana Jo asked.

"Dead." Ruby Mae shook her head. "So, out of desperation, she was trying to track down her father to see if he would consent to be a donor." She pursed her lips. "Although, he seemed like the type who was too wrapped up in his own career to think about anyone else. The poor child." Ruby Mae shook her head.

We sat in stunned silence for several moments.

"Well, on that sad note, I might as well go next," Dorothy said. "I didn't have a lot of luck with my Shady Acres list either. However, I did get one bit of information from Earl."

Ruby Mae frowned. "Who's Earl?"

"Earl, the bus driver who drove us to Chicago." Dorothy fidgeted with her napkin.

"And how did you happen to run into Earl?" Nana Jo asked.

Dorothy blushed. "Well, Earl and I spent some quality time together one night in Chicago."

Nana Jo clucked her tongue but said nothing else.

"Anyway, I was curious what happened to him. He did have a family emergency. His brother's appendix burst and he had to be rushed to the hospital."

"Is he okay?" I asked.

"Fortunately, he is." Dorothy released a sigh of relief. "Anyway, he was in a real pickle about driving us home. So, they had to get someone at the last minute to fill in." She paused.

"Well, what's wrong with that?" Nana Jo looked up.

Dorothy smiled. "The problem was, they didn't have time to go through all of the new procedures the board put in place after the debacle with the former administrator, Denise Bennett. She hired him, but no one double-checked his background until after he got back. Turns out Bob, our replacement driver, is an ex-con."

"Good Lord. Did Denise Bennett hire anyone who wasn't a criminal?"

We all shrugged.

"What was he in jail for?" I asked.

Dorothy leaned forward. "Armed robbery and murder."

CHAPTER 10

Dorothy dropped that bombshell and everyone immediately started firing questions at her. She held up her hands to fend off the onslaught. "Hold on." She turned to each person and responded to the questions she'd heard asked. "I don't know who he murdered. I don't know how long he was in prison. Nor do I know why Shady Acres would hire a murderer to drive our bus." She took a deep breath and turned to Nana Jo. "I was hoping Josephine could get Freddie to look it up."

Nana Jo, normally anxious to volunteer Freddie to use his influence or his son's to get information, was abnormally quiet. "I'll try, but his son, Mark, had to take the family to his in-law's in upstate New York for the holidays."

I raised my hand. "I might be able to help."

Everyone turned to me.

"I forgot to mention it, but I stopped by the police station and talked to Detective Pitt."

"What's Stinky Pitt been up to?" Nana Jo asked.

"I think he's a bit bored." I told them about my conversation and our deal.

"Why, the lazy parasite," Nana Jo said. "He's going to sit back and let you solve another murder for him while he takes all of the credit."

I could feel my grandmother's blood pressure rising. "Hold on. Let's be fair. Technically, this isn't his murder. It didn't even happen in the state of Michigan."

Nana Jo reluctantly agreed.

"Plus, he's going to be providing us with information we probably couldn't get anywhere else." I stared at her. "Besides, the last thing I want is 'credit' for solving anything."

"Well, okay, if you're going to put it like that, then I take back what I said." Nana Jo huffed.

I pulled out my notepad and made a note to ask Detective Pitt about Bob the bus driver.

Nana Jo was the last to report. "I didn't find out a lot of information. Most of the people on my list were too busy answering

163

the call of nature and didn't go near the bus until it was time to board." She looked disgusted.

"Well, you can't blame them for that," I said.

"Pshaw." She snorted. "I certainly do blame them. People should be more interested in their surroundings and their fellow man."

I took a sip to avoid laughing.

"I didn't get much from Velma." Nana Jo sighed. "Actually, I didn't get anything from Velma."

Irma snorted.

"Did you say something?" Nana Jo turned to Irma.

Irma muttered something that sounded like "cheap manstealing witch," but she broke out in a coughing fit and I didn't want to aggravate her throat unnecessarily by asking her to repeat herself.

"I thought you went to the jujitsu class specifically so you could talk to her?" I asked.

"I did." Nana Jo raised her hands.

"Well, what happened?" I asked.

She shrugged. "I tried several times to partner with her, but she always had another partner before I could get to her. Then, when we had our break, I made sure I was right beside her and I tried to strike up a conversation, but the woman is deaf as a doormat. She couldn't hear one single word I said. When class ended, she rushed out of that room so fast, I nearly got whiplash from watching her."

"Harrumph." Irma grunted. "There's nothing wrong with that woman's hearing. She's got ears like a bat."

Nana Jo looked skeptical.

"I'll bet if a single man whispered his telephone number in the middle of gale force winds, she'd catch every digit." Irma folded her arms and glared.

Ruby Mae grinned.

"Sounds like someone else we know," Dorothy joked.

Nana Jo narrowed her eyes and stared at Irma. "Are you sure?"

Irma nodded. "I promise you. There's nothing wrong with Velma's hearing." She used her finger to cross her heart and then confirmed her pledge by holding up three fingers in the Girl Scouts' salute.

"I guess I'm going to have to work harder to corner Velma." Nana Jo looked thoughtful.

I recognized that look and felt a momentary pang of pity for Velma. My grandmother was taking this as a challenge and

165

Josephine Thomas was a competitive woman who didn't like losing; even if the loss was only in her mind. I suspected Nana Jo's next encounter would end very differently than the last one.

We chatted a bit, and then I drove back to Shady Acres. Irma wanted to go to a bar to have a drink to memorialize Max, or so she said, but I suspected that was merely an excuse to party a bit. However, maybe I was being uncharitable. We vetoed Irma's request and I drove them back to Shady Acres.

I pulled up to the main building as usual and let the girls out, which was expected, but my surprise came when Nana Jo got out.

"Are you staying at your place tonight?"

"I'm going to corner that Velma Levington if it kills me." She stared at me. "Do you need my help at the bookstore?"

I shook my head. "No. Zaq and Christopher have everything under control."

She nodded, then looked closely into my eyes. "Are you sure you don't need my help?"

"I'll be fine. I'll probably talk to Stinky Pitt and see what I can find out. I'll see you at the meeting tomorrow night."

We had agreed to skip our noon meeting

and meet for dinner instead. Shady Acres was preparing for the big New Year's Eve party and everyone was signed up to help. They were going to use that as another opportunity to collect information.

Nana Jo accepted my response, and we parted with me promising to call if I needed her.

As I pulled away, I got a call from Frank. One of the things I loved about my new-to-me Ford Escape was Bluetooth, which enabled me to talk without holding my phone.

"Hey, beautiful."

I smiled even though he couldn't see me. "Hey, yourself."

"I'm thinking about taking a day off tomorrow and wondered if I could cash in that rain check you gave me."

"Time off during the day? I don't think you've done that since I met you." I laughed.

"I think I'm getting burned out working such long hours. I took Nana Jo's advice and hired an assistant."

I laughed. "Nana Jo was joking, but I think it's great. I knew you were looking for someone, but I didn't know you'd finally found someone you could trust."

"It wasn't easy, but actually, an old buddy of mine from my military days reached out and mentioned he was looking for a new start. He's a Catholic priest but needs a break, so . . . he's looking for someplace quiet where he can think."

Frank didn't talk much about his time in the military, and I knew better than to ask too many questions. However, I hoped I'd have an opportunity to meet his friend. "So, you're starting him tomorrow?"

He laughed. "No. I wouldn't do that to him. The mornings are pretty light, so I hoped I could spend a little time with you and then I'd work the evening shift. He'll be at the restaurant tomorrow, but just as an observer."

"Sounds great." I got an idea. "Hey, how do you feel about a quick trip to Chicago? There are a few people I need to talk to."

"I can't believe it. You're finally going to let me go sleuthing with you?" he joked.

"Well, usually I have Nana Jo with me, so you'll have some big shoes to fill."

"I'll do my best to live up to the high standard your grandmother has set." He laughed. "Actually, if you don't mind making a few extra stops, that would work out great. There's a restaurant distributor in Chicago and I could pick up a few things." He hesitated. "That is, if it's okay with you?"

"Of course."

168

We talked a bit more about tomorrow. By the time we hung up, I had made it home.

I took care of Snickers's and Oreo's immediate needs, which included a potty break and treats, and then I went upstairs.

I checked my email and was pleasantly surprised and a bit terrified to see an email from my agent, Pamela Porter, at Big Apple Literary Agency. For some reason, whenever I opened emails from her, my heart raced. I took a deep breath and clicked open.

The email was an update letting me know she'd just heard from one of the editors she'd sent a query about my manuscript. He requested a full. I met my agent briefly when I was in New York after Thanksgiving and received a crash course in the lingo. She'd explained a query was a high-level pitch about my book. If an editor was interested, they might request to read a partial, a specific number of pages or chapters, or a full, which was a request to read the entire manuscript. She cautioned me that this was a good thing but not to get too excited. He may still reject the manuscript and the timing was horrible because most of the publishers were closed for the holidays. However, she told me to remain "cautiously optimistic."

"Cautiously optimistic?" I picked up

Snickers. "She has got to be joking." I spun around in a circle and did a happy dance. Oreo pawed at my leg, but he wasn't nearly as good a dancer as Snickers. Nevertheless, I picked him up and did a two-dog happy dance. As soon as I stopped, he leapt out of my arms and gave himself a shake.

Snickers clung to my shirt for dear life. When she was sure I'd stopped spinning, she gave my face a lick.

I put her down and went back to my laptop. "My first full." I couldn't stop smiling, and knew I was too excited to sleep now. I said a silent prayer he, whoever he was, would like my manuscript and decided to spend a few hours in the British countryside. Maybe a few hours with Lady Elizabeth Marsh would help me make sense of Max Franck's murder.

"Aunt Elizabeth!" Lady Clara Trewellen-Harper ran to her cousin and engulfed her in a warm embrace.

Lady Clara was tall, slim, and stately. She had light brown curly hair, intelligent eyes, and a quick smile.

Lady Elizabeth smiled. Her cousin Mildred's daughter had always called Lady Elizabeth, Aunt Elizabeth. She'd grown up with Daphne and Penelope and picked up the habit from them. Lady Elizabeth hadn't minded and the familiar moniker had continued into adulthood.

She embraced her cousin warmly. "Hello, Clara. I'm so glad you were able to come."

"Wild horses couldn't have prevented me from joining in on the fun."

Lady Elizabeth withdrew from her young cousin and smiled broadly. "Detective Inspector Covington. Thank you so much for coming."

The detective inspector stepped forward and tipped his hat. "I had holiday time to use by year's end, so it worked out well." He smiled. "Plus, I like to keep an eye on things."

Lady Elizabeth turned to her cousin. "Clara, dear. I want you to meet a good friend of mine." She smiled warmly. "This is Detective Inspector Covington." She turned to the detective. "This is my cousin Lady Clara Trewellan-Harper."

Lady Clara's eyes widened and she smiled warmly at the detective. "A real policeman. How delicious."

Detective Inspector Covington smiled, tipped his hat, and bowed slightly. A careful observer would note the detective's eyes held a sparkle and a slight blush rose up his neck.

Lady Elizabeth was just such a careful observer.

"Please call me Clara." Lady Clara extended

171

her hand to the detective.

The detective inspector shook her hand but said nothing.

After an awkward moment of silence, Lady Elizabeth turned to her cousin. "Do you have luggage?"

Lady Clara turned and noted a porter struggling with several large pieces of luggage. "There's the porter now."

Lady Elizabeth smiled and led the small party through the small Dinsmore rail station and outside to the curb, where a car waited. Standing stiffly beside a Rolls-Royce Wraith was Thompkins, the Marsh family butler. He opened the rear car door.

Lady Clara smiled at the butler as she folded herself into the back. "Thompkins, I didn't know you were coming on this adventure too."

The butler bowed. "Lady Clara."

Lady Elizabeth instructed the porter to load the luggage into the boot of the car. She then turned to the detective inspector. "You're able to drive this beast, right?" She extended a set of keys.

Detective Inspector Covington looked stunned but nodded as he tossed his small duffle next to the driver's seat and accepted the keys. "Yes, m'lady."

"Thank heavens. I don't think Thompkins's nerves can handle much more of my driving."

172

She scooted into the back seat next to her cousin.

Once all the luggage was loaded, Thompkins tipped the porter and got into the front passenger seat of the car.

Detective Inspector Covington started the car and took one moment to caress the wood dashboard, then he turned to the back. "Where to?"

Lady Elizabeth pulled a notepad out of her purse and read. "I intended to stay at Dinsmore Inn, but as it turns out, Lady Alistair keeps a cottage here." She glanced at the notes. "Hapsmere Grange." She looked up. "She's graciously invited us to stay with her." She passed the directions up to the detective, who read them, put the car in gear, and pulled away from the curb.

The drive to Lady Alistair's cottage was short, only two miles from the train station. Despite the diminutive name of "cottage," Hapsmere Grange was a seven-bedroom, three-storied mansion spanning over ten thousand square feet on fifty acres of land.

When the car pulled up to the front, Lady Alistair Browning opened the front door and came outside to greet her guests.

Lady Alistair Browning was a tall, slender woman with piercing blue eyes and unnaturally blonde hair. She was always fastidiously dressed. Today she wore an elegant, and undoubtedly expensive, navy-blue, fur-trimmed suit with a matching cloche hat. The outfit was tubular with a drop waist. By her side was her companion, a Chihuahua named Bitsy.

Thompkins hopped out of the car as soon as the motor stopped and opened the back door to assist Lady Elizabeth and Lady Clara out of the car.

Detective Inspector Covington stared at the large estate and whistled.

The women embraced and headed toward the door. Lady Alistair turned to Detective Inspector Covington. "Nice to see you again, Detective Inspector."

Detective Inspector Covington tipped his hat. "Lady Alistair." He followed slowly behind, allowing Bakerton, Lady Alistair's stately but elderly butler to take his bag.

Lady Clara walked slowly behind the older ladies, allowing Detective Inspector Covington to catch up to her. "I do hope you're going to be reasonable and at least talk to me."

Detective Inspector Covington blushed. "Of course, your ladyship. What would you like to talk about?"

Lady Clara giggled. "Why murder. What else?" She stopped and grabbed the detective inspector by the arm. "I intend to be a world-famous writer some day and this could be just the thing for me to write about. Everyone loves a good murder."

Detective Inspector Covington smiled. "Hardly a proper topic for a lady to write about."

She huffed. "I can see you're going to be tiresome about that title." She dropped his arm and hurried ahead.

Standing at the top of the steps, talking, were Lady Elizabeth and Lady Alistair. They chatted while inconspicuously glancing at the younger people.

Lady Clara flounced through the door. Moments later, Detective Inspector Covington followed, nodding to the ladies as he entered the house.

Helene, Lady Alistair Browning, was the mother of James FitzAndrew Browning, the 15th duke of Kingfordshire and recently married husband of Lady Elizabeth's niece, Daphne. The women had known each other a long time, but the courtship and wedding had reconnected the women. Lady Alistair gave her friend a meaningful look.

Lady Elizabeth smiled. "Give them time."

CHAPTER 11

I woke up next morning with my head lying on my keyboard. I panicked for a moment, afraid I'd lost my manuscript. Thankfully, the document was still there, but there were 819 pages of gibberish where my chin rested on the keyboard. I deleted the excess pages and saved again to be safe.

I looked at the time. I had about thirty minutes until the time Frank and I had arranged to meet. Strapped for time, I hurried the poodles downstairs and put them out. It was chilly, but they were wearing sweaters and I knew Christopher and Zaq would be here shortly. So, I left them out while I showered. By the time I was out of the shower, I heard them barking and knew the twins had let them inside.

I still felt guilty about falling asleep on our date and considered putting on a skirt until I checked the weather app and saw it was eight degrees in Chicago. Instead, I put on jeans and a warm sweater. I took extra care with my hair and makeup. You could catch pneumonia trying to look cute in the winter in the Midwest.

When I emerged from my bedroom, Frank was having coffee with Nana Jo at the breakfast bar.

He winked. "Good morning, gorgeous."

"Good morning, handsome."

Nana Jo rolled her eyes. "Good grief. Let's not start that again." She sipped her coffee. "I can feel my blood sugar rising."

"Speaking of sugar." I turned to Frank. "Did you remember to bring the cake?"

Frank helped me on with my coat. "Yes. It's in the car."

"Cake?" Nana Jo looked up with a hopeful expression.

"Sorry. It's spoken for, but Dawson left some cookie dough in the freezer." I turned to leave.

"Wait." I turned back around at the stairs. "What are you doing here? I thought you were staying at Shady Acres to talk to suspects?"

She sipped her coffee. "When I got home, I remembered I had arranged to meet Elliott this morning. Your place is closer to MISU's library."

Elliott was a research librarian and one of

Nana Jo's old beaus. He still held a torch for her, even though Nana Jo had moved on.

I wished her well and hurried downstairs.

Frank navigated the Chicago traffic like a pro. About halfway there he asked, "Where to first?"

"Well, there's this mystery bookstore I'd love to visit. Then we can hit the restaurant supply store."

Frank smiled. "Let me guess. It's the mystery bookstore your grandmother pulled you out of the last time you were here."

I smiled. "Right the first time."

Frank navigated city traffic much easier than our taxi driver and dropped me off around the corner from the Murder Between the Pages bookstore. He drove around in search of a parking space.

Inside, the building was warm and the smell of books and freshly brewed coffee greeted me like an old friend. I stopped and inhaled the familiar aroma as my gaze traveled around the store. The mystery lover in me admired the colorful stocked shelves and something deep inside my soul rejoiced at seeing the shelves full of tales of mayhem and suspense. I smiled. The bookstore owner inside me couldn't stop myself from looking critically at the dusty shelves, dimmed lighting, and waterstained roof. However, the allure of books overpowered the bookstore owner and I got lost.

"Can I help you find anything?"

I nearly jumped out of my skin. "Dear God, you scared me." I was miles away in an Irish cottage following Alexia Gordon's enchanting sleuth, Gethsemane Brown, through the twists and turns of solving a murder.

"I didn't mean to frighten you." Linda Herald, the bookstore owner I met on my first visit, apologized.

When my heart stopped racing, I smiled and reassured her I was fine.

"Samantha, right?"

"You have a great memory."

"Not really. It's just that I don't meet many mystery bookstore owners." She smiled. "Anything in particular you're looking for?"

I shrugged. "I'm just browsing." I looked around. "You have a lovely shop and I may steal some of your ideas."

She laughed. "Feel free. I've probably stolen them from someone else."

"Do you remember a man and a woman having an argument in your loft the last time I was here? They got quite heated."

179

"Pity. That must have been Max Franck and his daughter, Rosemary."

"You know them?" I tried to hide my surprise.

She nodded. "Max Franck is a bestselling crime writer. He's done several book signings here."

I leaned closer. "You know he was killed?"

She nodded. "I saw it in the newspaper. I think he expected something like that. Well, maybe not murder, but he must have expected some type of trouble."

"What makes you say that?"

"Why else would he have hired a bodyguard?" She shrugged. "You must have seen him. He was here at the same time Max and Rosemary were arguing. The big guy with the mirror sunglasses."

"I saw him. He was pretty hard to miss."

She gave a half shrug and adjusted some books on a nearby shelf. "Actually, I think his agent or editor hired him, but I thought it was all just a big hoax."

I must have looked as puzzled as I felt because she colored slightly and shrugged. "Max was here for his last book signing about a week ago. His editor made a big deal about Max's next book." She stuck out her chest and puffed up her cheeks. " 'This next book is going to blow the lid off the theories about who killed Robert Kennedy.' " Linda tilted her head and gave a cocky chuckle. " 'Max is in so much danger. I'm concerned for his safety. I've gone so far as to hire a professional bodyguard to protect him.' "

I stared for a few seconds and then realized my mouth was open and closed it.

She nodded. "That's the same expression I had."

"You didn't believe him?"

She thought for a moment and then shook her head. "Honestly, I didn't believe him. At the time, I remember thinking it was a gimmick to get publicity and increase book sales." She sighed. "I mean, if you wanted to hire a bodyguard, why hire someone so . . . I don't know . . . so . . . ."

"Obvious," I volunteered.

"Exactly. I mean, he was so big and those mirrored sunglasses were over the top." She paused. "I guess maybe he was right. Maybe it wasn't just hype."

"Max was here a week ago?"

"Christmas Eve." She hurried to the counter and came back with a brochure. "This is the brochure advertising the book signing."

I quickly read over the brochure. "May I keep this?"

181

"Of course. They'll just go in the trash now."

"So, if Max was here Christmas Eve, why was he back the day I saw him here?"

"He said he forgot something," she said hesitantly.

"He said? You didn't find anything?"

She shrugged. "Only the brochures. I offered to mail whatever it was to him, but he wanted to get it himself."

"Did he say what it was?"

She shook her head. "No, but when he came in, he went up to the loft area." She pointed to the area where I'd seen Max on the day he died.

"Why was he arguing with his daughter? Rosemary is his daughter, isn't she?"

She nodded.

Someone entered the store and she excused herself to go and check on her customer. However, they must not have needed assistance because she returned quickly. "Sorry about that."

"No need to apologize. Customers come first."

"Where were we?" She was silent for a moment. "Rosemary. I think he must have arranged to meet her here because she came not long after he arrived."

"Do you know why they were arguing?"

She shook her head. "Honestly, I wasn't paying attention."

We chatted a little longer, but her customer selected a book and was waiting at the counter.

Frank had entered the store while Linda and I were talking but had maintained a discrete distance. I found him glancing through a thriller near the back of the store.

"Find something you like?"

He grinned and the look he gave me made the heat come up my neck.

I giggled. "I'm talking about the book."

He returned it to the shelf. "I like to patronize my local mystery bookstore." He leaned close and whispered, "I'm kind of sweet on the owner."

I grinned. "I hear she's kind of sweet on you too."

I waved at Linda Herald as we left the store.

Frank had found a great parking space a block away and we were quickly on our way to the restaurant supply store.

Similar to the way I could spend hours in a bookstore, Frank could spend hours looking at ginormous pots, pans, and commercial bakeware. I wandered around while he picked out the items he wanted. Surprisingly, we were on our way in less than an hour.

Back hatch fully loaded, Frank got into the car and turned to me. "Where to now?"

I pulled out the list Caroline Fenton gave me with the names and addresses of the bus passengers. I looked for Rosemary Lindley's name and saw she lived in Lake Forest. I went to college in Evanston, Illinois, so I was familiar with many of the suburbs and recognized the city as one of the more exclusive areas where a lot of professional athletes bought large homes. "Rosemary Lindley is Max Franck's daughter." I glanced down the sheet.

"How are you going to question her?"

I smiled. "That's why I asked you to bring your delicious sour cream cake."

He chuckled. "I should have known you weren't planning snacks for us to enjoy."

"If we run into traffic like we did the last time I left Chicago, we might have to dig into that cake and pick up some flowers for the grieving daughter," I joked.

Traffic cooperated and we made it to Rosemary Lindley's home midmorning.

As I suspected, the suburb was north of Chicago, not far from the northern border of the state. The street was called Lake Road, and we got a glimpse of Lake Michigan through the trees as we drove.

Frank pulled his car in front of the address his GPS indicated was our final destination, and we sat outside and admired the architecture. Rosemary Lindley lived in what I could only describe as a large brick mansion. The homes on this street were all massive and set on enormous lots well away from the street. Mature trees shaded the yards and, combined with the lush landscaping, created an atmosphere that screamed wealth. Unlike Chicago and the immediate suburbs, where houses were conjoined to each other or so close together you could stand between them, extend your arms and touch them, these homes were much farther apart. The lawns were vast and landscaped to provide maximum privacy from prying eyes, while providing the owners with plenty of elbow room.

Rosemary Lindley's house had a semicircular drive with brick pavers that looked wider than the interstate we'd just exited. The front façade had three arches, which welcomed invited guests and intimidated the uninvited.

I wasn't easily awed by ostentatious demonstrations of wealth, but this house was impressive. I was grateful Frank drove. His Porsche fit perfectly with the neighborhood whereas my Ford Escape would have been a red flag to the neighbors that we didn't belong and to call the police.

He whistled. "Looks like Max Franck's daughter did pretty well for herself."

I stared at the brick and stone mansion for a few seconds and then took a deep breath and opened my door. "Let's do this before I lose my nerve." For a half second, I wondered about the many ways money could intimidate but decided it would only work if I allowed it to.

We got out of the car and Frank handed me the cake he had brought. Together, we walked through the middle archway to the large, double front door. Once there, I quickly rang the doorbell before my nerves came back.

I expected a butler or maid to answer but was pleasantly surprised when a woman, who was obviously the homeowner, answered.

"May I help you?"

"My name's Samantha Washington and this" — I pointed to Frank — "is Frank Patterson. We were acquainted with your father and —"

"If you're friends of my father, you can just go to hades, where I'm sure you'll no doubt run into him." She stepped back and prepared to push the door closed but was halted as Frank put out a hand and stopped the door.

She flushed from her angry outburst and, like the steam in a teakettle, looked as though she was revved up for an explosion.

I quickly collected my wits. "Mrs. Lindley, I didn't say I was friends with your father. In fact, I barely knew him. However, I was acquainted with him and I wanted to provide my condolences to you and your family." I extended my peace offering. "I hope you'll accept this cake." I turned to Frank. "Frank Patterson is an excellent chef and owns a small restaurant in North Harbor, Michigan." I thrust the cake into her hands. "Or, if you prefer not to eat it, maybe you would give it to someone else at a hospital or nursing home rather than let it go to waste." I nodded to Frank and turned to leave.

We were down the stairs before she spoke.

"Wait. Please. I'm so sorry."

We turned around.

"Please, I'm sorry. Won't you come inside?"

Frank looked at me. I shrugged and we returned to the door.

She stepped aside and we entered.

If I thought the house was impressive on

the outside, the inside was even more so. We entered the two-story foyer with black and white marble tile floors and a chandelier overhead. There was an elegant curved staircase that led upstairs and, to the right, a curved doorway led to a wood-paneled room that looked like a study. I would have loved to explore the library but followed my host to the left to a formal living room.

The first home that Leon and I bought would have fit in that one room. The room was furnished with traditional sofas, chairs, and dark wood tables. A marble fireplace was centered in the middle of one of the walls, with doorways on either side. The back end of the room had a curved window and built-in window seat that looked out onto the backyard, pool, and, through the distance, the faint blue of Lake Michigan.

As we were about to sit, a faint voice called, "Mom."

Mrs. Lindley paused. For a split second, she hesitated, but only for a split second. Her loyalties were clear. She handed me back my cake. "Excuse me." She hurried out of the back of the room.

Frank and I glanced at each other.

"I'm going after her." I passed the cake to him and hurried after Mrs. Lindley, straining my ears to hear conversation. The house was so large; I was afraid I'd get lost. I went through a massive kitchen, which would have made Frank drool with envy, before I heard two voices.

I peeked into a long, narrow sunroom on the back of the house. The room had one wall of windows and French doors that led outside. The floor was blue and white tile, and the décor continued the theme with blue-and-white striped sofas and comfortable chairs. Sitting on one of the sofas, covered in blankets, was a small, thin little waif of a girl with large, dark eyes. She looked very pale and frail.

The girl was connected to several machines. One provided a drip that went into her arm. Oxygen tubes went into her nose.

Mrs. Lindley adjusted one of the machines, which was beeping, and had her back to me.

The girl looked up and caught sight of me. I backed up and turned to leave.

"No, please."

I turned and saw the girl smiling at me.

"Please. I don't get much company."

I smiled and took a few steps into the room. I hesitated and looked to Mrs. Lindley. "I'm sorry. I didn't mean to intrude. I . . . I was just really curious about your beautiful house and I let my curiosity take

189

control over my manners."

Mrs. Lindley shrugged. "It's okay."

I decided to take that as an invitation to stay and walked over toward the girl and smiled. "Hello. My name is Samantha but everyone calls me Sam."

She smiled. "I like that. My name's Isabelle, but everyone calls me Isabelle." She giggled. "I wish I had a nickname." She glanced at Mrs. Lindley, who was replacing one of the fluid bags. "Why don't I have a nickname, Mom?"

Mrs. Lindley glanced lovingly at the girl. "Don't you like your name? Isabelle was your grandmother's name." She placed the bag onto the hook and stood. "Every time I say your name, it reminds me of her." She gently caressed the young girl's cheek.

"That's okay, then. I don't mind not having a nickname." She leaned back against her cushions. "Can you stay a bit and talk to me?"

"I'd love to." I looked at Mrs. Lindley.

She nodded.

I smiled and moved to one of the comfortable chairs and sat down. "Great." I looked at Isabelle and, for a moment, I was unable to think of anything to say. After spending more than two decades as a high school English teacher, I usually felt very comfortable talking to young people. However, this little girl with the big eyes had me dumbstruck.

She smiled at me again. "Are you friends with my mom? Have we met before?"

"No. Actually, I've just met your mom." I started to tell her I came to give my condolences but didn't know if hearing her grandfather was dead would upset her. I hurriedly shut my mouth.

Mrs. Lindley must have sensed what I was thinking because she relieved my mind by stating, "Samantha came to tell me how sorry she was about your grandfather." She swallowed hard. "She even brought a yummy cake."

Isabelle's eyes got even larger and a huge smile illuminated her face. "CAKE." She clapped her hands.

Frank stuck his head around the corner. "Did I hear someone say cake?" He held up his cake.

I looked to Mrs. Lindley, and she smiled and nodded.

"Why don't I take that and bring us some tea." She reached out her hands and Frank handed over the cake.

"This is my . . . friend Frank."

Frank smiled and bowed to Isabelle.

She giggled.

He looked around and noticed a chess-board in the corner. "Do you play chess?"

Isabelle nodded vigorously. "I love chess, but my mom doesn't play and my dad isn't here." She looked sadly at the chessboard. "My granddad played, but he's in heaven with my grandmother now. So, I don't have anyone to play with."

Frank smiled and went to the corner, picked up the chessboard, and brought it to the table next to Isabelle. "Well, you do now." He sat down and smiled. "Black or white?"

"White."

He spun the board around so the black pieces were in front of him. Then he removed his jacket.

The two of them talked quietly and were quickly engulfed in a game I never learned to appreciate. After watching for a few moments, I removed my jacket and went in search of our somewhat-reluctant hostess.

I followed the clinking of dishes and the familiar sounds of water filling a teakettle back to the kitchen.

Mrs. Lindley opened multiple cabinets as she searched for the items she needed to fill the large tea cart on the granite counter.

The kitchen would have made a commercial chef like Frank extremely happy.

While I was no expert, I recognized the distinctive red knobs that adorned the massive eight-burner stainless steel gas stoves. There were two of them. Glancing around the kitchen, I noticed there were also two refrigerators and an incredible amount of cabinets.

A large island was situated in the center of the space, and I pulled out a barstool and perched on one of the stools. "Your house is beautiful, Mrs. Lindley."

She continued collecting coffee mugs. "Please, call me Rosemary."

"Thank you, Rosemary. I hope you'll call me Sam."

She put the kettle on the stove and turned to face me. "I'm very sorry for the way I behaved earlier." She leaned against the cabinet. "My father and I didn't have a very good relationship, but that's no reason for me to take out my anger on you."

"No apologies necessary." I thought for a brief moment. "I didn't know your father. I only met him a few days before he died. However, he was very friendly with one of my grandmother's friends . . . with my friend Irma." I smiled. "She was the reason he was on the bus to North Harbor. They were going to . . . spend some time together."

Rosemary laughed. "You don't have to sugarcoat it. I know my dad fancied himself as a Don Juan. It's the reason he and my mother divorced." She smiled. "My mom called him a tomcat."

I smiled. "My students would have called him *a playah.*"

She laughed for a long time. "I haven't laughed in a very long time." She sighed. "I find it hard to think of my dad as anything as hip as that, but I suppose the label fits."

The kettle whistled and she turned off the stove and filled a teapot. "Would you or . . . Frank, prefer coffee?"

I shook my head. "Tea's fine." I hesitated. "We're planning a bit of a memorial for your dad at Shady Acres. We're hoping it will help Irma and some of the other people who were on the bus get some closure." I took a deep breath. "I was hoping you might have seen or heard something that might help."

She tilted her head and stared. "Help how?"

"Help figure out who might have wanted to murder your dad."

She laughed. "That list would be way too long."

I was silent for a moment. "Well, maybe you noticed something that seemed . . . odd.

194

It might be able to lead the police to the killer."

She turned away and fidgeted with the cups on the tray. She took the kettle from the stove and started to fill the cups.

On a whim, I asked, "Why were you arguing with your dad at Murder Between the Pages, and why were you on the bus?"

Her hand pouring the water into the teapot faltered and she spilled water onto the counter, but she quickly recovered.

I hopped off the barstool and got a paper towel and helped to clean up.

"How did you know about the bookstore?"

"My grandmother and I were there."

She sighed. "I called him to talk . . . about Isabelle." She swallowed hard and paused. "He said he couldn't meet me because he was going out of town on this bus trip and needed to pick up something from the bookstore. I thought I could talk to him . . . reason with him." She stopped. "Plead with him, but it didn't do any good."

"Why did you need to plead with him?"

"Isabelle is sick. She has aplastic anemia."

I must have looked puzzled because she sighed. "I recognize that look. Most people have never heard of it. Basically, her body doesn't produce enough red blood cells." She paused. "She needs a bone marrow transplant." She looked at me. "That's why I was arguing with my dad. Neither my husband nor I are matches. I pleaded with him to get tested." She sniffed. "For Isabelle's sake."

"He wouldn't?"

She shook her head. "At first he said he would, but he never did." She rolled her eyes and slammed the kettle on the stove. "He was too busy. Too busy? Can you imagine? He was too busy to take a quick test that might possibly save his granddaughter's life." She cried.

For a brief moment, I looked on in disbelief. Then, I collected my wits, walked over, and hugged Rosemary Lindley. Initially, she stood very stiffly, but, after a few seconds, her shoulders shook and she sobbed. We stood that way for several minutes while she cried. Eventually, she pushed away.

She walked to the sink, turned on the faucet, and splashed water on her face.

When she turned the water off, I handed her a paper towel.

"Thank you." She wiped her face. "I'm sorry. It's been a while since I've cried like that. I didn't think I had any tears left."

We heard laughter from the sunroom and she smiled. "We better get this tea into our chess masters before it gets cold."

She picked up the tray and carried it through the entry toward the sunroom at the back of the house, and I followed.

At the entry to the sunroom, Rosemary paused. We stood for a moment and listened. Isabelle was laughing.

"Wait. How did you do that?" Frank asked.

Isabelle laughed. "It's called winning."

The two laughed.

"It's been a long time since I've heard her laugh like that," Rosemary whispered.

"It's not too much excitement for her, is it? Maybe we should go."

She shook her head. "No. It's not too much." She whispered, " 'A merry heart doeth good like a medicine.' "

"Proverbs, seventeenth chapter, twenty-second verse." I released a heavy sigh. "That was one of my husband's favorite scriptures."

She tilted her head toward the sunroom.

I shook my head. "No, my husband, Leon, died of cancer." I pointed toward the sunroom. "Frank is a new . . . friend." I smiled.

She nodded knowingly. "You're a lucky woman." She walked into the sunroom.

I thought for a few moments and smiled. It was true. I was a lucky woman. I followed her into the room.

We stayed another hour talking, eating cake, and laughing. Frank requested and was granted a replay, which he also lost.

Isabelle yawned and we made our exit.

Rosemary walked us to the door, where she thanked us, profusely. "It's been a long time since I've seen Isabelle that happy. Thank you."

Frank looked confused. "No thanks necessary. I enjoyed myself."

Rosemary's eyes and her body language reflected an internal conflict. One second, she looked as though she wanted to talk, but then a few seconds later, like she had changed her mind. I was curious how the battle would end. Eventually, she took a deep breath and blurted out, "You asked if I saw anything unusual on the bus."

"Yes." I didn't want to seem too eager, but I sure hoped she was going to tell me she saw someone murdering her father.

"I did notice something."

"Anything that seemed odd to you might be important." I gave her my most encouraging smile.

"It's just that when I walked down the aisle to my seat, I noticed his face and something struck me as odd." She pondered for a moment and eventually shook her head. "It was an impression more than anything. I felt like he saw someone he recognized."

I waited, but that was all she said. She shrugged and shook her head. "I know it's probably nothing, and I almost —"

"No, I'm glad you mentioned it."

She sighed. "It was probably me." She laughed. "I thought I was so clever in that floppy hat with the big glasses, but I guess he saw right through me."

She was probably right, but I didn't want to discourage her. "Well, if you remember anything else, please call me." I gave her one of the business cards my nephew Christopher had created for Market Street Mysteries, and we made our exit.

It didn't take long to get back on the interstate. We drove a few miles in silence before Frank added, "That little girl is a chess shark."

I laughed. "You're going to have to learn to lose gracefully."

He grumbled, "Easy for you to say."

Our last stop was to the address listed for Sidney Sherman. When Frank pulled up to the address, it was a small commercial storefront on the south side of town. The lights were out and the building had bars across the windows and doors. It was obvious it was closed, so we quickly moved on.

I filled Frank in on my conversation with Rosemary Lindley. He listened quietly.

"Sounds like Max Franck was a real piece of work."

I was glad he'd come to the same conclusion I had. "I know. It seems so bizarre. I mean, I didn't know him long, but he didn't seem like a jerk."

He smiled. "Sometimes it's not easy to tell how big of a jerk someone is until they say or do something . . . or, in this case, fail to do something important."

Despite the cake and tea we'd eaten, we were both hungry and decided to stop for a late lunch in Michigan City, Indiana.

Senior Kelly's was a Mexican/Irish pub. Neither ethnic group was authentic, but the margaritas were large and the atmosphere was always festive. Just as we finished eating, I got a call from Nana Jo.

"Sam, you better get back here."

"What's happened?"

"Someone just tried to kill Irma."

CHAPTER 12

A few probing questions revealed that Irma had taken a tumble down a flight of steps. I tactfully questioned whether Irma's tumble down the stairs could have been an accident. After all, she did wear six-inch hooker heels on a daily basis, and it was possible she merely tripped.

Nana Jo's response was that Irma'd been wearing stilettos for more years than I'd been alive and she would fill me in more when I got back.

I relayed the conversation to Frank and we quickly left and headed back. During the short ride from Michigan City, Indiana, to North Harbor, Michigan, we discussed the latest developments.

"Do you think someone really tried to kill Irma?" he asked.

"I don't know why they would. It seems so far-fetched." I shook my head. "If anyone other than Nana Jo told me someone tried to kill Irma, I wouldn't have believed it, but . . ."

"Your grandmother is usually a very reliable source." Frank turned into Shady Acres.

One glance at the parking lot sent my heart racing. There were at least four fire trucks, two police cars, and several ambulances. I gasped.

Frank reached over and gave my hand a squeeze. Then he navigated around the vehicles and pulled up as close to the curb near the door to the lobby as he could and let me out.

I hurried inside. The scene in the lobby was pure chaos. Irma was strapped onto a gurney in the lobby. Dorothy and Ruby Mae were shouting orders at the emergency technicians. Caroline Fenton looked as though she'd been crying. If she'd had a run-in with my grandmother, then she probably had. There was a crowd of residents gawking nearby. I recognized Sarah Jane Howard, who seemed as though she was trying desperately to get Nana Jo's attention. However, Nana Jo and Velma Levington had Bob the bus driver in a choke hold. Sidney Sherman was arguing with Detective Pitt, and the decibel level was unreal. Everyone was shouting.

I stood for a few seconds and watched in openmouthed wonder.

Frank whispered in my ear, "What's going on here?"

I shook my head. "I have no idea, but I'm going to find out." I reached into my purse and pulled out a whistle Nana Jo had given me when we went to New York for Thanksgiving. My grandmother was amazed to learn I had never learned to whistle, so she'd picked up a police whistle to help me hail a taxi.

I gave the whistle a long blow, which produced an eardrum-bursting sound that stunned the crowds into silence and had the desired effect of stopping the commotion.

"What on earth is going on here?" I asked.

Unfortunately, everyone started talking at once and I was forced to give the whistle another toot. "One at a time."

Nana Jo started. "Velma and I caught the murderer when he tried to kill Irma."

"I didn't kill anyone," Bob croaked, and squirmed under the pressure applied around his neck by the two women.

Irma moaned from the gurney. "Someone pushed me." She pointed her finger at Bob. "Why'd you do it? Why'd you kill poor Max?" She burst into tears, and Ruby Mae handed her a handkerchief.

Frank walked over to the EMTs and had a quick word and then they moved forward and wheeled Irma out of the building.

Dorothy and Ruby Mae followed hot on their tails. "We're going too."

I turned to Detective Pitt.

He stared at me. "Don't look at me. I just got here."

I tilted my head and narrowed my eyes and gave him a look that said, *aren't you going to take control?*

A tall, handsome African American man dressed in full firefighter gear came up and whispered something to Detective Pitt.

I recognized the man as the North Harbor Fire Chief. Something in the way he glanced around the lobby made me wonder if he was another of Ruby Mae's relatives. After a few moments, he motioned for the other firefighters to leave and gave the all-clear for the residents to go back to their rooms.

Larry Barlow, the security guard, helped usher the residents, many of whom were wearing lightweight clothing and slippers, which explained a bit of the chaos. It was too cold to go outside without proper winter wear, and, from my days dealing with fire drills as a teacher in the public schools, I was aware the firemen weren't going to allow anyone to return to their rooms for appropriate clothing.

Apparently, even Detective Pitt was constrained by the fire department. Only after the whispered conversation from the fire chief did he act. "All right, everyone is clear to return to your rooms. Clear the lobby." He glanced at Bob, still under the control of Nana Jo and Velma Levington. "Everyone except you." He motioned for one of the uniformed officers to take control of their prisoner. Then he looked around. His gaze landed on Caroline Fenton.

Caroline Fenton's eyes looked wild. She looked on the verge of collapse, and I hurried to her side just in time. She collapsed and would have crumpled to the ground if Frank hadn't been there.

Frank scooped the woman up and looked around for a place to take her.

"In here." I led him to her office.

He placed her on the small sofa.

Nana Jo and Velma followed us into the room.

Velma announced she'd been medically trained in the military and immediately sat down and checked her pupils. "She fainted." She turned to Frank. "Get a cold compress and a glass of water." She grabbed a pillow and propped it under her legs to elevate them.

Frank hurried out of the room. He was back so quickly with the items requested, I knew someone must have anticipated the orders and had them already prepared.

Velma put the compress on Caroline's forehead and gave her cheeks a light tap.

Caroline's eyes fluttered.

I glanced around at Nana Jo as she breathed a sigh of relief.

"Drink this." Velma reached behind her neck to help Caroline lift up enough to drink the water.

After a few sips, Caroline Fenton laid her head back against the cushions. "I'm sorry. It's just been such a crazy day, and I don't even remember if I ate anything."

"Well, that's the first thing we need to take care of." Nana Jo turned to Frank. "Would you ask Gaston to prepare some scrambled eggs and toast?"

Frank nodded and hurried out of the room.

I glanced at Detective Pitt, who looked a bit pale. I remembered how he panicked the last time a woman fainted and had to turn away to keep him from seeing the twitch of my lips as I struggled to keep from smiling. Once I had control of my face, I turned back around. "Detective Pitt, is it true that he tried to kill Irma." I pointed at Bob, who was handcuffed.

The prisoner struggled. "I didn't try to kill anyone."

Nana Jo looked as though she would wring the bus driver's neck. She took a step in his direction. "Maybe I should have walloped you a bit harder to help jar your memory."

I stepped in front of my grandmother.

"That's enough of that." Detective Pitt pulled a notepad out of his pocket. "The district attorney frowns on prisoners coming in bruised."

I detected the first glimpse of humor in the detective's eyes.

He sat behind the desk and looked from the handcuffed man to Nana Jo and then to Velma Levington. "Now, does someone want to tell me what happened?"

Nana Jo opened her mouth, but Velma Levington beat her to it. "He pushed her. I saw it."

Detective Pitt held up his hands to stop the flood of words. When he had quiet, he turned to Nana Jo. "Perhaps Mrs. Thomas can explain what happened."

Nana Jo nodded. "We were upstairs. I was . . . hoping to talk to Velma about what she saw on the bus." Nana Jo blushed and I knew there was more behind her words, but I'd ask her about it later. "I had just approached her when we heard Irma scream. Her apartment is down the hall from Velma's."

"Was that when he pushed her?" Detective Pitt asked.

"I never pushed anyone. I swear, I —"

Detective Pitt held up a hand. "Allegedly pushed."

"No. Actually, that happened later. I rushed down the hall when I heard Irma scream." Nana Jo scowled at Bob. "Someone had broken into her room and ransacked it."

"What?" Detective Pitt stood up. "No one mentioned there had been a break-in."

"In all of the commotion, we forgot," Nana Jo said.

Detective Pitt walked over to the door and yanked it open. "Cooper."

The uniformed policeman who'd handcuffed Bob hurried to the door. Detective Pitt whispered something to him and he nodded and hurried off.

Detective Pitt closed the door and returned to his seat. "You amateurs have probably trampled all over the evidence," he mumbled.

Nana Jo narrowed her eyes. "We didn't touch anything." She took a deep breath. "Every dodo knows better than to interfere with a crime scene."

Detective Pitt muttered, "Dodo is about right."

The look in Nana Jo's eyes made me reach out a hand to prevent my grandmother from throttling a policeman.

Detective Pitt must have sensed his life was in danger because he thankfully stopped the insults. "Now, anything else *important* you want to tell me."

Nana Jo cleared her throat. "As I was saying, Irma's apartment had been ransacked. Just as we were *about to enter,* the fire alarm went off."

"The fire department should be able to tell us which alarm was pulled," Detective Pitt said.

"Yes, they can do that," Caroline Fenton mumbled from the sofa. "Plus, Larry can check the security cameras."

Detective Pitt made notes. "I'll get Cooper on that as soon as he finishes with the break-in."

Bob started to speak and Detective Pitt added, "Alleged break-in." He looked at Nana Jo.

"When did the attempted murder occur?"

She sighed. "A crowd gathered in the hallway after Irma screamed. So, it was a bit chaotic. When we heard the alarm, we all headed for the stairs." She glanced at Caroline Fenton. "The elevators don't work when the fire alarm goes off."

"It's the law," Caroline Fenton said.

There was a knock at the door.

Detective Pitt tapped his pen in frustration. "Enter."

Frank returned with a Styrofoam container, which smelled delicious. He walked over to Caroline Fenton, who was sitting up on the sofa now.

She thanked him and took the container. She opened the lid. Gaston had outdone himself. Inside was an omelet, toast, and a few slices of fruit. She tucked into the food.

Detective Pitt glanced in her direction with a bit of envy. Perhaps he was remembering the delicious breakfast he'd had when he investigated a murder here previously. However, he sighed and quickly returned to the task at hand. "What happened after the alarm went off?"

Nana Jo shrugged. "We all hurried to the stairs. We were just headed down the stairwell when Irma went careening down the stairs." She glared at Bob.

"Did you see him push her?" Detective

Pitt asked.

Nana Jo paused. "No, but Velma did." She turned to Velma Levington, who was standing quietly in a corner.

"That's right. I was standing very close to Irma and I saw his hand extended toward her back. That's when I reached out and grabbed his arm," Velma Levington said.

"I reached out to catch her. I saw the lady flying down the stairs, and I reached out my hand to catch her. That's when these crazy old bats tackled me." Bob tilted his head to indicate Nana Jo and Velma.

Detective Pitt wrote in his notepad. "So, you saw him actually reach out his hand and push Mrs. Starczewski down the steps?"

"Well . . ." Nana Jo stammered. "I didn't see it, but Velma did. She was a lot closer to Irma than I was."

"Yes. I saw him. He reached out his arm and shoved her in the back," Velma Levington said with confidence. "And furthermore, I'm sure he must have been the one who killed Max Franck. I fell asleep on the bus and was one of the last ones to get off when we stopped. When I did, I saw him standing over Max Franck. He jumped when he saw me."

"You're crazy." Bob tried to stand. "It's a setup. I didn't kill anyone."

211

"Well, we know that's not true," Nana Jo said. "You went to jail for murder."

"WHAT?" Detective Pitt smacked his notepad down on the desk.

I explained what Dorothy had found out from her friend Earl.

Detective Pitt looked from me to Nana Jo to Caroline Fenton. "Why didn't someone tell us sooner?"

"I didn't hire him." Caroline Fenton swallowed hard. "That was my predecessor's doing, Denise Bennett."

Detective Pitt groaned. "Not her again."

"I was going to tell you when we met," I whispered.

He scowled at me and then turned to Bob.

The blood drained from Bob's face, and he sat still for a second. "I was set up before and now it's happening all over again."

"It's always a setup with you people." Detective Pitt leaned across the desk. "Everyone is innocent. You never killed anyone."

"Wait." Bob shook his head. "It's not like that." He scooted to the edge of his seat. "I was young and stupid. I fell in with the wrong crowd and when they suggested we rob a bank, I agreed." His voice shook. He paused for a moment. "No one was supposed to get hurt. We were just going to take the money and get out."

"But, that's not what happened, is it?" Detective Pitt added sarcastically.

Bob shook his head. "No. There were four of us. Lenny drove the get-away car. Jack and Carl were brothers." He shook his head. "Carl was the brains. He planned the entire thing." He sighed. "Carl and I were supposed to burst in and wave our guns around. Jack was supposed to get the money."

I looked at the pitiful creature in the chair. His eyes filled with tears. "One of the tellers pushed the silent alarm, and Jack flew into a rage. He pistol-whipped her." He looked at me. "He hit an old woman." He swallowed hard. "I was in shock. I couldn't move. That's when Carl started yelling. 'Get out! We gotta get outta here,' but I couldn't move. The security guard reached for his gun and Jack raised his arm. He pointed his weapon. He was gonna shoot him."

"What did you do?" I asked.

He shook his head. "I couldn't let him shoot that man. I saw the look in his eyes, and I knew he was going to shoot." He lowered his head. "I don't even remember raising my gun. I just remember the sound it made."

"You shot your partner?" Detective Pitt asked.

He nodded. The tears flowed down his face. "He was a hothead. He had a record and had been in and out of jail. He said he'd never go back inside. So, that's how I knew he'd kill them rather than go back to prison."

"You killed him?" I asked.

He nodded. "Carl and Lenny got away, but I just stood there. I couldn't move."

"So, you went to jail for murder?" Nana Jo asked.

He nodded.

"Doesn't sound like an innocent person getting set up to me. It sounds like cold-blooded murder." Detective Pitt scowled.

Bob sat in the chair and cried.

Detective Pitt closed his notebook. "I've heard enough." He walked over to the crying man. "Come on. I'm arresting you for the attempted murder of Irma Starczewski and suspicion of the murder of Max Franck." He grabbed him by the arm. "Let's go."

Bob's gaze traveled around the room like a trapped animal. "Please, I swear I didn't do it. Please." He gazed into my eyes. "Please. You have to believe me."

Detective Pitt led him out of the room, none too gently.

For a few moments, we all looked on in shock.

After a few seconds, Velma walked toward the door. "I'm glad they were able to catch that dangerous killer before he killed anyone else." She grabbed the doorknob and then walked out of the room.

Caroline Fenton swiveled her legs off the sofa and stood. "I've got a ton of paperwork to fill out. Today has been one crazy day, and we have that memorial service tomorrow." She moved over to her desk, and we all took the message and made our way out of her office.

Outside, Nana Jo turned to me. "What are you thinking?"

"I'm thinking something doesn't feel right."

She nodded. "I'm thinking the same thing."

Frank shook his head. "You two just feel sorry for him because he seemed remorseful, but Detective Pitt had no choice. There's a lot of evidence against him."

"What evidence?" Nana Jo asked.

Frank ticked off the answers. "He was seen on the bus standing over Max Franck. He was on the stairs when Irma fell. He was seen with his arm outstretched toward her just as she tumbled down the stairs."

215

"Circumstantial evidence," Nana Jo added.

Frank shrugged. "It may be circumstantial, but it may be enough to convict him." He paused. "Plus, he's a convicted murderer." He looked from me to Nana Jo. "He may just be a great actor. He may have turned on the tears to make himself seem innocent." He reached out a hand and rubbed my arm. "He might be playing on your emotions."

Nana Jo looked at me. "What do you think?"

I thought for a moment. "I think I believe him." Frank started to speak, and I hurriedly continued, "Look, I may be wrong. He may be a cold-blooded murderer, but something about this whole thing doesn't feel right."

Frank smiled. "Then let's get to work."

CHAPTER 13

Irma's tumble down the stairs wasn't nearly as bad as it could have been. Thankfully, she only had some bumps and bruises and a badly sprained ankle. However, the hospital decided to keep her overnight for observation.

Frank dropped Nana Jo at the hospital and then took me home. We were gone a lot longer than we originally planned. There was still a couple of hours before the bookstore closed, but traffic was light. I needed to distract my mind and had been missing time in the bookstore, so I let my nephews leave early and took over. It was wonderful to get back into the swing of things. I loved walking around my bookstore and helping customers, especially new customers, find just the right book, which I hoped would open their minds to the genre I loved.

During a lag in customer traffic, I reshelved books and couldn't help thinking about how much my life had changed since I opened Market Street Mysteries.

"Mrs. Washington."

I jumped at the unexpected intrusion into my dream world. "My goodness. You scared me." I turned around and saw a familiar face. "Taylor?"

"I can't believe you remembered my name." Taylor smiled.

"You're hard to forget." I smiled. "You have such a beautiful face."

She blushed.

I looked at the Goth goddess dressed in black from head to toe, with black lipstick, black fingernails, and hair dyed so deeply it looked purple under the lights. "Come for more Charlaine Harris?"

Taylor was a student at MISU and a member of a book club started by a couple of students, Jillian Clark, who was Dorothy's granddaughter and was dating my assistant Dawson, and Emma Lee, who was dating my nephew Zaq.

"I can always use more Charlaine Harris." She laughed. "But the main reason I came was to thank you."

I had just reached up to get the latest book in the Harper Connelly Mystery series, which had enough paranormal activity that I knew Taylor would love it, when her words sunk in. "Thank me? For what?"

She smiled. "You suggested I talk to my guidance counselor about combining my love of writing and video games with my dad's desire for me to become a computer programmer." She grinned so large and rocked on the balls of her feet.

"And?"

She squealed. "It's so awesome. There's this special course I can take and get a certificate and my guidance counselor actually knows one of the founders of Vamps." She waited expectantly, as though the name would mean something.

I shook my head. "Sorry. I've never heard of Vamps."

She jumped up and down. "Ohmygodohmygod. Vamps is *the* number one gaming company. They have the *best* graphics. I absolutely *love* their games." She took a deep breath and steadied herself. "It's just too amazing for words."

She was so excited; I was afraid she'd pass out. There'd been enough of that for one day, so, I suggested we go to the back of the store and sit down.

The store traffic was virtually nonexistent, and I knew the seat that would give me a clear view of anyone entering or leaving. We went to the back and I brought two cups of tea to a small bistro table. Dawson had prepared a host of goodies to keep the store stocked before he left. Today, my nephews had defrosted the dough for peanut butter cookies, Zaq's favorite. A few cookies had escaped the twins' notice, and I brought them over to the table.

By the time I sat down, Taylor had calmed down enough to tell me her news.

"My guidance counselor, Mr. Leonard, knows one of the guys who started Vamps. So, when he found out what I wanted to do, he called him." She started breathing heavily again.

I reached out a hand. "Breathe."

She stopped and took a deep breath. "Bottom line, he's going to give me a summer internship with the company."

"That's fantastic. How did your dad take it?"

She smiled. "At first, he thought I was crazy. He said, 'It's just a fad and it'll die out like the' " — she used air quotes — " 'dot com bubble.' " She puffed up her chest and tilted her head in a cocky manner. Then she laughed. "That was until he heard how much money I'm going to be making."

"I'm really happy for you, Taylor. I hope you have a great internship."

She spent a few minutes gushing about Vamps and how jealous her boyfriend was when he heard where she was going to be working.

When she finished, we chatted about books for a bit and then she selected and paid for some and left.

I couldn't help smiling as I closed the shop and tidied up. Taylor was a smart young girl, and I was glad she was having an opportunity to pursue her dream. Working with kids and seeing them achieve things they never knew they could was one of the things I missed about teaching. Seeing the excitement on Taylor's face filled a void I didn't know I had.

Christopher and Zaq had let the poodles outside before they left, but I took them down again. Snickers was old and took advantage of the opportunity to go potty every time it presented itself. Oreo took the opportunity to play in the snow until his underbelly and paws were cold. Then he tried to get back inside. However, I had learned to harden my heart against his sad poodle eyes and stood firm behind the closed door until he gave up, went to a nearby bush, and hiked his leg.

Mission accomplished, I opened the door and wiped the excess snow from him.

Thankfully, Oreo didn't hold a grudge and gave my hand a lick.

Upstairs, I wasn't hungry. The events from earlier today were tumbling around in my mind, and I needed a way to sort through everything.

So, I sat down and fired up my laptop.

Despite the massive size of the house, the drawing room of Hapsmere Grange was small. There was an oversized marble fireplace on one wall and a crystal chandelier that hung from the center of the coffered ceiling. There was also a large overstuffed sofa and several cushioned chairs — too many chairs.

Bakerton, the ancient butler who'd served the duke's family for decades, opened the double doors that led into the room and Thompkins pushed in a tea cart laden full of cakes, pastries, sandwiches, and tea.

Once the items were distributed, Bakerton and Thompkins turned to leave.

"Thompkins, I would appreciate it if you'd stay," Lady Elizabeth said.

Bakerton bowed and left while Thompkins, who was accustomed to her ladyship's odd requests, walked over to a corner and stood stiffly.

Lady Elizabeth knew Thompkins well

enough to know he would never sit in her presence, so she smiled and hurried on. "Now, I think we all know why we're here." She looked around.

Everyone nodded, although Detective Inspector Covington frowned. The tall, gangly man looked puzzled. "Well, your ladyship. To be completely honest, I know why I'm here." He looked around. "You think Mrs. Forsythe's death may have been murder rather than an accident."

Lady Elizabeth nodded.

"I'm a policeman, so it makes sense for me to be here. I get paid to investigate things like this." He leaned forward and scratched the back of his neck. "What doesn't make sense to me is why the rest of you are here."

Lady Clara huffed and made a very unladylike snort. "It's rather obvious why we're here." She leaned toward the detective inspector and glared. "We're here because your bloody lot didn't believe Aunt Elizabeth when she said she thought poor Mrs. Forsythe had been murdered. Now, she's here to find the evidence to prove that she was. She's doing the job you should have done in the first place."

Blood rushed to Detective Inspector Covington's cheeks and he looked like a teakettle about to blow.

Lady Elizabeth raised her hands and halted

the storm, which looked about to explode in the Hapsmere Grange drawing room. "That's not entirely true, dear." She turned to her cousin. "The police at the tube station were very kind and attentive; however, they have to work with facts."

Lady Clara snorted.

"Scotland Yard does a wonderful job and we've had the pleasure of working with Detective Inspector Covington several times in the past. He's always been very good about listening to our ideas." She turned to the young man. "There's absolutely no evidence that Mrs. Forsythe was murdered. Nothing, but a . . . feeling."

Lady Alistair reached across and squeezed her friend's hand. "Your feelings have been pretty accurate."

Detective Inspector Covington gave Lady Elizabeth a sheepish look. "Your feelings have been pretty bang on, and I'm sorry."

She smiled. "Thank you, Detective Inspector. That means a great deal coming from you." She paused for a moment. "However, the truth of the matter is, we don't have any proof whatsoever that Mrs. Forsythe didn't have an accident." She put down her teacup and picked up the knitting bag she'd set by her side. She took out a ball of pale yellow wool and a pair of knitting needles. "Mrs.

Forsythe might be exactly what Mrs. Sanderson accused her of being, a batty old dear."

"You don't believe that." Lady Clara stared at her cousin.

Lady Elizabeth knitted a few stiches and then smiled. "No. There was something about her that didn't seem like she'd lost her wits. No. In fact, I think she was quite clever." She knitted a few more stiches. "The way she managed to sneak away from the house when her cousin and his wife were out and how she slipped away from Mrs. Sanderson. That took some cunning."

"Okay, what do you want us to do?" Lady Clara asked eagerly.

Lady Elizabeth knitted. "We don't have much time. The cousin wants something." She paused. "I don't know what, but I intend to find out."

"What do you want the rest of us to do?" Lady Alistair asked.

"Well, I was hoping we could divide and conquer." She smiled. "I couldn't help but notice Mrs. Sanderson seemed a bit . . . awed by my title." She glanced at Lady Alistair. "I was hoping we could both tackle her."

Lady Alistair took a bite from her scone. "Shall I pull out one of my tiaras for the occasion?"

Lady Elizabeth smiled. "I don't think we'll

need to go to that extreme, but if you have your chauffeur, I think we could definitely borrow him." She looked from Detective Inspector Covington to her cousin. "Now, I have noticed that men are often more receptive to a pretty woman." She turned to Detective Inspector Covington. "While women are often more responsive to a handsome young man. I was hoping that you" — she looked at her cousin — "if the opportunity presented itself, could talk to Desmond Tarkington alone." She turned to the Scotland Yard detective. "While you could have a talk, informally of course, with his wife, Constance."

Detective Inspector Covington frowned. "I've noticed that murderers aren't usually very forthcoming with information when they find out I'm with Scotland Yard."

Lady Elizabeth smiled. "Exactly. Which is why I was hoping we could introduce you as a friend of the family." She looked slyly at her young cousin. "I hoped we could explain your presence as a close friend of Lady Clara."

The two young people glanced at each other and color rose up both of their necks. However, neither objected.

Lady Elizabeth turned to the butler. "Thompkins, I was hoping you might see what you could find out about Mrs. Forsythe's maid, Dora."

Thompkins bowed.

She smiled. "Mrs. Forsythe mentioned they'd had to cut back on expenses. I gathered they may not have many servants, so I was hopeful that tomorrow you would accompany us and . . . well, perhaps you could help find out what's going on below stairs."

Thompkins nodded stiffly.

Lady Elizabeth knitted. "I want to caution everyone to be very careful. If I'm right and Mrs. Forsythe was murdered, then someone believes they got away with murder. If they think there's someone nosing around who suspects the truth, well . . . he or she could prove very dangerous." She paused and gazed into the fireplace. "Yes. It could prove very dangerous indeed."

CHAPTER 14

Often, writing provides clarity and helps me put things into perspective. Tonight's writing didn't accomplish this task. In fact, if anything, I felt more confused. However, I had learned to try not to force things. Instead of staying up worrying, I went to bed and surprised myself by sleeping through the night. It was only when Snickers pounced on my chest, causing momentary panic and temporary loss of breath, that I woke up.

I rolled over, forcing the poodle off my chest, remembering to keep my mouth closed to prevent her attempts to lick my teeth.

I took care of my call of nature first and then quickly took the poodles downstairs to allow them to answer theirs.

Snickers stepped over the threshold and executed a circus-worthy maneuver where she balanced all of her weight on her back right leg, enabling her to keep three paws off the ground while she took care of her business.

Yet again, Oreo jumped around in the snow for several moments and spent extra time playing before he remembered why he was there and went over and hiked his leg.

Inside, I cleaned the excess snow off his belly and looked him in the eyes. "You might want to skip your romps through the snow and follow your sister's lead."

He gave my hand another lick, similar to the previous night, and I couldn't help but laugh. "You have such a zest for life, don't you, boy." I dried him and scratched that place behind his ear that made his eyes roll back into his head and caused his leg to jiggle.

Eventually, Snickers had had enough of me playing with the boy dog and gave my legs a scratch.

I hadn't bothered to put on pants, so it was a painful lesson to learn. *Don't keep the girl poodle waiting while I played with the boy poodle.* "Message received." I put the dogs down and hurried upstairs, making a mental note to take them to get their nails trimmed.

I showered, dressed, and cooked breakfast. By the time I finished, I heard Christopher and Zaq coming upstairs.

"Hey, Aunt Sammy," Zaq said.

"You boys want some bacon?" I asked the question even though I already knew the answer. It wouldn't matter how many times or how much my nephews ate, the answer was always going to be *yes* when the question involved bacon. Nana Jo said we had a bacon gene.

I took three pieces of bacon and left the rest for the twins. They each grabbed bread and stacked it with the remaining bacon. Mouths full, they descended the stairs, mumbling, "Thanks."

I was just about to load the dishwasher when I heard my nephew's call. "Aunt Sammy!"

One glance at my watch showed me the store wasn't opened yet, and I gave a silent prayer of thanks that my nephews hadn't yelled for me with a store full of customers. Rather than yelling back, I went downstairs.

"You yelled?" I joked as I walked around the corner. I stopped with the smile frozen on my face when I saw Detective Pitt. Based on the scowl on his face, and the pacing he was doing around the small bistro tables in the back of my bookstore, he wasn't happy.

"Detective Pitt, I wasn't expecting —"

He marched to within inches of me and pointed his finger in my face. "You're behind all of this. What have you gotten me involved in?"

I was shocked into silence for several seconds. Detective Pitt and I hadn't always gotten on like best friends, but he'd never taken such a hostile attitude toward me. From behind the steaming detective, I saw my nephews watching. Both were over six feet and, based on their stances and the frowns on their faces, they were prepared to protect me. It was clear to me that this situation was about to get out of hand quickly.

I channeled my school teacher attitude and stood tall and straight. "Detective Pitt, stop shaking your finger at me and sit down."

The detective dropped his hand instantly. He took a deep breath and pulled out a chair and flopped down.

My nephews' shoulders relaxed, although their eyes indicated they were still on high alert.

"It's okay, boys. I'm fine. Detective Pitt and I are going to have a *friendly* conversation. You both can get back to work."

The boys hesitated for a moment. Zaq nodded and turned and walked away first.

Christopher stayed a few seconds longer. "We'll be right up front if you need us."

I nodded. When they were both up front,

I turned my attention to the detective. I glared at him. "Now, it's obvious you're upset and your mind isn't functioning properly or you would never have marched in here and yelled at me like that." I took a deep breath. "I know you've got better manners than that, so I'm going to excuse your behavior."

A flush rose up his neck, and his eyes flashed. However, the spark quickly vanished and the detective took a deep breath. "I'm sorry."

I pulled out the chair across from the detective and sat. "Would you like a coffee?"

He shook his head. "No . . . thank you." He ran his fingers over his head. Unfortunately, this action served to dislodge the hairs he'd combed over his bald spot and now, rather than bending over his dome, they stood straight up.

I tried not to stare, but the hairs were so rigid, it took a lot of control not to stare. "What can I do for you?"

He leaned forward. "You got me involved in this murder business and now, I've got Sergeant Alvarez, the district attorney, and the Justice Department asking questions."

I raised an eyebrow. "Really? Why so much interest?"

232

He banged his hand on the table. "You tell me."

"Well, I told you it would be a high-profile case, but —"

"High profile is one thing, but the bleeding Justice Department is another thing altogether."

I stared across the table. "What's the real problem?"

Detective Pitt glanced at me but then reached inside his coat and pulled out a folder. He slid the folder across the table while looking over his shoulder. "That's the coroner's report about Max Franck, and getting a copy of that nearly cost me my job."

I suspected the detective was exaggerating. His job had been in jeopardy for quite some time, if my sister, Jenna's, sources were to believed. I scanned the file. However, Detective Pitt leaned across the table and stared the entire time. I found myself distracted not only by his eyes but the strands of hair, which seemed to stand at attention, atop his head, as well as the scrambled eggs that he'd dropped on his shirt. "Look, I can't read this if you're going to stare at me. Why don't you get yourself a cup of coffee and a cookie?" I pointed to the counter.

Detective Pitt walked over to the counter, giving me a little breathing room.

I sighed and read through the report as quickly as possible. Max Franck had been killed by a thin knife to the kidneys. I reread that several times to make sure I understood.

"What's got you so engrossed?" Detective Pitt said around a mouthful of chocolate chip cookies and dropped crumbs on my shoulder.

"The murder was caused by a thin stiletto-type knife wound to the kidneys." I flicked the crumbs off my shoulder and the table. "Would that cause a lot of blood?"

He shrugged. "Beats me."

I sighed. "Does this mean they're going to let you work the case?"

He flopped back down in his seat and leaned close. "That Alvarez wants to take me prisoner. He's madder than a wet cat." He grunted. "I'd be fine if it was just a matter of Alvarez, but the Justice Department is an entirely different matter. I've got a meeting with my chief in" — he pulled up his sleeve and glanced at his watch — "in an hour." He looked at me. "What am I supposed to say? Did this bus driver . . . Bob Marcus . . . did he kill Franck? If so, why?"

I thought for a few minutes. "I don't think

he did kill Max Franck. I'm not even convinced he pushed Irma down a flight of stairs." Detective Pitt started to talk and I held up a hand to stop him. "Look, I don't think Sergeant Alvarez has anything connecting Bob Marcus to Max Frank's murder. If he did, he would have arrested him at the rest stop."

He rubbed his chin. "Yeah, that's a good point."

I nodded. "Look, if it were me, I'd go into this meeting and say you were just responding to a call for an attempted murder. If Sergeant Alvarez believes the attempt on Irma's life is connected, then it makes sense for you to investigate. It's your territory, after all."

He nodded. "Yeah, you're right."

It took a little more pumping up, but, by the time I finished, Detective Pitt was chomping at the bit and ready to take on Sergeant Alvarez and the entire United States Justice Department.

I, on the other hand, felt drained. Something about the coroner's report bothered me, but I couldn't figure out what it was. I sat for a few moments, but customers started to come in.

I helped my nephews for a few hours. When it was close to lunchtime, I went upstairs and put on my winter gear and then walked down the street to Frank's restaurant to pick up lunch for my nephews.

When I walked into Frank's place, he was behind the bar. He smiled and I walked over and hopped onto a barstool.

He finished providing beverages for one of his waitresses. There was another man behind the counter who came over. However, before he could ask for my drink order, Frank sidled up next to him. "Sorry, Benny, I've got this one." He leaned across and kissed me on the cheek.

Benny grinned. "I'm sorry. I get it." He held up both hands. "Off limits. I got it." He winked at me.

Frank laughed. "Exactly."

Heat rose up my neck, but I smiled and extended my hand. "Hello, Father. I'm Samantha, but everyone calls me Sam."

He looked at Frank. "Is it okay if I shake?"

Frank gave him a playful punch.

Benny wiped his hands on a towel and then shook my extended hand. "Hello, Sam. I'm Bernard Lewis. You can drop the 'Father.' Just call me Benny."

"Nice to meet you, Benny."

He smiled and then walked a discrete distance away.

Frank poured me a glass of lemon water.

"Are you here for lunch?"

"Yes, and I need lunch for my nephews too."

He nodded and took our orders. Once he placed those, he leaned across the counter and smiled. "It's great to see you."

I smiled. "It's great to see you too, but . . ."

He stood up. "You've got that look in your eyes."

I tilted my head. "What look?"

He leaned closer. "The look that says you're investigating and need information." He whispered, "When I was hoping you just wanted me for my body."

I had just taken a drink of my water and spit it out as I laughed.

Frank laughed and grabbed a towel and wiped up the water I'd spewed across the counter. "What can I do for you?"

Once I was able to talk again, I looked around. Thankfully, the restaurant wasn't very crowded and we had a bit of privacy. "I just saw the coroner's report on Max Franck." I quickly explained the little bit of information I'd gleaned from the file. "I remember you mentioning once that the best way to kill someone quietly was a knife to the kidneys."

He nodded. "It's a technique that was used by military during World War II."

"Is that something that's common knowledge? Or is it specialized." I noted the confused look in his eyes and tried to explain. "I guess what I'm asking is, whether this is something you'd have to be in the police or military to know? Or, is that something that anyone could know?"

He stood still for a moment and then shrugged. "Honestly, in this day and age, anyone with access to the Internet could figure it out. Heck, there's probably a video demonstrating the technique if you look long enough."

I sighed. "Well, that's a bummer."

Frank's brow was furrowed.

"What?"

He took a deep breath. "It's just that most of the people on that bus trip were seniors. Many of them may have been in World War II or Korea, Vietnam . . . anything. Men and women all served and were trained to kill silently. Between that and the Internet, your killer could have been just about anyone."

I sighed. "That's what I was afraid of."

We chatted until my order arrived.

"Will I see you tonight?" He smiled. "You still owe me dinner."

"I'm going to the memorial service for Max Franck. Wanna come?"

He grinned. "Not exactly the romantic evening I was thinking about."

"Well, we're still on for New Year's Eve, right?"

He nodded. "Definitely."

I worked in the bookstore while my nephews ate lunch, although there weren't very many people. Afterward, I went upstairs and ate my lunch while I sat at my laptop.

I tried to make sense of the information, but nothing made sense. It would be so easy if Bob was the murderer, but no matter how much I wanted it to be over, I knew in my heart he wasn't the murderer. He wasn't cold and calculating enough to have stabbed Max Franck in the kidneys. If he was the killer, that would eliminate Rosemary as a suspect. She'd fought with her father twice and seemed like a really good suspect, but she was in Chicago when the attempt was made on Irma. Although, I had to wonder, why try to kill Irma? Was it attempted murder? Or did she simply lose her balance and stumble? I really wanted to believe Irma tripped and the entire thing was merely an accident. Because if it wasn't an accident, if someone really had tried to kill Irma, then the killer must believe she knew something, and her life was in danger.

CHAPTER 15

I couldn't stop thinking about Irma. Was she really in danger? Why was her room searched? I never asked if anything was stolen or not. Why Irma's room? I made a mental note to ask Nana Jo if any other rooms were broken in to. As I thought about my grandmother, my cell phone rang and her picture appeared on the screen.

"Sam, I'm at the hospital. They're releasing Irma in a couple of hours."

"Would you like a lift?"

Nana Jo released a breath and I could hear the smile through the phone. "That's what I was hoping you'd say."

She promised to text when it was time to go and then said she needed to go stop Irma from flirting with the medical students making rounds with the doctor and hung up.

I took out a notepad and wrote down what I remembered from the coroner's report so I could fill Nana Jo and the girls in when I saw them later. I also jotted down a few questions that kept running through my mind. *Was the break-in at Irma's apartment a coincidence? If not, what was the killer looking for? Was she pushed? Or, did she trip? If she was pushed, why? What does the killer think Irma knows?*

I looked over my notes. "Those are good questions. I wish I had the answers."

Oreo barely glanced up from his nap. Snickers yawned, stood, turned around in a circle, and lay down with her back to me. I guess my talking was disturbing her nap. Perhaps a little writing would help.

Battersley Manor was a large home but looked quite demure when compared to Hapsmere Grange. The house sat back from the road, and Lady Alistair's chauffeur pulled the Rolls up to the front steps. Before he could get out, Thompkins, who was on the front seat, promptly hopped out and opened the doors for Lady Alistair and Lady Elizabeth.

Detective Inspector Covington pulled up behind. Lady Elizabeth felt it would be better if the two younger people arrived together.

The front door of the manor was opened, and Mrs. Sanderson hurried down the steps to greet the guests.

"Your ladyship." She curtsied and nervously

241

bounced around as though unsure if she should walk in front, behind, or simply stand silently.

Lady Elizabeth smiled fondly and offered her hand. "Mrs. Sanderson, let me introduce you to my dear friend, Lady Alistair Browning."

Mrs. Sanderson bobbed and smiled. "Your ladyship."

Lady Alistair smiled. "I was so sorry to hear of the death of Mrs. Forsythe. Please accept my sincere condolences."

Mrs. Sanderson blushed and nervously turned from one woman to the other.

Detective Inspector Covington and Lady Clara approached the small party.

"This is my cous . . . ah, niece, Lady Clara Trewellen-Harper and her friend, Peter Covington." Lady Elizabeth hoped her faux pas went unnoticed. They'd agreed previously it would be easier to introduce Lady Clara as her niece, especially since Lady Clara had the habit of calling her "aunt" anyway. They'd also agreed to say as little as possible about the detective inspector. He was a close friend of Lady Clara's, spending his holiday with them.

Mrs. Sanderson seemed overwhelmed by the number of visitors but bobbed to Lady Clara and the detective inspector.

When it seemed Mrs. Sanderson had met

everyone, she looked up and noticed Thompkins.

"This is my butler, Thompkins," Lady Elizabeth announced.

Another decision made previously was to say as little as possible about Thompkins' presence. The butler had, in fact, suggested people might not question his presence. He reminded them it had been quite common in the past for aristocrats to travel with maids, valets, and butlers.

Apparently, the butler had been correct because Mrs. Sanderson merely nodded to the butler and asked no other questions.

A dark-haired woman with a birdlike face stood in the doorway. "Sanderson, don't leave our guests waiting outside in the cold."

Everyone followed Mrs. Sanderson up the stairs. At the door, the introductions were made again.

The woman introduced herself as Constance Tarkington. She was a large-boned woman with an athletic build. She looked to be the type who spent a great deal of time outdoors and was more comfortable in the company of horses than people.

On the outside, Battersley Manor was a classic English Edwardian manor house. The inside was a completely different matter. Once you stepped over the threshold, you stepped into the Orient. From the large Oriental rugs that covered the floors to the silk screen, blue and white vases, and silk draperies. There were large collections of swords, teacups, and even what appeared to be a collection of Buddhas, which varied in size from tiny miniatures to a massive one near the front door.

Constance led the group into a dark, dusty sitting room, where they were joined by her husband, Desmond Tarkington. Desmond was a dark-haired man with a weak chin. He had dark eyes and a theatrical air. He wore a smoking jacket and cravat and carried a pipe, although it wasn't lit and was clearly for effect.

Desmond struck a thoughtful pose and leaned against the fireplace. "Welcome to Battersley Manor." He nodded.

Lady Elizabeth smiled. "Thank you, Mr. Tarkington. I'm so glad you were able to accept a visit during your time of mourning."

Desmond looked confused for a few seconds but quickly regained his composure. "Yes. Yes, well, the old dear was rather old and we knew it was coming."

"You knew she'd fall down the stairs?" Detective Inspector Covington asked innocently.

"Well, no, of course we didn't know that." He waved away the comment. "However, she'd been sick and she was subject to . . . well . . .

244

to . . . accidents," he said casually. "These things happen when people get old, don't they?"

Constance Tarkington frowned at her husband but soon turned back to her guests. "Did you know Eleanor long? We never heard her mention you."

Lady Elizabeth sat very straight and forced a smile. "Your cousin was a very old and dear friend." She paused as though trying to remember but, after a few seconds, she simply shook her head. "It's no use. I can't recall the last time we saw each other."

Constance smiled. "What a coincidence you two running into each other that way."

"A coincidence?" Lady Elizabeth asked.

"Of all the days of the year, what are the chances that two old friends who haven't seen each other in . . . a long time would both be at Harrods having tea at the same time."

Lady Elizabeth smiled. "I don't know that it's too much of a coincidence. Not really." She smiled. "After all, who wants to miss a Boxing Day sale at Harrods?" She laughed.

Lady Alistair smiled. "I intended to go myself, but, at the last minute, something came up."

There was an awkward silence for several seconds. Lady Clara stared at Desmond Tarkington and then scooted to the edge of her seat. "Haven't I seen you someplace before?"

Desmond Tarkington hemmed and blustered for a few moments. "I've had the great pleasure to be featured in several . . . small roles on the stage."

"That's it. I knew your face looked familiar." She smiled. "How exciting to meet a real-life actor in the flesh."

Desmond puffed out his chest.

Constance rolled her eyes.

Lady Clara stood. "Would it be possible for me to get your autograph?"

Desmond smiled. "Of course, my dear girl." He turned to leave. "If you'll accompany me to my office, I'm sure I have a photograph that I'll be more than happy to sign to you."

Lady Clara gushed and followed Desmond out of the room.

Taking his cue, Detective Inspector Covington turned his attention to Constance Tarkington. "I couldn't help but notice your stables when we drove up. Do you ride?"

Constance Tarkington gave the first real smile since their arrival. "We do have some rather fine horses. Would you care to . . . ?"

Detective Inspector Covington nearly leapt from his chair. "I'd love to see them."

Constance headed out of the room but turned back to her guests. "If you'll excuse us, we're just going to run down to the stables unless . . ."

"Don't mind us. We'll be perfectly fine here talking to Mrs. Sanderson." Lady Elizabeth smiled.

"Yes. Please take your time," Lady Alistair said.

Constance Tarkington and Detective Inspector Covington left, and Mrs. Sanderson looked nervous and picked imaginary pieces of lint from her skirt.

Lady Elizabeth smiled at the woman. "Now we can have a nice chat."

In the kitchen, Thompkins met Dora, the maid. She was a plump, freckled girl. She wasn't attractive, but she had an honest face.

Thompkins stood stiffly in the kitchen and watched as the girl worked. She appeared to be cooking over an ancient wood-burning stove while tending to a kettle. "Are you the only servant?"

Dora chopped vegetables. "Yaw."

The butler removed his jacket and rolled up his sleeves. He reached out and removed the knife from the young girl's hand. "Let me."

Dora stood back in shocked silence. She watched as the butler expertly peeled and then chopped the carrots.

After a few seconds, she nodded her approval and went over to the pot simmering on the stove. "Well, I thank you for that." She stirred.

"Don't tell me they expect you to cook *and* clean."

She nodded. "Plus, I tended to Mrs. Forsythe when she was alive. May she rest in peace." She stirred. "But I didn't mind because the mistress was a wonderful woman. Always saying please and thank you." She snorted. "Not like that other one."

Thompkins glanced back at the maid. "Mrs. Sanderson?"

"Pshaw. Good Lawd, no. That other one. Mrs. High and Mighty Tarkington."

"Not a very good mistress?"

"Naw, and I won't be staying much longer now that Mrs. Forsythe is gone. I won't be staying to work for that stingy cow."

Thompkins continued peeling and cutting. "Tell me about your mistress."

Dora's face lit up as she talked about Mrs. Forsythe's kindnesses to her, which included a lot more than just saying *please* and *thank you*. Apparently, Mrs. Forsythe was generous and sent old clothes to Dora's ailing mother and often paid her younger brother to do odd jobs around the house. "But, when Mr. Desmond came, he put a stop to that." She stirred the pot and then set a tray with cups for tea. "Fired all of the other servants. We used to keep a cook and manservant and then there was Mrs. Bolton, who came in twice a week to do the washing."

"Don't tell me they expect you to do that too?"

She nodded.

"What about Mrs. Sanderson. Doesn't she help?"

Dora laughed. "That one? She couldn't tell a chicken from an egg unless someone gave her instructions." She shook her head. "She wasn't hired to help with the work. She was hired to keep an eye on the mistress. She's some distant cousin or something." She shook her head. "No, she's just one more mouth to feed as far as I'm concerned."

Thompkins stared. "But why would you put up with that? Why stay?"

She sighed. "I stayed for her . . . for Mrs. Forsythe. I could see clear enough they wanted to get rid of me too, but that was where the mistress put her foot down. 'No,' she said. She wouldn't allow them to fire me." She smiled. "So, they went about trying to force me to quit. More and more work they piled up on me, but I did it." She sighed. "But, now that the mistress is gone, well, I don't have to put up with the likes of them no more." She took a kettle of boiling water off the stove and filled the teapot. "I've given my notice and

I'll stay my thirty days so she can't try to send me off without a notice."

Thompkins finished the chopping. He watched while the maid prepared the tea tray and transferred the vegetables to the pot. "Was Mrs. Forsythe . . . a bit addled?"

Dora slammed the teakettle onto the table, spilling hot water onto the table. "No, she was *not* and don't you dare say she was."

Thompkins stepped back. "I didn't mean any offense. It's just I heard my lady say someone told her that she was."

Dora wiped up the water she spilled. "Well, whoever said the mistress was daft musta been daft themselves, that's what. Mind, she was a bit queer about her Oriental treasures." She smiled. "That's what she called them, her treasures, but that don't mean she was balmy. It's just that China was where she and her husband were happy."

"They weren't happy here?"

Dora sighed. "I don't think so. Not like they was in China. Missionaries they was." She paused for a few moments. "But I think it was more about being free. They didn't have nobody telling them what to do and which way to go when they was in China, but then Mr. Forsythe's father got sick and they had to come back." She shook her head. "I don't think they was ever really happy again, not

250

really. But if you asked me, wasn't nothing wrong with her, except too much money and too many relatives."

"Was Mrs. Forsythe wealthy?"

"She wasn't as wealthy as your ladyship out there, with her fancy car and that fur coat and all them jewels." Dora tilted her head toward the sitting room. "But her husband left her real comfortable and she was generous, but she wasn't wasteful. She was always careful with her money." She smiled. " 'Dora,' she used to say to me. 'One day, I'm gonna take care of you because you've done such a good job taking care of me.' " Dora sniffed. "But that was before Mr. Desmond arrived."

"Maybe she left you something . . . a legacy in her will."

Dora sniffed. "That's just the thing. She didn't leave a will."

"No will? Surely her solicitors . . . have a copy."

Dora shook her head. "You better believe Mr. Desmond called the very day she died. But Mr. Danvers, that was her family solicitor, he said she didn't leave a will with him." She paused. "Which is really odd considering her husband used to be a solicitor. You'd have thought she would have been sure to make a will."

"Her husband was a solicitor?"

251

Dora nodded. "When he come back from China, his mother talked him into doing something 'sensible.' Well, I ask you, what could be more sensible than helping heathens in foreign parts?"

Thompkins shrugged.

Dora nodded. "Anyways, he studied to become a solicitor and they became sensible about everything, except their Oriental treasures. Crazy about their Oriental knickknacks and furniture they was." She shook her head. "Mr. Forsythe goes into business with his friend. It used to be called Forsythe and Danvers, but after Mr. Forsythe died, he chucked the Forsythe and shortened it to Danvers."

"What happens to her money without a will?"

Dora shrugged. "I don't know. I guess Mr. Desmond gets it. The house is . . . some funny name . . . like fairy tales."

"You mean entailed?"

"Yaw, that's it." She stared. "That means Mr. Desmond gets it?"

"It means, the house goes to a particular relative, usually a male."

She nodded. "I thought so. More's the pity." She shook her head. "That's the last person she would have wanted to have it. 'Dora,' she says to me. 'I think I'd rather burn my money in a bonfire than see Desmond and his greedy wife get it.' "

"What makes you think they're greedy? I mean, if Mrs. Forsythe was family, then it would make sense for the money to stay in the family."

Dora snorted. "I ain't saying that's not true, but that Mrs. Tarkington was always trying to get Mrs. Forsythe to spend money on them horses and redo the stables and such. One day I admired a pretty red box with one of those dragons on it that Mrs. Forsythe had. She collected the boxes . . . Chinese puzzle boxes they was. Well, Mrs. Forsythe gives it to me. Says she wants me to have it. I was showing it to Cook before they let her go and Mrs. Busybody comes in and accuses me of stealing and gives me the sack." She huffed. "Well, I tells her Mrs. Forsythe gave me that box. I ain't never stole nothing in my life." She took several deep breaths to steady her nerves. "Well, just then, Mrs. Forsythe come down the stairs and tells her she did give me the box and she didn't have the authority to fire me, not so long as she was alive." Dora smiled at the memory.

"I'll bet that didn't sit very well with Mrs. Tarkington."

Dora laughed. "You got that right. She was furious. Stomped out of the room. Well, the next thing you know, that box comes up missing. Well, I didn't think too much about it, but then later that night, in waltzes Mrs. Tarkington smiling like the cat that got the last of the cream. She plops that box on the table and says she took it into town to a friend of hers. Says it's just a cheap piece of junk and not worth more than two quid." She stared at the butler. "I tells her plain as day, I don't care if it wasn't worth but two pence, it was a gift and she didn't have no right to take it."

"What did she do then?"

"She just laughed and waltzed out." She shook her head. "The house was entailed and he gets that regardless, but the money doesn't go with the house. It was Mrs. Forsythe's money, not her husband's." She shrugged. "Well, I guess Mr. Desmond and that woman is gonna get Mrs. Forsythe's money regardless of what she wanted." She sighed. "It's a pure shame too, but I guess if she didn't want him to get the money, then she shoulda made a will."

Thompkins watched the maid finish the tea and wondered. That was very odd indeed.

CHAPTER 16

Nana Jo texted that Irma had been discharged and I needed to get my butt to the hospital before she ended up committed to the psychiatric ward for being a nymphomaniac. I grabbed my notebook and hurried downstairs.

My nephews had things well under control and promised to lock up and take care of the poodles before they left.

When I arrived, Nana Jo, Irma, Dorothy, and Ruby Mae were waiting in the lobby. Irma was in a wheelchair, being pushed by a small, dark-skinned woman with a short afro. She was petite with smooth skin and had a big smile.

Ruby Mae got in the car. "Sam, this is my granddaughter Francesca. She's a medical student at JAMU."

I smiled. Ruby Mae had nine children and her extended family was larger than the population of North Harbor.

The ride to Shady Acres was uneventful, apart from the bickering between Nana Jo, Irma, and Dorothy.

I pulled up to the front of the main building and let everyone out and then parked and went inside to check on the arrangements.

A memorial service was a fairly simple affair to arrange. Gaston was providing some appetizers and light refreshments. Most of the residents weren't familiar with Max Franck, but they would attend for the refreshments, if nothing else.

Caroline Fenton had reserved the main living room area and several people were already there. Irma had a compression boot on her left foot, which was only slightly shorter than her hooker heels. She had one arm in a sling. Other than that, she looked pretty much the same. However, she walked up to the first man she saw and stared up with large doe eyes and milked her injuries for all she was worth.

"Gerald, would you help me to the sofa, please. I'm not used to this boot, and I need a strong man to hold on to." Irma grabbed hold of Gerald's arm.

"That poor man should have run. With one good leg and an arm in a sling, she could still calf wrestle a grown man to the ground in less than five seconds," Nana Jo said.

There were a couple of lovely floral arrangements near the picture of Max at the front of the room.

"Who sent flowers?" I asked.

"My sister's art gallery is next to that florist shop, so I ordered one arrangement, but I have no idea who the other one is from." She walked over to the flowers and looked at the card. When she returned, she said, "Rosemary Lindley."

I hadn't had an opportunity to fill them all in on everything I'd learned in Chicago, but we planned to get together for drinks following the memorial.

The girls split up and mingled. One thing I'd learned from these ladies was that the best way to get information was to divide and conquer. Ruby Mae took her knitting and sat down on the sofa. It wasn't long before someone came and sat down next to her. She had one of those faces that people felt comfortable confiding in. Irma was flirting with Gerald on the sofa at the other end of the room. Irma was the world's biggest flirt, but she wouldn't forget to pump Gerald for information. Dorothy was also a flirt, but she was subtler than Irma, which wasn't saying a lot. At close to six feet, Dorothy managed to attract men of all ages.

Nana Jo had a steady boyfriend, Freddie, but he was nowhere to be found. She headed toward Velma Levington. "I never did get a chance to question Velma."

That left me standing alone. I was probably the most awkward of the bunch. I smiled as I remembered the first time I went with my grandmother to a reception after a funeral and drank several glasses of champagne on an empty stomach and ended up puking and humiliating myself. I bypassed the glasses of white wine and grabbed a small plate of appetizers. I spotted Sidney Sherman standing nearby and casually walked over so I was standing next to him. "I remember you from the bus. You were the bodyguard."

Sidney Sherman stood in his tight jeans and leather jacket. Although he wasn't wearing the mirrored sunglasses, he might as well have been. His face and his eyes were stone and gave away nothing of his thoughts or feelings.

"Perhaps I should introduce myself." I wiped my hand on my napkin and extended it. "I'm Samantha Washington."

Sidney Sherman barely glanced at my hand.

After a few moments, I dropped it. "If you

weren't going to talk and just wanted to stand around and be rude, why did you bother to come?"

He barely moved, but a muscle at the corner of his jaw pulsed.

"Surely now that the person you were guarding is dead, your assignment is over."

The jaw clenched and a slight flush of color rose up the side of his neck.

"Unless, of course, you're the one who killed him."

The blood from his neck hit his ears and he turned to face me. His eyes were slits and the muscle on the side of his face was pulsing like crazy. He pushed a finger in my face and glared. "Are you accusing me of murdering my client?"

Nana Jo walked up beside the bodyguard. She was taller than him and she looked like a mother bear protecting a cub. "I've got a .38 pointed at your side, and I'm a darned good shot. Now, you've got three seconds to get your finger out of my granddaughter's face before I redecorate this room with your guts." She pushed the barrel of the gun into his side. "And, just in case you're wondering, I wasn't making a pass. I removed your gun from your waistband." She smiled and passed me her purse and another gun, which I assumed from the look in Sidney

Sherman's eyes, he recognized.

Sidney Sherman lowered his fingers from my face. He gritted his teeth. "What do you want?"

"My granddaughter wants to ask you a few questions. So, we're going to sit down in these chairs, nice and friendly, like human beings. She's going to talk and you're going to answer." Nana Jo inclined her head toward several Queen Anne chairs in a quiet corner of the room.

We walked over slowly, smiling the entire time. Nana Jo walked next to Sidney Sherman with her gun in his side. She used her body to conceal the weapon from view.

Sarah Jane Howard approached us, but Nana Jo turned. "Not now, Sarah."

"I really need to talk to you, Josephine."

"Sure. I just need to talk to this gentleman first. Why don't you wait for me over there?" She inclined her head to the lobby. "I'll be there in just a minute."

Sarah Jane Howard looked reluctant but eventually left.

Once we were seated, she glanced at me. "Now, Sam, why don't you ask your questions?"

I took a deep breath. "Who hired you to guard Max Franck?"

Sidney Sherman clamped his jaws closed,

but, after a few seconds, he said, "I was hired by Mr. Franck's agent, John Goldberg."

"Why?" I asked.

He sighed. "Obviously, he believed he was in danger. Why else would he hire a bodyguard?"

"In danger from whom?"

He was silent but eventually shrugged. "I don't know."

Nana Jo's eye narrowed. "Now, why do I get the impression you didn't take this threat seriously?"

He shrugged. "I dunno what you're talking about."

"Look, you were hired to protect Max Franck and someone killed him. That can't be good for business," Nana Jo said.

He huffed. "Okay. You're right. I didn't believe he was in danger." He paused but rushed on. "I thought it was a publicity stunt." He adopted an attitude. " 'Mr. Franck's next book is going to rock the world. It's so dangerous I'm hiring a bodyguard to protect him.' " He shook his head. "He was just trying to sell more books."

"Well, obviously, not, since the man is dead," Nana Jo said.

Sidney Sherman turned and Nana Jo leveled her gun.

Sherman stopped and raised his hands. "All right. Could you drop the gun? I'm talking. I'm answering her questions. I don't want you getting nervous and that thing going off and killing someone."

Nana Jo smiled. "Look, I'm not suffering from the palsy and my hands are still steady. So, as long as you don't make any sudden movements, you'll be safe."

He sighed.

"Why do you think hiring you was merely a publicity stunt?" I asked.

"Because he told me it was. He said I just needed to look the part and stay close to him for a couple of days."

"Why didn't you?" I asked.

"Why didn't I what?"

"Stay close to him? What happened?"

He sighed. "When everyone got off the bus, he said he wanted to stretch and take a leak. When I got up to go with him, he said he didn't need help." He sighed. "He got off the bus. There was one old lady asleep in the back and then he got into an argument with his daughter. I hung around for a bit, but I could see she wasn't a threat." He paused for a few minutes. "So, I went to the bathroom and, by the time I got back . . . well, you know."

I couldn't think of anything else to ask. I

turned to Nana Jo.

"Why are you here now?" she asked.

He sighed. "I wanted to pay my respects." He looked down. "I thought maybe I could remember something that would help the police."

"Did you?" I asked.

He shook his head. "Nothing."

Nana Jo looked at him for several seconds. Then she lowered her gun. "Sam, you can return his gun."

I made sure no one was watching and then slid the gun across.

He took it and slipped it inside his jacket. "Are we done?"

I nodded.

He stood. He glared at Nana Jo and then turned and walked out.

A few seconds later, we heard a scream.

"That sounded like Irma." Nana Jo stared at me.

We rushed toward the direction of the scream. In a corridor off the lobby near the elevators, lying in a heap, was the body of Sarah Jane Howard.

Irma screamed once more and then fell down in a dead faint.

CHAPTER 17

If I thought the murder of Max Franck on a chartered bus between North Harbor, Michigan, and Chicago, Illinois, was chaos, I was wrong. Between the police and the ambulance and Irma's hysterics, this was an absolute circus.

Detective Pitt marched through the lobby and glared at me as though I was responsible for murdering Sarah Jane Howard. He glowered. "Come with me."

He marched off in the direction of Caroline Fenton's office.

I looked around for Nana Jo but remembered she was comforting or threatening Irma, depending on what the situation called for. After a brief moment's hesitation, I decided to suck it up and followed Detective Pitt to the office.

In Caroline Fenton's office, he paced. "Shut the door."

I closed the door behind me and stepped

up to the desk. "Detective Pitt, you seem to be angry, but, for the life of me, I can't —"

He halted. "Angry? Angry? You think I'm angry?" He glared. "I haven't even begun to get angry. What the —"

I held up a hand. "I didn't kill her. For some reason, you seem to believe this is all somehow my fault, but you're wrong. All I did was arrange a memorial for Max Franck."

He paced, but I could tell he'd lost some of his steam. "I don't know how, but I'm sure you or your nutcase of a grandmother are somehow responsible for this mess." He paced a bit more and then flung himself into a chair. He leaned back and then made a sweeping gesture indicating I should sit.

I sat down on the guest chair across the desk from the detective.

"Now, will you tell me what's going on?"

I took a deep breath and recounted what I knew of the events.

Detective Pitt watched me but said nothing until I was done. "That's it? That's all you've got?"

I nodded. "That's all I've got."

He rubbed his hand through his comb-over. Just like before, the few strands stood at attention as though electrified. "Well, I'm going to need something to go on. When

265

the chief heard there was another murder here, he went crazy. He insisted I call in Sergeant Alvarez."

"Why? I thought Sergeant Alvarez thought Bob Marcus was responsible for Max's death? Since you have him in custody, it can't be him and that blows his theory out of the water." I smiled. However, I should have known better than to get excited too early. One look at Detective Pitt's face told me my assumptions were wrong.

Detective Pitt shook his head. "Had to let him go."

I dropped my head. "You let him go? Why?"

"He made bail."

I stared openmouthed. "Does Sergeant Alvarez . . ."

He was nodding before the words left my mouth.

"Well, fiddle sticks."

Detective Pitt smiled. "You better be careful. Your grandmother might just wash your mouth out with soap."

I tried to smile at the detective's joke, but my heart wasn't in it. "If Bob left jail and came here, I haven't seen him." I thought for a moment. "Are you sure it was murder?"

He nodded. "We'll have to wait to hear

from the coroner, but she's got the same type of wound."

"That wound seems rather specialized, don't you think?"

He shrugged. "A sharp object to the kidneys is pretty effective." He looked hopeful. "Are you asking if the murderer would have had medical training?"

I told Detective Pitt what I'd learned from Frank about quiet kills.

A flash of what I would call respect crossed his face but was quickly replaced by the anxious expression he'd started this round of conversations with. "So, basically anyone with any type of medical or military experience or anyone who has access to the Internet would have known how to kill quietly."

"True, but . . . why would they?"

He stared. "What do you mean?"

"Okay, so maybe Max Franck knew something. Maybe during the course of researching his next book, he stumbled across something that made him dangerous to someone. Or maybe he made his daughter angry for not getting tested or maybe he was just a plain jerk who was responsible for someone committing suicide. Whatever the killer's motive for killing Max Franck, why kill Sarah Jane Howard?" I paused.

"I remember her from that other murder,

when that Romanov woman was murdered." He colored slightly.

I guessed he was remembering how he nearly arrested my grandmother for that one but chose to remain silent.

He hurried on. "That Sarah Jane Howard was a nosy old busybody."

"Exactly."

He looked surprised. "What?"

"She was nosy. Nana Jo said Sarah Jane Howard was the nosiest person she'd ever met." I thought back for a moment. "I remember Ruby Mae saying she used to sit at her window with binoculars and spy on people." I paused, but Detective Pitt didn't seem to be catching on.

"What are you saying?"

I sighed. "I'm saying, maybe Sarah Jane Howard was being her normal, nosy self. And, what if she saw something she wasn't supposed to see?"

He shook his head. "Naw, that's no good."

I was crestfallen. "Why not?"

"Because busybodies like that Howard woman are all the same. What's the good of knowing something if no one knows you know it?" He gave me a knowing look.

I thought about what he was saying.

He leaned across the desk. "Trust me. If that woman knew something, or even if she

268

thought she might possibly *know* something, she would have told someone. She would have reported it."

I scooted to the edge of my seat in excitement. "What if she didn't *know* she knew something?"

He rubbed his forehead. "You're making my head hurt."

"Stay with me. What if she didn't realize what she saw until later?" I gasped in excitement. "Or, what if she didn't know anything about Max Franck's murder, but what if what she knew was related to the attempt on Irma's life?"

"I thought you didn't believe Irma was pushed?"

I thought about it. "I don't believe Bob pushed Irma. But what if it wasn't Bob? What if she saw the person who really did push Irma?"

He shook his head. "She still would have wanted someone to know. She would have told someone."

I nodded. "What if the person she told was the real killer?"

CHAPTER 18

Detective Pitt didn't look convinced, but he shrugged. "Okay, I'll bite. Who did she talk to?"

Heat rose up my neck. "I don't know that she actually *talked* to anyone."

He squinted. "Who did she attempt to talk to?"

I squirmed in my seat. "I don't know who she talked to, but I do know she wanted to talk to Nana Jo."

Luckily, Nana Jo had an ironclad alibi for the time of the murder. Although she wasn't thrilled when Detective Pitt pulled her into the tiny office to ask her about her movements.

"Listen here, I was too busy putting the drop on that Sidney Sherman character and preventing him from getting violent with my granddaughter to be going around killing Sarah Howard," Nana Jo exaggerated.

After a good fifteen minutes of yelling,

Nana Jo made her point and stomped out of the office.

Detective Pitt looked as though he'd been working out. He had beads of sweat on his forehead and, unfortunately, under the pits of his arms.

It was several hours later before we were released to leave. By the time I got home, I was exhausted. It wasn't until I made my way upstairs that I realized part of my problem was that the only thing I'd had to eat was appetizers.

I looked in my refrigerator and smiled when I saw a pint of Frank's taco soup. He must have dropped it off earlier. I smiled as I put a generous serving into a bowl and heated it in the microwave while I changed into yoga pants and a warm sweater. By the time I was comfy, my food was ready.

I crushed several saltines and dumped them into the soup. While I sat at the breakfast bar and ate, I marveled at the wonders of technology, which allowed me to heat dishes in seconds and send text messages of gratitude, which I knew would be received almost instantly. Technology was a wonderful thing. At least it was when it worked. Unfortunately, the cameras in the stairwell at Shady Acres hadn't been working. Although, it wasn't necessarily that the cameras weren't working but that they weren't pointed in the direction to capture Sarah Jane Howard's murder. Which I found interesting. Either the killer knew the exact location where he or she could murder someone without being caught on camera or our murderer was extremely lucky. The truth was probably a combination of both.

After dinner, I let the poodles outside and decided to spend some time writing in the hopes that I could collect my thoughts.

Detective Inspector Covington traipsed through the cold, damp ground to the stables and tried to smile and not think of his wet shoes, although the squishing he heard each time his foot hit the ground made it extremely difficult to think of anything else. In the stables, he was assaulted by the stench of damp horse flesh and manure. He tried not to think of Lady Clara sitting in the office with smiling Desmond Tarkington or even Lady Elizabeth sitting in front of a warm fireplace sipping tea.

Constance Tarkington walked up to a tall beast of a horse that seemed taller than any horse he'd seen. Although, granted, growing up in the streets of London meant he hadn't seen many. Not up close and personal, anyway. He forced a smile and took several deep breaths to steady his nerves. He'd always heard animals could sense fear.

"What a magnificent animal," he said with what he hoped was the right amount of enthusiasm in his voice.

Constance opened the stall door and led the beast out.

"What's his name?" He asked more for something to say rather than a desire to know. He had no intention of addressing the creature.

"Satan."

"Excuse me?"

Constance laughed. "His name is Satan." She caressed the animal's back. "My husband's idea of a joke."

The animal stomped his feet and snorted in a manner that indicated the name might not have been a joke after all.

"I know what you want." She reached into her coat pocket and held up a carrot, which the beast quickly chomped. When he finished, he used his head to push her forward. She would have fallen had Covington not reached out to catch her.

He helped to right Constance, who clutched his arms, forcing him to hold her closer and longer than necessary. When he looked at the woman, he recognized a hungry look in her eyes.

The detective forced himself to smile and

hoped the smile extended to his eyes. "Mrs. Tarkington."

"Constance."

He looked around. "You have very nice stables . . . Constance . . . but I don't see any helpers. Surely your husband doesn't do all of the work himself."

She snorted. "Him? You must be joking. Desmond isn't into horses or riding or anything fun." She released the detective's shoulders and walked around the stables. "This is all mine." She raised her hands to encompass the entire stables.

"But surely it's too much for one woman . . . even a woman such as yourself."

She smiled, accepting the comment as a compliment. "My husband doesn't believe in 'wasting money.' " She used air quotes. "At least not on anything that interests me. However, he can waste plenty of money on plays."

The detective tsked. "Surely your husband's cousin could afford to pay for someone to run your stables."

"Eleanor wasn't fond of horses either." She sighed. "More's the pity."

The detective inspector chuckled. "Well, now that she's gone . . ."

Constance smiled. "Yes, now that she's

gone, we shall be able to afford some improvements."

Constance Tarkington glowed. She spent the next five minutes telling the detective inspector exactly what improvements she planned for the stables. Even to someone unfamiliar with animals or construction, the plans sounded expensive. Clearly, Constance Tarkington had put a lot of thought into how she would spend Eleanor Forsythe's money. The question that crossed the young detective's mind was how long she'd been making plans.

Lady Clara Trewellen-Harper sat in Desmond Tarkington's study. The conceited old bore had been talking for what felt like hours about his roles in various theatrical performances. Fortunately, Desmond Tarkington, like many men, didn't really need or expect much from her, other than the occasional coos of awe and "Oh my, aren't you amazing," and "How fascinating." Recalling her days in finishing school, she was highly skilled at small talk and pretending to listen to conversations she knew nothing about.

Lady Clara glanced out the window and wondered what Detective Inspector Covington was talking about with Constance Tarkington.

"Is anything wrong?"

"No, why do you ask?"

"You were frowning and I wondered if I'd said something to offend you."

Lady Clara laughed. "I'm sorry. I was just thinking about your wonderful career. I find it so fascinating, and I was thinking how wonderful that you can live in such a grand home and go on the stage and meet fascinating people."

Desmond Tarkington chuckled. "Well, I suppose it is fascinating to an outsider."

Lady Clara nodded. "Indeed, I mean, if I lived in a beautiful house like this, I don't think I would ever want to leave."

The frown on Desmond Tarkington's face indicated that wasn't exactly the direction he expected the conversation to go. "Yes, well, the house is rather nice, I suppose. Although, it's not really my taste."

"I suppose a famous actor like you would rather be in a modern house in London or . . . Hollywood," she whispered with enthusiasm.

He sat straighter in his seat. "I suppose so . . . One of these days I'll make a film or two, but I have to say, I prefer the stage. There's nothing like a live audience to bring out the best in an actor's performance." He stuck his prop pipe in his mouth and put his other hand inside the front of his smoking jacket.

Lady Clara thought he looked like Napoleon and found it rather difficult to take him seriously. But she'd been entrusted with the task of getting Desmond Tarkington to talk and she refused to go back and have that arrogant Scotland Yard detective providing clues and solving the murder while she sat listening to dreary Desmond Tarkington talk about his glory days on the stage. "I suppose now that your cousin has died, you'll be famous *and* rich."

Desmond Tarkington frowned. "Well, I hardly think that's a proper conversation to have." He looked at Lady Clara but eventually smiled. "However, I suppose it's true that I'll inherit. My cousin was very wealthy, and I am her closest relative." He bit the end of his pipe. "We were very close." He smiled but quickly looked away and frowned.

Lady Clara batted her eyelashes. "Why, Mr. Tarkington, is there anything wrong?"

At first, Desmond Tarkington denied anything was wrong, but with just the slightest bit of prodding from Lady Clara, he admitted something was bothering him.

"Desmond . . . you don't mind if I call you Desmond?" She smiled.

Desmond smiled in a way that indicated he didn't mind the least bit that Lady Clara called him by his first name. "Well, there's nothing

277

wrong . . . not really. I've just been concerned about my cousin's will."

"Her will? You don't mean to tell me she's done something silly and left all of her money to a cat or something?"

Desmond chuckled. "No. Nothing like that. It's just that she indicated she had a will but no one can seem to find it. In fact, I rather hoped she might have said something to your aunt, Lady Elizabeth, when they were in London."

Suddenly, all was clear to Lady Clara. "Did you indeed?"

Lady Elizabeth and Lady Alistair sat in the sitting room with Mrs. Muriel Sanderson. The woman had barely said anything and spent the majority of the time gaping at Lady Alistair's jewels and the fox stole she wore around her neck.

"How long have you been with Eleanor?" Lady Alistair asked.

"About two months."

"What brought you here?" Lady Alistair smiled at the tedious manner they were having to pull information out of the frightened woman.

"Eleanor was my cousin," the woman mumbled. "A distant cousin, but . . . family."

"So nice to have family." Lady Elizabeth,

who was highly skilled at small talk, smiled and took a sip of the tea Thompkins had brought them. "Now that Eleanor is gone, will you stay on here?"

Muriel Sanderson dropped her spoon. She reached down and picked it up. "I . . . don't . . . I suppose . . ." She dropped her napkin. "It depends on the . . . I mean . . . I'm sure they wouldn't . . ." She choked back a cry and pulled a handkerchief from the sleeve of her dress and dabbed at her eyes.

Lady Alistair and Lady Elizabeth exchanged glances.

"Surely Eleanor provided for you? Some type of . . . legacy perhaps?" Lady Elizabeth asked.

Muriel Sanderson choked back tears. "I don't know. I just don't know. I assumed there would be something, but with no will . . ."

"No will?" Lady Alistair asked. "You don't mean to say she died without making arrangements for her family and the servants?"

Muriel nodded. "Nothing. If she had a will, no one knows where it is. There's only one servant, Dora, and she's going to give her notice."

"I suppose you've tried her solicitor?" Lady Elizabeth asked.

Muriel nodded. "Desmond called him first thing."

"How odd." Lady Alistair sipped her tea.

"We wondered if maybe she hid it somewhere or . . ." She stared at Lady Elizabeth. "Or perhaps, she gave it to someone close to her."

Lady Elizabeth sipped her tea. "I wonder the same thing."

CHAPTER 19

At some point during the night, I stopped writing and got in bed. Although, I couldn't remember actually going through the motions. I knew it must have happened since I was in bed. I received a jolt when I recognized the noise that woke me was the sound of snoring in my ear. I sat up straight in my bed, wide-awake. When I realized the snoring was coming from Snickers, who was curled up asleep on my pillow, I relaxed. Apart from Snickers' snoring, which was amazingly loud for a ten-pound poodle, the house was quiet. Nana Jo had wanted to keep Irma company, so she spent the night at Shady Acres. Regardless of whether I believed Irma was pushed down a flight of stairs or tripped, she had found two dead bodies, sprained an ankle, and fainted twice. That was a lot for anyone.

A hot shower provided some time for me to think through recent events. I kept going back to my conversation with Detective Pitt and asking, *why would someone want to kill Sarah Jane Howard?* It seemed obvious that the murder was connected to Max Franck's murder in some way. The method used to kill both people was too similar for the two deaths not to be connected. By the time I finished my shower, dressed, and took the dogs downstairs to take care of their business, I still didn't have any answers.

I wasn't in the mood to cook today, so when my nephews arrived, I sent a message to my sister, Jenna, asking if she wanted to meet me for breakfast. I even offered to treat. Being the trusting soul that she was, her reply was, What do you want?

I took her snarkiness as acceptance and typed the location of her favorite breakfast spot.

As usual, I arrived before my sister, who was known for always being ten minutes late, and she didn't disappoint.

Jenna and her husband, Tony, were both attorneys, although Jenna was a criminal attorney and Tony practiced corporate law. Roughly the same height as me, Jenna was four years older, although you couldn't tell by looking at her. She was also known within law enforcement circles as "The Pit Bull," a label she embraced.

Jenna flew into the restaurant wearing her lucky suit, which indicated she would be heading to court when she left the restaurant. She sat down and the waitress immediately brought her a cup of hot tea. "Can I have a butter croissant to go and a take-out cup, please? I won't be staying long."

The waitress smiled. "You just enjoy that one and I'll bring you a fresh tea in a to-go cup. Same kind as usual?"

Jenna nodded. "Yes, English Breakfast."

The waitress nodded and hurried to take care of Jenna's order.

My sister sipped her tea and looked at me. "What's up?"

"Nice to see you too."

She looked at her watch. "I have to be in court in thirty minutes. Make it quick."

"I'm offended that you think the only reason I would call you is because I want something. I've left you alone because I know you've been busy, but maybe I just missed spending time with my older, wiser big sis."

Jenna glanced over her cup. "My clock is ticking. In ten minutes, I'm going to be walking out so I can get to work. If you want something, you better make it quick."

"All right." I knew my sister and she'd

walk out in ten minutes regardless of what I said. I quickly told her about Bob Marcus.

The waitress brought Jenna's croissant in a bag along with another tea, this time in a paper cup.

Jenna stood. "What do you want me to do?"

"I don't think Bob killed Sarah Jane Howard, and whoever killed Sarah Jane Howard more than likely is responsible for killing Max Franck. Sergeant Alvarez wants to wrap this thing up, and I'm afraid he's going to arrest Bob and charge him with both murders. He'll take him to Chicago and no one will do anything, and an innocent man will spend more time in jail."

She glared. "So, how does this affect me?"

"You're a lawyer . . . a pit bull. Don't let them railroad an innocent man. At the least, don't let them take him to Chicago until we can find the real killer."

Jenna stared for several seconds and then lifted her cup. "I've gotta go. Thanks for breakfast." She held up her cup and the bag with the croissant, turned, and walked out.

My sister got into her car and I wondered why I had bothered. Obviously, I didn't know my sister as well as I thought. I slumped down in my seat but nearly jumped when my phone vibrated, indicating I'd gotten a text message. I lifted my head and pulled my cell phone out of my pocket.

The text was from Jenna. Text me Bob's full name. No promises.

A smile spread across my face as I replied. Maybe I knew my sister after all. The waitress returned and I smiled. "I'm ready to order."

After I left the restaurant, I went back to the bookstore. Today was New Year's Eve, and I planned to close the store early. The twins would be going out to celebrate later, so I thanked them for helping out, paid them, so they'd have plenty of spending money, and let them go. Traffic in the store was light, and I was well able to handle things myself until noon, when I closed down.

I got a text message from Nana Jo instructing me to meet at her house for a noon meeting. Her message was immediately followed by a message from Frank saying Nana Jo had ordered lunch and told him I'd bring it with me. Unlike the mystery-book shoppers, his customers were there in droves. He didn't have a lot of time, but if I pulled up to the back of his restaurant, he would load the food into my truck. He was a good man.

I went upstairs and noticed Snickers and

Oreo asleep in their beds. My poodles were getting older. Their muzzles were filled with white and their once-dark chocolate coats were now more café au lait than espresso. I also noted they spent a lot more time sleeping and wondered how many more years I'd get to spend with them.

Those dark thoughts made me sad, and I picked up Snickers and gave her a tight squeeze. She was the older of the two and held a special place in my heart. "I need to spend more time with you, girl, don't I?"

She yawned and then licked my nose.

Nana Jo and the girls would want to ring in the new year with drinks, dancing, and fun, which meant a late night for me. "Wanna go to Nana Jo's house?"

She yawned again. Obviously, she'd had a busy day.

Oreo scratched at my legs. I'd neglected to make their grooming appointment.

I grabbed my coat and purse and a handful of dog biscuits. "Come on." I needn't have bothered speaking. The treats were enough to get them to follow me. Outside, I waited while they took care of business. Today was one of those days where I was grateful for automatic start. I used it to make sure the car and the seats were nice and warm by the time the poodles finished and we were ready to leave. I might not have a luxury vehicle like Frank, but I was definitely fond of my Ford Escape with its bells and whistles.

I loaded up the poodles and sent Frank a text before I pulled out of the garage, letting him know I was on my way.

It was a short drive to his restaurant, and he was waiting as soon as I pulled up, which let me know he had been looking out for me.

One button on the dashboard opened my back hatch and I didn't even have to get out of my car. Frank had a large cardboard box, which he quickly loaded into the rear, and then pressed the button to close the hatch.

I pushed the button that rolled down the window when he hurried toward my window. "Thank you, but you'll catch a cold out here with no coat."

He stuck his head inside and kissed me. After a few seconds, when he pulled away, I felt a bit dizzy.

He smiled. "I'm warm enough now."

I grinned like a silly schoolgirl. "I wish you didn't have to work tonight, but I understand." We'd talked about not being able to ring in the new year together.

Frank released a heavy breath. "I know

it's our first New Year's Eve, but I don't want to leave Benny here alone or —"

I held up a hand to stem the explanation. "I know. It's okay. I absolutely understand and it's okay."

He gazed into my eyes with intensity. "Are you sure?"

I smiled and nodded. "I'm very sure."

Benny came to the back door of the restaurant. "Frank, we have a problem."

"You better get back to work." I crooked a finger and beckoned for him to lean close. When he did, I kissed him again. "Thank you."

He fanned himself. "You're welcome."

I smiled most of the way to Nana Jo's. In fact, I was so distracted by Frank Patterson, I nearly forgot that Snickers and Oreo were in the car until I glanced in the rearview mirror and saw them cuddled up together in their dog bed on the back seat of the car.

At Nana Jo's I pulled into her driveway and blew the horn. After a few seconds, the door lifted and I pulled into the garage.

Nana Jo helped me bring the food from the back of the car into the house, where the others were waiting. Snickers and Oreo trotted in like they owned the place. Of course, everyone petted them, so they were very happy. Eventually, Nana Jo found the extra food dishes that we kept at her house and the poodles were distracted by food.

We took thirty minutes and ate lunch without talking about murders or crime. However, when everyone had finished eating, Nana Jo picked up her iPad, which signaled it was time for business.

I got up and let the dogs out to take care of business and quickly came back inside and got them settled down by my feet.

"Okay, who wants to go first?" Nana Jo looked around and her gaze landed on Irma. "Irma, maybe you should go first. I think you should tell us everything that happened."

Irma was wearing a lot more makeup than usual, which was saying a lot. "I told Gerald I wanted a throw and he'd gone to get one." She smiled demurely. "He's such a thoughtful man."

Nana Jo squinted and looked as though she would strangle Irma.

"Actually, I'd like you to go back to the other day, when your room was searched and you fell down the stairs," I said.

Irma nodded. "Of course. I forgot you weren't there when the killer made the first attempt on my life."

Nano Jo rolled her eyes at Irma's *first attempt.*

Irma recapped the incident from the other night, which was very similar to what Nana Jo had said.

"Who was in the stairway?" I asked.

Everyone exchanged glances. Irma shrugged. Nana Jo frowned for several seconds as she tried to remember. "Sam, honey, everyone was in the stairwell. The fire alarm was blaring and flashing like a strobe light at a disco." She paused. "I know all of us were there. I'd just been trying to track down Velma Levington." She shook her head. "That is one woman who's hard to reach. I spotted her down the hall and headed that way, and that's when I got distracted because Irma screamed." Nana Jo frowned at Irma. "You've been doing a lot of screaming lately."

Irma sniffed. "The next time you find two dead bodies and someone tries to kill you, we'll see if you scream."

"Don't get your panties twisted in a wad." Nana Jo tapped her stylus on the table for several seconds but eventually gave up and shook her head. "I'm sorry, but I can't remember who was in the stairwell."

"Where was Bob?" I looked around. "Was he near Irma's room?"

Everyone looked around. Eventually, Dorothy shook her head. "No, I don't think he was."

Ruby Mae looked up from the knitting she had just taken out of her bag. "I know he wasn't because Bob came upstairs with me."

Everyone turned to Ruby Mae and started hurling questions at her. "Are you sure?" "How do you know?" "Why didn't you say something sooner?"

She huffed. "Now, y'all are gonna need to stop firing questions at me and let me tell you." Ruby Mae took a few deep breaths. "I had been downstairs talking to Melvin."

"Melvin Cooper?" Irma asked. "He's so handsome. I didn't know you were interested in Melvin."

Ruby Mae looked at Irma out of the side of her eyes. "Honey, I ain't interested in no pretty boys like Melvin Cooper. Ain't no way a man that good looking is going to be satisfied with one woman, and I don't believe in sharing." Ruby Mae looked down her nose at Irma. "I was talking to Melvin Cooper to see if he had any information about Max's murder." She glanced at Irma again. "You remember him. Max, the man you were gushing over just a few days ago."

Irma stuck out her tongue but started coughing. She reached into her purse. Usually, she pulled out a flask, but she felt around and didn't seem to find one. Eventually, she dumped the contents of her purse on the table and started sorting through them.

Ruby Mae continued, "We were in the elevator together. We had just gotten off the elevator when we heard Irma scream and we rushed to your room to see what had happened." She turned to me. "Does that help?"

I thought for a moment. "Not really. Unless Bob was with you the entire time, it doesn't mean he couldn't have ransacked Irma's apartment earlier."

"What's this?" Irma held up a key.

"I know you pretend to be a ditz sometimes, but now isn't the time." Nana Jo turned away from Irma.

"I know it's a key," she said sharply. "I mean why is it in my purse?"

I stared at Irma. "Isn't it yours?"

She shook her head. "I've never seen it before."

I held out my hand and Irma gave me the key. I turned it around. "It looks like a key to a locker." The key had a cheap circular tab with a number written on it. "Eight one nine."

Nana Jo leaned across the table. Then she

looked at me. "You don't suppose Max put it in her purse."

I shrugged. "Who had access to your purse?"

Irma thought for several seconds but then shook her head. "Beats me."

"Did you leave it on the bus when we stopped at the rest area?" I asked.

Irma's eyes grew larger and she nodded. "I left it on the bus because Max said he wasn't going and I knew it would be safe."

The excitement grew as we examined the key.

"Anything else in there?" I asked.

Irma sifted through the items scattered across the table.

My gaze landed on a picture. I pointed. "What's that?"

Irma leaned across. She picked it up and stared. "It looks like a picture of Robert Kennedy."

That got our attention. We all crowded around Irma and stared at the picture for several seconds.

"Who's that with him?" Ruby Mae asked.

We stared harder. It was an old black-and-white Polaroid photo that had seen better days. The photo was approximately three and a half inches by four. There was a white border around the outside. One corner was missing, and the photo had a bend that went straight across. However, the image showed Robert Kennedy lying on the floor of the kitchen in the Ambassador Hotel in California where he had been shot. I had seen a similar photo in textbooks. However, something was different about this photo. I couldn't figure out what. It appeared to have been taken immediately after he was shot, which would have been in June 1968. Crouched beside the body was the busboy who had been shaking Kennedy's hand when he was shot. However, this photo showed several people standing nearby.

We passed around the photo, but no one recognized anything particular about the photo.

Nana Jo stared at the photo for a very long time. "Something seems familiar about this, but I just can't put my finger on it."

"Are photos like this rare?" I asked.

"I can ask my sister. She'd know." Dorothy shrugged. Her sister owned a gallery in downtown South Harbor and she'd been instrumental in finding information previously.

I sighed. "Most likely he had it for research for his book. He was writing a book about Robert Kennedy's assassination."

"What do you think we should do with

it?" Ruby Mae asked.

I looked around the table. "As much as I hate to say it, I think we need to give the key and the photograph to Sergeant Alvarez or at least Detective Pitt."

Everyone started talking at once, which made it hard to understand.

"I don't see why we have to turn this stuff over to the police," Irma said. "It was in my purse."

"Besides, we don't know for certain Max is the one who put those items in Irma's bag," Nana Jo argued.

"Right. I mean, she's had that bag in a lot of places. Anyone could have put that stuff in there," Dorothy said.

"We don't even know what the key opens," Ruby Mae said.

I scowled. "You've got to be joking. Who else would put a picture of Robert Kennedy on the day he was assassinated in Irma's purse, along with a locker key, except the man who was writing a book about the subject?"

I looked from one of them to the other. "Look, you may be right. Maybe it is some grand coincidence. Maybe the key fell into her purse and it has absolutely nothing to do with his murder, but *if* it is important, then it's against the law to withhold evidence to a crime."

"But we don't know it's evidence. So, if you don't know it's evidence, then you can't be held accountable."

Something about the way Nana Jo looked when she said that made me wonder if she was serious. I stared at her. "Are you making that up?"

She hesitated for a few seconds but eventually shrugged. "I'm sure I saw it on *Law and Order* or maybe it was *Perry Mason.*"

I sighed. "I tell you what, I'll run it by Jenna and see what she says." I glanced around the table.

They weren't happy, but eventually everyone agreed.

I held out my hand and Irma turned over the key and the picture.

The rest of the meeting was relatively uneventful. I updated everyone on my conversation with Detective Pitt and my conversation with Jenna.

Nana Jo filled the group in on our conversation with Sidney Sherman.

"Do you think he's telling the truth?" Ruby Mae asked.

I glanced at Nana Jo, and we both shrugged. After a few minutes, though, I added, "I think he was telling the truth. I mean, if he was going to lie, he would have tried to make himself look better, don't you think?" I glanced around.

"Well, he sure didn't help his reputation as a bodyguard to admit he permitted his client to get murdered while under his protection, did he?" Nana Jo tapped her stylus.

Irma turned to me. "You do believe the two murders are connected, don't you?"

I nodded. "I do. I can't see why anyone would kill Sarah Jane Howard unless she knew something about the first murder."

"Well, heck, I can think of a lot of people who would want to murder that nosy busybody," Nana Jo said.

"Me too," everyone added.

"She was a nosy busybody, that's true, but she's been at Shady Acres for how long?" I glanced around.

"Ten years?" Nana Jo looked at the others, who nodded.

"Well, I think that means you all found a way to either ignore her or shun her, but, in the past ten years, no one has killed her."

"I sure wanted to," Nana Jo mumbled.

"Especially after the way she tried to cast suspicion on you after Maria Romanov's murder," Dorothy said.

"That's all true, but you didn't murder her." I looked at Nana Jo.

She sighed. "I get what you're saying."

"Good. So, back to Irma's original question. Do I believe the two murders are connected?" I looked around. "My answer is yes. I do."

Nana Jo read back through her notes from the conversation I'd had with Sarah Jane. "What about the argument she overheard between Rosemary and Max?" She looked up. "I mean, the woman was furious about him not at least getting tested to see if he could donate bone marrow. I know I would have killed someone if I thought it would help my daughter."

I looked at my grandmother, who had the mother bear look in her eyes again. "I know that just sounds so coldhearted. Christopher and Zaq aren't my children, but I think I could easily kill if it meant saving their lives." A chill ran down my spine, and I shuddered.

Everyone agreed, although Ruby Mae seemed distracted.

"Ruby Mae?"

She knitted a few more stitches before she looked up. "I agree with what everyone said. Y'all know I have nine children and I would do whatever I have to do to make sure my children are safe. I was just wondering . . . is this Rosemary a smart woman?"

I squinted and stared at Ruby Mae. "Yes. She seemed like a very intelligent woman."

She nodded. "I thought so too. I can't see her killing him and not getting the bone marrow." She glanced around. "I mean, if you're going to kill him, at least make sure you take his body to the hospital and get what you need."

"I'm not sure you can take someone's bone marrow without their permission. Even if they're dead," I said.

"I know that." Ruby Mae knitted a few stitches. "But, if it were me, I'd make sure there was a note or something that gave me permission to take the bone marrow."

I thought about it. "I think you're right."

The only new information anyone had learned was that Caroline Fenton had submitted her resignation and was planning to leave Shady Acres. Rumor had it, she said her nerves were shot after all of the murders, but no one knew for sure.

"I don't think Caroline Fenton's the only person who thinks Shady Acres is dangerous. I've heard several people are planning to leave." Ruby Mae knitted.

"Anyone we care about?" Nana Jo asked.

Ruby Mae glanced at Irma. "I've heard Melvin Cooper is one."

Irma gasped. "Why that dirty son of a —"

"Irma!" everyone yelled.

Irma coughed and began looking for her flask in the dumped contents of her purse. She sifted through all of the items on the table. When she found it, she took a swig.

"I heard Velma Levington was another one," Dorothy said.

Now it was Nana Jo's turn to look surprised. "Velma Levington? That is one busy woman. Every time I try to get close to the woman to talk to her, something happens. Either fire alarms go off or people are murdered."

"Maybe you need to stop trying to talk to her." Ruby Mae shuddered. "I can't handle no more murders right now." She looked down her nose at Nana Jo. "I know that isn't grammatically correct, but you know what I mean."

We chatted a bit longer, and then Irma said, "It's New Year's Eve and I want to go party."

"I thought Shady Acres was having a New Year's Eve party?" I asked.

"Caroline Fenton canceled it," Dorothy said.

I must have looked puzzled because Nana Jo added, "She said, with Sarah Jane's murder and the police crawling around everywhere looking for clues, it was irreverent and too much of a hassle."

I blinked to try to clear my confusion. "But today is New Year's Eve. How can she wait 'til the last minute to cancel your party?"

Everyone shrugged.

"Let's go to the casino," Irma suggested.

I wasn't ecstatic about a trip to the casino. My hair and clothes always reeked of cigarette smoke afterward, however, the idea of sitting home and watching the ball drop on Times Square wasn't appealing this year either, especially alone.

I nodded and the girls packed up their belongings.

It had been quite a while since the poodles had stayed at Nana Jo's, but, in addition to extra food and water dishes and dog food, she also kept an extra crate and dog bed for what she referred to as her "great-grand poodles." So, we made another trip outside. When they were done, I cut a piece of string cheese into small toy poodle-sized pieces and put them in one of Nana Jo's spare bedrooms. I turned on the radio and gave them the treats. Then I quickly left and closed the door, a habit I'd developed since they were puppies. If they had an accident in the house, at least it would be contained. Thankfully, Nana Jo didn't stress about the dogs the way Jenna did. She had a host of rules, which included no poodles on the furniture, no accidents in the house, and no table food for the dogs. I suspected between Jenna's husband, Tony, and the twins, they'd broken nearly every rule. However, at least at Nana Jo's, I knew I wouldn't hear about it.

Once the poodles were taken care of, I found Nana Jo and the girls waiting for me in the car.

The drive to the Four Feathers Casino wasn't far. The casino was located in a small nearby town, with a population less than two thousand five hundred people. For a small town, the Four Feathers Casino and Resort, owned by the Pontolomas, a recently recognized Native American Tribe, was surprisingly grand. Just off Interstate 94, the uninformed traveler might have passed by the casino without giving it a second look. It appeared to be in the middle of nowhere. A winding road snaked around a picturesque woodland environment, which was the home to many deer and other animals that drivers learned to watch for as they traveled the winding road. There was a man-made lake and the drive was designed to showcase the natural landscape. At the end of the drive, there was a massive pillared entrance that led to the 150,000-square-foot casino and 500-room luxury hotel and resort. Inside, the casino had three bars, seven restaurants, retail shops, and an event center that drew big-name entertainers from all over the world.

Normally, I parked in the attached parking garage. However, I was concerned the crowds would be large and parking might be challenging. Instead, I pulled up to the valet parking lane and let the casino deal with parking.

Once we were inside, we had a set routine that involved eating at the buffet and then splitting up for a few hours of gambling. Ruby Mae's expansive family generally meant we didn't have to pay for our meals. Tonight was no different. Ruby Mae had sent a text message to a niece, great-niece, cousin, or some other relation while we were traveling. So, when we arrived and approached the hostess station, our names mysteriously had already been added to the list and our table was ready and waiting for us.

I didn't glance at the crowds of people standing waiting for tables.

Once we were seated in a prime location, close to Ruby Mae's favorite buffet table, I leaned across the table and whispered,

"Don't you feel bad about getting in front of all of those people?"

All of the girls looked at me with the same, "you must be joking" expression and said in unison, "No."

I'd eaten a big lunch just a couple of hours ago, so I wasn't starving, but I did enjoy the casino's fried chicken and the smell enticed me to load up my plate. I also loved the casino's dessert bar. They had lime tarts that were amazing.

When we were done, the hostess told us they had some bags for us that we could pick up when we were ready to leave. Normally, I would haul everyone's boxes to the car. However, Ruby Mae must have sent a message to her grandson, third cousin twice removed, or nephew-in-law, letting them know I valet parked. For that, I was grateful.

The casino was elaborately decorated, and I marveled at the hours and manpower it must have taken to transform the space into what appeared to be a mystical wonderland.

Nana Jo enjoyed playing poker and headed to find a game. Dorothy, who was wealthier than the rest of us, liked to play blackjack or high-limit slots. She went in search of a blackjack seat. Irma, as usual, went to the bar to pick up men. Ruby Mae, who was rarely without her knitting bag, ran into someone she knew as we were leaving the buffet and they went off to catch up on old times.

I wandered around the penny slots, looking for an interesting game with an empty seat. I wouldn't call myself a big gambler; although, since I'd started hanging out with my grandmother and her friends, I'd certainly gambled a lot more than I had before. I found a seat near a game I recognized, with cute panda bears, and sat down and put twenty dollars in the machine. I could bet a minimum of fifty cents, and that was just about my limit. I set a maximum of fifty dollars and, at fifty cents per spin, I could play for quite some time.

In addition to the New Year's Eve festivities, the Four Feathers was also giving away a thousand dollars every hour, and, at the end of the night, they would give away two sports cars parked in the lobby. This meant there was a lot more noise and excitement as the announcer randomly selected names of people who had their Four Feathers's Rewards cards in the machines. Names were called and people were given five minutes to make their way to one of the stations to claim their prize. Failure to claim your prize in the allotted time meant another name would be selected.

You didn't have to be a statistician to realize you stood a better chance of getting struck by lightning than having your name called. So, I tuned out the buzz and enjoyed the monotony of pushing the button. Honestly, playing the slot machine required very little brain power since the machine did all of the work. If I went into a bonus, the machine told me. After a while, I was lost in the spin of the wheels and the routine of pushing the button. There was something therapeutic about watching the wheels spin, and I allowed my mind to wander. I thought about Max Franck and Sarah Jane Howard. Solving one murder was challenging. Solving two murders should be more challenging. However, part of me felt the second murder helped to narrow things down. Instead of just figuring out who murdered Max Franck, I could eliminate people who wouldn't or couldn't have also murdered Sarah Jane Howard. I thought through the list of suspects.

I thought about Bob Marcus, the bus driver. Technically, he could have killed Max and since he'd been released from jail, he could have also killed Sarah Jane Howard. I made a mental note to check with Jenna on his alibi for the second murder. He didn't really have a reason that we knew of for killing Max. Just because he'd killed before didn't automatically mean he'd kill again. Besides, deep inside, I didn't believe he killed Max and, try as I might, I couldn't picture him killing an old woman.

Sidney Sherman was next. Him, I could imagine killing both Max and Sarah Jane Howard, but I couldn't believe he'd be so sloppy as to do it when he knew it would reflect negatively upon him. Sidney Sherman seemed like the type of man who would always look out for number one. Besides, I didn't see a motive.

Caroline Fenton was a tough one. She definitely had a strong motive and desire for killing Max Franck. She believed him responsible for her father's downfall and death. She admitted she hated the man. But, could she kill him? Could she kill Sarah Jane Howard? I thought and thought about that one through multiple spins and several bonus games. Still, in my mind, the answer was no. Although, I couldn't deny the fact she was leaving was suspicious. Something flashed across my mind and, for an instant, I felt a jolt like lightning. However, just as quickly as the jolt appeared, it vanished. Try as I might, I couldn't get whatever thought had appeared to reappear. I knew better than to keep trying. I pushed the button for my slot machine and nothing happened. When I checked my balance, I realized there was nothing left. No need putting more money into a losing machine. So, I got up and wandered around. The next machine that caught my eye advertised X-Men. I sat down and inserted twenty dollars. I'd never played the game before, but, again, it wasn't rocket science and the machine did all of the work. I was intrigued by the graphics and thought briefly about Taylor, the MISU student who'd be working for the video game company, Vamps. I shook my head.

"Did you say something?" the lady sitting next to me asked.

"No. I'm sorry. I was just trying to figure out how this machine works," I lied.

She smiled. "It's very simple. If you get three Xs, then you get into the Free Spin bonus."

"Thank you."

I pushed the button and watched reels of X-Men characters like Magneto, Charles Xavier, Wolverine, and Storm appear. After a few spins, I was able to allow my mind to wander again.

Rosemary Lindley was harder for me. She had the best motive for wanting to kill Max Franck. But I couldn't see her killing Sarah

Jane Howard. Plus, Ruby Mae was right when she said Rosemary would have made sure, if she did kill her father, she could have gotten his bone marrow.

Who was left? I pushed the button and three *Xs* appeared on the screen.

"You've gotten into the bonus now. It'll keep giving you free spins, but if you get a wild on the middle reel, then it switches in between heroes and villains," my helpful neighbor explained.

I stared at the *Xs* and again felt that jolt of lightning through my mind. *X . . .* who was *X*? Could there be another person, someone else on the bus that we just hadn't found yet? I pushed the start button and watched the reels roll by. Who were we missing? Nana Jo and the girls had interviewed everyone. Well, everyone except Velma Levington. Nana Jo had yet to corner her. We'd have to make sure we questioned her. My phone vibrated. I had a text from Frank.

Where are you?

Four Feathers Casino.

I miss you.

Ditto.

I waited, but there wasn't another text. So, I put my phone back in my pocket. I had won two hundred fifty dollars in my bonus spin, and that was good enough for me. I cashed out and took my ticket, indicating I'd won.

"You're smart to leave while you're ahead," my helpful neighbor said.

I smiled. "I think this noise has given me a headache. I'm going to find a quiet place to sit and think."

I passed one of the waitresses dressed like a stereotypical Hollywood rendition of an Indian squaw in a short brown dress and got a Diet Coke. Then I walked to the hotel section of the resort, which I knew from past experience was quieter and a lot less smoky.

I found a comfortable seat and sat down. After a few seconds, I pulled out my notepad and a pen and started to write.

Lady Elizabeth sat on the sofa in the drawing room at Hapsmere Grange. Lady Alistair sat next to her. Detective Inspector Covington warmed his hands in front of the fireplace. Lady Clara stood nearby.

"You look dreadful," Lady Clara declared. "Your face is flushed and —"

Detective Inspector Covington sneezed. "Thank you, Lady Clara. I get the picture."

"I was only trying to be helpful. You shouldn't have gone traipsing through those fields out to the stables with Mrs. Tarkington without

310

wellies." Lady Clara glanced at the detective's feet. "Your shoes are ruined, and your feet must be soaked."

The detective inspector sneezed again. "Yes, I have realized that, but I didn't know I'd have to walk through wet grass when I agreed to holiday here, so I didn't pack my Wellingtons."

Lady Clara pushed the bell, which summoned Bakerton. When the butler arrived, she gave an order. "Please bring a large tub of hot water, towels, a warm blanket, and a huge pot of hot tea and lemon."

Bakerton bowed. "Yes, m'lady."

"Look, I'll be —" Detective Inspector Covington sneezed again.

Lady Clara pulled a handkerchief from her sleeve and handed it to the detective inspector.

He took the dainty handkerchief and promptly put it to use. When he was done, he looked sheepish. "Thank you."

Lady Clara pushed a chair behind his knees. "Now, sit down and take off those wet shoes and socks and put your feet in front of the fire."

The detective gave Lady Elizabeth an alarmed look that begged for assistance.

However, Lady Elizabeth merely shook her head. "I think you'd better do as you're told.

311

You'll catch your death of cold and I'll never forgive myself."

Lady Clara gave the detective inspector a stern look, and he sneezed three times in succession and then sat down and did as he was told.

Lady Elizabeth and Lady Alistair exchanged a triumphant glance.

Thompkins opened the doors and entered, carrying towels and a blanket. He glanced at Lady Elizabeth, who gave a slight nod in the direction of Lady Clara, who promptly took the blanket and ordered Thompkins to assist the detective inspector.

Thompkins placed the wet shoes and socks in front of the fireplace to dry and put the towels down near the hearth. By the time they were done, Bakerton entered with a large plastic tub filled with steaming water. He and Thompkins placed the tub in front of the detective.

The embarrassed detective attempted to get up. "Maybe I should take the train back to London. I don't want to inconvenience anyone. I'm —"

Lady Clara glared. "Sit!" She pointed to the chair.

The detective inspector sat.

"Now, put your feet in that water, or so help me, I'll have Thompkins tie you to that chair."

Lady Elizabeth nearly burst out laughing at the look on the detective inspector's face but covered it by coughing.

The defeated Scotland Yard detective did as he was told.

Bakerton turned to Lady Alistair. "Tea for everyone?"

Lady Alistair nodded. "Yes, that would be nice."

Bakerton left.

Thompkins turned to go but was halted when Lady Elizabeth said, "Thompkins, I'd like for you to stay."

The butler bowed. "Yes, m'lady."

Bakerton brought the tea and left, closing the doors behind him.

Lady Alistair poured and Thompkins assisted in distributing the tea. When everyone was served, the butler stood quietly near the wall.

"Now, who would like to go first?" Lady Elizabeth asked.

Detective Inspector Covington sneezed twice and then pulled out his notepad. "Maybe I should go before I'm sent to my bed like a child." He glanced at Lady Clara, who merely raised an eyebrow but remained silent.

He told them about the conversation he'd had with Constance Tarkington and her desires to expand the stables.

313

Lady Clara picked at an imaginary piece of lint on her skirt. "Is that all that you two talked about?"

If Detective Inspector Covington hadn't been ill, he might have noticed that Lady Clara avoided making eye contact and had a very pretty flush in her cheeks. However, the detective didn't seem as observant as usual. Instead, he merely said, "Pretty much. The woman is obsessed with horses and riding. She hardly talked of anything else." He shivered. "She's got some beast of a horse named Satan, who she's particularly attached to." He muttered silently, "Which seems fitting."

Lady Clara smiled and glanced at the detective. "Well . . . that's . . . why that's splendid," she said a bit breathy.

Detective Inspector Covington sneezed again. "What did you find out from Desmond?"

Lady Clara sighed. "Not much. He's such a bore. I sat there for what felt like hours while he nattered on about himself and his career on the stage. No one understands him. His wife doesn't appreciate him. His cousin didn't understand the artistry involved in going on-stage and wouldn't shell out money to put on productions, which would guarantee him good roles and gain him the recognition he deserved." She recited. "However, he has high hopes that things will change now that Mrs.

Forsythe is dead."

"Did he say that?" Lady Alistair paused with her cup midway to her mouth.

Lady Clara shook her head. "No. He was careful." She bit her lip. "But he does seem concerned about the fact that no one can find Mrs. Forsythe's will. He thought she might have given it to you." She turned to Lady Elizabeth.

"Does he indeed?" Lady Elizabeth knitted.

Lady Elizabeth shared the information she and Lady Alistair heard from Mrs. Sanderson.

Lady Clara paced. "What do you suppose it means? I mean, why would they kill the old lady if they didn't know for certain they'd get the money? I wonder where she hid the will."

Thompkins coughed discretely. "M'lady, I think I might be able to shed some light." He recounted what he'd learned from the maid and told them about the red lacquered box.

Lady Elizabeth sat up straighter in her chair. "That's very interesting. Those boxes often have multiple hiding places." Lady Elizabeth stared into space for several moments.

Detective Inspector Covington stared at Lady Elizabeth. "You're concerned about something. What is it?"

She sighed. "To be completely honest, I'm worried. I'm very worried about that maid, but as long as none of the others realize that the lacquered box could have multiple hiding places, she should be safe."

Lady Clara gasped and covered her mouth with her hand.

"What is it, dear?" Lady Elizabeth asked.

"When I was in the study with Desmond, I noticed the collection of Chinese boxes." She paused and her eyes went from one person to the other. "I went to a lecture about Chinese artifacts at the National Museum, and I mentioned about the different hiding places." She stared like a deer caught in headlights at Lady Elizabeth.

Lady Elizabeth turned to Detective Inspector Covington. "We need to get to Battersley Manor at once."

The Scotland Yard detective stood up. "You believe the maid's in danger?"

"I'm afraid I do. I believe she may be in a great amount of danger."

The detective dried off his feet and grabbed his socks from the mantle.

"I believe if we don't act quickly, that poor girl will be murdered," Lady Elizabeth said.

Lady Clara looked stricken but stared at Detective Inspector Covington. "You can't possibly put those wet things back on."

"If you think I'm staying here" — he sneezed — "while you all go after a murderer, then you're batty."

Thompkins walked over. "Perhaps you would permit me." He handed the detective a pair of clean, but more importantly, dry socks. "I believe I can find you a pair of dry boots, but, if you will permit, I have a bit of information to report." He turned and left.

Thompkins returned with the boots and the detective donned them. He sneezed several more times. Thompkins also reached inside his jacket and pulled out a red lacquered box with a gold filigree dragon on top.

Lady Elizabeth took the box the butler extended to her. "How did you get this?"

Thompkins coughed. "When Dora mentioned the box, I wondered if there might be more to it and asked if she would permit me to borrow it for a short time."

Lady Elizabeth stared at the butler with wide eyes filled with admiration. "Thompkins, you're wonderful."

The door to the drawing room opened and Bakerton entered slowly. The butler seemed stiffer than normal. He stood silently for several seconds.

Lady Alistair looked with confusion. "Bakerton?"

The door opened wider to reveal Constance Tarkington with a gun pointed at Bakerton's back. "You can hand over that box."

Lady Elizabeth stood very still. "Where's Dora?"

Constance Tarkington gave a mad laugh. "Sleeping, very soundly at the moment, thanks to a double dose of sleeping draught."

Detective Inspector Covington moved toward Constance Tarkington, who pushed the gun into Bakerton's back. "Keep moving and I'll be forced to use this relic as a shield."

"Please, don't," Lady Alistair pleaded.

"Then give me what I want and no one will get hurt." She extended her hand to Lady Elizabeth.

"I don't believe that," Lady Elizabeth said. "You pushed Eleanor Forsythe down a flight of stairs. Why should we believe you won't kill us too?"

Constance Tarkington sneered. "That old woman had it coming. Her and all her blasted Chinese vases and boxes. She didn't care about anything except her *Oriental treasures.* The bloody cow didn't give two pence for me and my comfort. I asked . . . no, begged her to upgrade the stables, but no. She wouldn't and Desmond doesn't care about anything but the theatre and trying to pursue a career on the stage." She turned to Lady Elizabeth. "Do you know that sniveling idiot had the nerve to tell me he plans to sell the house as soon as he can." She took a step into the room toward

Lady Elizabeth. "After all the years I've put up with his droning on and on about the stage . . . I've put up with living in that damp, dark mausoleum and all I asked was for a little money to go into the stables and the horses." She was now standing directly in front of Lady Elizabeth.

"Surely, you didn't have to kill her," Lady Alistair said.

Constance Tarkington shrugged. "I'd waited long enough and I'm done waiting." She leveled her gun at Lady Elizabeth. "Now, give me that box."

Detective Inspector Covington inched closer to Constance. One of the floorboards squeaked and Constance Tarkington turned her gaze to the side.

Lady Elizabeth tossed the red box across the room to Lady Clara, who reached up and caught it.

Constance Tarkington turned toward Lady Clara just as Detective Inspector Covington leapt across the room. He wrestled the gun away from Constance Tarkington, who wiggled and squirmed. Eventually, the detective inspector managed to wrap both arms around the woman and hold her until she stilled.

Lady Elizabeth turned to Thompkins. "Please call the police to come pick up Mrs. Tarkington and send the doctor to Battersley

Manor to check on Dora."

"Yes, m'lady." Thompkins turned to leave.

Bakerton, who was visibly shaking, did the first unprofessional thing in his entire career. He sat down in the presence of his mistress.

CHAPTER 20

My phone vibrated and brought me away from 1938 England. I glanced down and saw a message from Frank. What are you doing?

Sitting in the hotel lobby, writing.

I waited, but there was no response. I stretched and glanced down at the time. We always met in the lobby, but tonight, we would wait until after the New Year's festivities. I yawned.

"Tired?"

I looked up. "Frank? What are you doing here?" I stared in shocked surprise.

"I really wanted to ring in the New Year with you. So, I left Benny in charge and drove here." He stared into my face. "Is that okay?"

I sprang from my seat, threw my arms around his neck, and squeezed him.

He nuzzled my neck. "I'll take that as a yes."

I responded with a passionate kiss.

Frank pulled away. "Wow." He tugged at his shirt collar. "Is it just me or did it suddenly get warm in here?"

I laughed. I reached down and grabbed my purse and notebook. "How about I buy you a drink with my winnings?"

He raised an eyebrow. "If you think you can ply me with liquor and then have your way with me, then I just have one thing to say."

I waited. "Well?"

"Don't waste your money on the liquor."

We laughed and walked hand in hand.

The Four Feathers had recently added a piano bar to the hotel area of the resort. This allowed those staying at the hotel, who wanted a drink in a slightly quieter locale, to relax. We headed there in the hopes that it would be a little less congested.

At the bar, we found Irma leaning against the bar with men on either side of her. Dorothy was perched atop a baby grand piano belting out a song while a middle-aged man with vibrant red hair and a beard, who was dressed in a tuxedo, accompanied her.

Frank paused for a moment when he recognized Dorothy. He stopped and looked at me.

I shrugged and hurried toward a small

table I spotted in the corner.

Seated, he leaned over. "I knew you said your grandmother's friends were a bit . . . uninhibited, but I didn't expect . . . I mean, are they like this all the time?"

I shook my head. "No. They aren't like this all the time, but you should see them when they really get revved up."

His eyes widened, but he merely smiled.

Dorothy was a surprisingly good singer. She had a deep, throaty voice, and her style matched the bar's atmosphere. When she finished, everyone applauded.

It looked as though Dorothy was going to slide down off the piano, but her audience was having none of it. The small crowd applauded and yelled and cajoled until she agreed to sing more. Her response was met with enthusiastic applause. Dorothy and the pianist consulted for a few seconds and then decided on their next song, which was Nat King Cole's "Unforgettable."

We sat in silence for a few seconds and listened along with everyone else. Then our waiter broke the spell by asking what we wanted to drink.

Frank ordered a bottle of champagne, which I recognized as being expensive. Our waiter smiled and left to get the order with a bit more pep in his step than when he'd first come to our table, perhaps sensing the expensive bottle of champagne meant a higher tip.

I raised an eyebrow, but Frank merely shrugged. "You only live once. This is our first New Year's together, I thought it should be special."

I smiled at the thoughtfulness and wished I'd taken more care in my attire. However, I decided to let those thoughts of insecurity stay in the past and focus on the moment and the future.

The waiter returned quickly with our champagne, a bucket of ice, and two glasses. He popped the cork, which made a momentary interruption to Dorothy's song, and then quickly filled our glasses with the bubbling elixir before rushing away.

We toasted to the future and then sipped our champagne.

We talked about nothing important, drank champagne, held hands, and enjoyed each other's company until the announcer announced five minutes until the new year. Frank quickly paid the bill, poured the remaining champagne into our glasses, and indicated we should leave.

I grabbed ahold of his arm and followed. I was surprised when he led me outside. It was December in Michigan, which meant cold, but I followed.

Outside of the main doors was a covered porch with large overhead heat lamps. He guided me there, then passed me the glasses. He took off his jacket and put it around my shoulders and held me close and rubbed my arms to keep my blood circulating. He leaned down and whispered in my ear, "You okay? If you're freezing, we can go back inside, but I love to watch the stars every New Year's Eve."

I smiled. "Actually, I feel rather warm."

I felt his laughter and he held me tightly to his chest with his arms around me.

We heard the announcer and everyone in the casino begin the countdown. When they got to five, I handed Frank a glass of champagne.

I looked at the night sky and marveled at the vastness of space. The countdown continued. When they reached one, there was an uproar of cheers, noisemakers, and what sounded like fireworks. I looked at Frank, prepared to toast, but the look in his eyes indicated he had other ideas. He bent down and kissed me. When he pulled away, he smiled. "I hope we can spend every New Year's Eve this way."

I nodded. "Me too."

We toasted the new year and watched the

stars a bit longer until some of the casino patrons started to wander outside, breaking the lovely mood.

We finished our champagne and then went back inside.

Ruby Mae was sitting by one of the enormous fireplaces that flanked either side of the casino lobby. She was surrounded by several people, who I assumed were relatives. We decided not to disturb them and waited near the other fireplace.

Eventually, Nana Jo made her way to the lobby. She was wearing a paper hat and had a noisemaker. She smiled when she saw Frank. "Glad you made it." She looked around. "Where are Irma and Dorothy?"

I told her we left them in the piano bar and she left to go get them.

Frank looked concerned. "Maybe I should go give her a hand. I don't think Irma and Dorothy may be too anxious to leave."

I smiled. "Trust me, Nana Jo will drag them out if she has to."

About five minutes later, Nana Jo returned. She and Dorothy were on either side of Irma, who was quite tipsy.

Frank took Nana Jo's place as Irma's prop while Nana Jo took our tickets to the cash machine to cash out. Irma flirted with

Frank, who looked uncomfortable but endured.

When Nana Jo returned, she divided up the winnings, which amounted to five hundred dollars each. I gasped at the money when she handed it to me.

"Somebody won big tonight. I only contributed two hundred and fifty to the pot."

We always pooled our winnings at the end of the night and divided them. That way, everyone usually left with something. If one person lost, someone else usually won. Rarely had we ever left with nothing.

"I had a great night on the poker table and Dorothy hit it big on the blackjack table."

Since I valet parked, I gave the parking ticket to the attendant so they would bring my car around.

Ruby Mae's family had made sure our to-go bags were brought to the front and before long, we loaded up and prepared to go.

Frank saw us all into the car. He bent down and kissed me. "Are you okay to drive home?"

I smiled. "Absolutely."

"Maybe I should follow you."

I shook my head. "That's sweet but completely unnecessary. I'm fine."

The drive back to Shady Acres was uneventful. Irma slept the entire way. The others were tired and talked about the fun they'd all had at the casino. When I complimented Dorothy on her singing voice, she explained she used to sing at nightclubs on the weekends while she was in college to earn extra spending money.

"I guess that's where Jillian gets her talent." I glanced in the rearview mirror and was rewarded by Dorothy's smile.

I went inside Nana Jo's to collect my poodles, who were fast asleep in the guest room. In fact, turning on the lights didn't even wake them. I had to shake them.

Snickers looked around as though confused and yawned.

"Some watchdog. I could have been a robber and neither of you bothered to bark," I joked.

Snickers stretched several more times and yawned.

Oreo stretched and pranced around as though to say, *I wasn't sleeping.*

I let them outside to potty and went back in to say goodbye to my grandmother.

"It's almost two in the morning. Why don't you all just sleep here tonight. You can go home later." She yawned.

I thought about it but decided I'd rather

sleep in my own bed. I was grateful I'd made that decision when, just a few seconds later, we heard a key in the lock.

Freddie, Nana Jo's boyfriend, walked in. "Is everything okay? I saw the light on."

"When did you get back?" Nana Jo asked.

He released a deep breath. "Just now. I'm worn out." He glanced over at me. "Hi, Sam." There was a moment of indecision when he looked as though he was going to leave.

I smiled. "Hello. I'm glad you're back. I was just leaving." I turned and gave my grandmother a kiss. "Happy New Year."

"Happy New Year."

The poodles and I drove home. When we left the garage, I couldn't help pausing to look at the stars. I smiled as I remembered the moment outside of the casino, looking up into that same night sky with Frank. It was a lovely memory. Snickers took advantage of being outside to answer the call of nature, while Oreo sniffed and played in the snow.

Inside, I dried off the poodles and we hurried upstairs.

I was exhausted and got ready for bed. However, something kept tickling the back of my mind. Just as I dozed off to sleep, I remembered what it was. I picked up my phone and dialed my sister. The phone rang several times before she answered.

"Are you in jail?"

I paused. "No."

"The hospital?"

"No."

She sighed. "Then you better have a really good reason for calling at this time of the morning."

I glanced at the clock. "Sorry."

She grunted. "What do you want?"

I quickly explained about finding the photograph and the key.

She was silent for a long time and I was afraid she'd fallen asleep.

"Jenna?" I whispered. "Are you still there?"

"Yes. It's evidence and you need to turn it over to the police."

"Okay, but we were hoping maybe we could . . . Jenna?" I glanced down. The phone was black. She'd hung up. "Happy New Year."

I called Nana Jo. I knew she'd be awake. She picked up after just a couple of rings.

"Did you ever get a chance to interview Velma Levington?"

"Not yet, but I plan to tackle her first thing."

"Well, maybe you should get to it. Remem-

330

ber what Ruby Mae said." I paused. "Or was it Dorothy? Well, one of them mentioned that several people were planning to leave Shady Acres."

"You think she knows something?"

I paused. "I'm working on an idea . . . it's a crazy idea, so I want to think it through a bit more."

I heard Freddie ask a question and Nana Jo whispered a response, which reminded me of the time.

"Look, I want to mull this idea over a bit more. In fact, I might bounce it off Detective Pitt first. I'll call you in a few hours and let you know."

I needed to make one more call, but Chicago was an hour behind and decided I had better wait. I put my cell phone down and thought over what I knew of Max Franck and the other suspects. I thought I was right, but how to prove it?

As tired as I was just a short time ago, there was no chance of sleep now. I was wired. I tossed and turned for close to an hour before I gave up on sleep and went to my computer to write.

Detective Inspector Covington kept a firm hand on his captive, but Constance Tarkington had spent all of her energy and sat quietly in the chair.

When Thompkins returned, he brought a tea cart.

Lady Elizabeth smiled. "I think Bakerton might need something a little stronger than tea." She turned to Lady Alistair, who nodded. "In fact, I think we might all do with something a bit stronger."

Thompkins nodded. He left the room and returned with a bottle of brandy and several glasses. He poured a bit of the amber liquid into the glasses and turned to leave.

"I think you should stay, Thompkins." Lady Elizabeth sipped the liquid. "After all, if it weren't for your quick thinking, Constance Tarkington might have gotten away with this."

The butler bowed stiffly and stood silently in the corner.

"Nice catch, by the way." Lady Elizabeth smiled at Lady Clara. "Do you think you can open the box?"

Constance Tarkington looked up but said nothing.

Lady Clara turned the box around in her hands while she talked. "Well, I've been looking at this dragon on top and I think if you . . ." She put the box onto a table and pushed down on both of the eyes of the dragon and a panel opened. She looked inside, frowned, and continued to stare at the box. After a few seconds, she slid the dragon's tail and another panel flipped down.

Constance Tarkington gulped.

Lady Clara examined the opening. After a few seconds, she reached in and pulled out a folded sheet of paper. She passed the paper to Lady Elizabeth.

Lady Elizabeth unfolded the paper and read it. "Eleanor Forsythe's will." She perused the document. "Desmond Tarkington gets the house, but that's it. She left her favorite red lacquered Chinese puzzle box and a small legacy to her maid, Dora . . . Bakerton." She turned to the butler.

"Dora's my granddaughter," he said with a quiver in his voice. "I nearly passed out when she said she'd put her to sleep."

There was a timid knock on the door and a maid stuck her head inside. "Constable Redmond." She stepped back and the door opened to a constable, who looked around nervously. He spotted Detective Inspector Covington and walked over to him. He whispered something to the Scotland Yard detective.

Detective Inspector Covington smiled. "The maid is okay. The doctor said she'll be fine."

Bakerton put his face in his hands and wept.

The Scotland Yard detective handed Constance Tarkington over to the constable and announced, "I'm going into the village with Constable Redmond." He glanced around the room, but his gaze lingered longest on Lady Clara. Then, the two policemen left with their prisoner.

After a few minutes, Bakerton pulled himself together and stood. "I'm terribly sorry."

"No apologies necessary," Lady Alistair re-assured the butler. "Thompkins, perhaps you could —"

"Of course, your ladyship." Thompkins bowed and then assisted the older butler out of the room.

Lady Clara continued to examine the red lacquered box.

Lady Alistair sipped her brandy. "That was certainly astonishing." She turned to her friend. "What on earth put you on to her?"

Lady Elizabeth took a sip of her brandy and then placed her glass on a nearby table and picked up her knitting. "Several things, actually. First, I thought it was suspicious that Constance just happened to be in the subway at the same time when Eleanor Forsythe had a fatal fall. Mrs. Sanderson mentioned she'd called them, but it bothered me she had the fall after she'd talked to me. I also thought it odd Mrs. Forsythe mentioned she'd had an accident with the soap. She might have fallen, if it hadn't been for Dora. At the time, I didn't put together the fact that Desmond had been gone." She pursed her lips. "Maybe, if I'd been quicker . . ."

Lady Alistair reached across and squeezed her friend's hand. "You can't blame yourself."

Lady Elizabeth sighed and smiled weakly. "I know you're right, but . . ." She shuddered.

"Is that all?" Lady Clara asked while she continued to examine the lacquered box.

Lady Elizabeth knitted. "I remembered Eleanor Forsythe mentioned how much she loved puzzles and Chinese artifacts." She paused and thought for a few moments. "She kept saying how she loved puzzles when we were at tea. Then, when Thompkins mentioned how Constance Tarkington always seemed to be listening, well . . . I just felt it had to be her. Desmond seemed too timid to have killed his cousin." She glanced over at Lady Clara. "Clara, you seem absolutely intrigued by that box."

Lady Clara picked up the box and stared at it. "There's a very strange symbol on the corner that really seems out of place." She reached out a finger and pressed. "I just wonder if we've uncovered all of the box's secrets."

A very small drawer popped open and Lady Clara gave a small cry of surprise. Her eyes grew wide and she tilted the box and out came

335

several brightly colored stones. "My goodness."

Lady Elizabeth nodded. "If I'm not mistaken, that's the real treasure Eleanor Forsythe and her husband had. She couldn't leave the house to Dora because it was entailed to Desmond. However, if you recall what Dora said to Thompkins, Eleanor Forsythe and her husband loved China, but his family wanted him to be sensible." She smiled. "This was their way of rebelling. They took their money and put it into gems and hid them in that box, which she knew neither Desmond nor Constance would appreciate."

"Goodness gracious." Lady Clara held up one of the stones. "This appears to be jade."

Lady Alistair said, "Do you think Dora will get to keep them?"

Lady Elizabeth nodded. "I believe that's what Eleanor intended." She nodded. "I think Dora will be an excellent steward."

CHAPTER 21

As soon as the clock hit a decent hour, I called Detective Pitt. There was so much to go over, I asked if he would come to the store so I could fill him in. My second call was to Rosemary Lindley. I had two pressing questions. The first one was easy. Did she know if her father had a gym membership or if he had a locker anyplace?

Surprisingly, she didn't ask why I wanted to know. The idea of her father working out made her laugh, but eventually she sobered up and thought for a few minutes.

"When I was small, he used to like to box. If he went anywhere, it would have been the gym. There used to be one near the newspaper where he worked. It was a terrible neighborhood, but he loved it."

"Great." My second question was a little harder. I filled her in on the events that happened at her father's memorial. I asked if she would call and ask Caroline Fenton if she would be willing to try again, this afternoon, with a brief Mass. Even her silence sounded reluctant, but I'd had hours to work up a counter. "I know it's a holiday and last minute. However, I think it's important. In fact, I think it would be really awesome if you could come too."

"It's New Year's Day. Can't this wait until tomorrow?"

"Actually, there are several people who I know are planning to leave and won't be here tomorrow. I know it's a huge inconvenience, but I wouldn't ask if it wasn't important." I waited.

She was silent for so long I actually looked at my cell to make sure she hadn't hung up, but the call was still engaged. Eventually, she said, "Yes. I'll do it." She released a heavy sigh. "But you need to know something. I'm not doing it for him or for me. I'm doing it for Isabelle. I think she needs this. She needs to say goodbye."

I said a silent prayer of thanks and worked to keep the glee from my voice. "Great. Leave the details to me. I'll take care of it, but I need you to call Caroline Fenton to get permission. It'll hold more weight coming from you."

While I was on a roll, I called Frank. "Happy New Year. Can I borrow Benny for a few hours today?"

"Happy New Year to you." I could hear the laughter in his voice. "If I didn't know you better, I might be worried about that request."

"Don't be silly. I just need a priest to do a Mass at the last minute, and he's the only one I know."

"Should I ask why?"

"You probably don't want to know. Can you check and text me and let me know?"

We chatted for a few minutes about nothing, but my cheeks got warm and I remembered I needed to get showered before Detective Pitt arrived.

I hung up with Frank and showered, dressed, and grabbed a cup of coffee and some scones from the freezer and headed downstairs. The poodles trotted along beside me and, by the time Detective Pitt arrived, we were all set.

Frank sent a text message while I was walking downstairs that Benny agreed. So, I gave him the time I'd worked out with Rosemary Lindley for the Mass and told him I'd meet him there.

When I opened the door, Detective Pitt growled, "This better be good."

"Happy New Year."

He grunted and walked to the back of the store.

Since we were officially closed, I locked the door and followed him to the back.

"Coffee?"

He grunted again.

I took that grunt to mean yes and handed him a mug of coffee and a scone.

I waited for him to sit before I started.

"I think I know who killed Max Franck and Sarah Jane Howard, but I'm going to need your help to prove it."

He glared over the top of his coffee mug but said nothing.

He was definitely grumpy in the morning.

"What I'd like to do is have a big reveal, like in Hercule Poirot books, where you bring all of the suspects together and then the sleuth" — I pointed to him — "can reveal whodunit."

The glare he gave me earlier became a scowl. "Why don't you tell me whodunit and I'll go arrest them and we can skip this 'big reveal.' "

I was afraid he'd go there. "Because I don't really have any proof."

"What good is bringing people together and accusing someone with no proof?"

I took a deep breath. "Well, I'm hoping someone will remember something or say something to help. Or maybe the killer will say or do something to give themselves away."

He laughed. "Are you joking? This isn't television. Real killers don't crack under the pressure of hearing the evidence against them. Real killers laugh in the face of overwhelming mountains of evidence and deny to their dying day that they're guilty."

"If that's the case, then I doubt you'll ever be able to arrest the killer."

The scowl came back. "Who's the murderer?"

I hesitated. "Before I tell you that, I need to give you something." I reached in my pocket and handed over the locker key and the photograph.

"What's this?"

"Irma found them in her purse."

Like a pot that bubbled up on the stove, I could see the steam bubbling up inside. His face grew red. His eyes were huge, and his nostrils flared.

Before he blew a gasket, I held up a hand. "Look, we weren't withholding evidence in a murder investigation. She just found these items last night."

He huffed. "How is it possible she had these items in her purse for an entire week and just now noticed them?"

"Have you seen the inside of her purse? Nana Jo says it's where sick elephants go to die. Honestly, you're lucky she found them at all."

He took several deep breaths. "Okay," he said slowly. "What are they?"

I reminded Detective Pitt that Max Franck was a writer. "I suspect the photograph was research for his book."

He picked up the photo and stared at it for several seconds and then put it down and picked up the key. "And this?"

I shrugged. "I called Rosemary Lindley this morning and she said her dad used to have a locker at the gym near his newspaper." I gave him the address I'd googled after talking to Rosemary. "I don't know if he still has a locker there or if this key is even Max Franck's key." I stared at him. "However, I think someone" — I looked pointedly at Detective Pitt — "should go and check the locker."

"It's New Year's Day. Can't this wait until tomorrow? I have plans."

"We don't have time to wait. Caroline Fenton is leaving and so is Velma Levington. Sergeant Alvarez is trying to extradite Bob Marcus to Chicago, and Sidney Sherman could be in Timbuktu in a couple of days."

342

Detective Pitt stared at me and then ran his hand over his head and ruined his comb-over. "Fine." He took the key and put it in his pocket, finished his coffee, and shoved the last bits of scone into his mouth. Then he got up and walked out.

I called Nana Jo and gave her instructions and then hurried upstairs. I was antsy and nervous. I'd never tried anything like this before, and it could end up being a big mess. However, no matter how I played things in my mind, I couldn't think of any other way to prevent the killer from getting out of town without at least trying.

I let the poodles outside and gave them treats when they came in. I then grabbed my purse and left. I stopped at the grocery store and picked up the food I'd ordered for the MISU football tailgate party we'd planned for Nana Jo's. There was plenty of food, and I was able to buy extra chicken wings, dip, and chips. The food would have to do double duty — tailgate/memorial Mass.

Caroline Fenton was clearly not happy about the last-minute Mass for Max Franck and Sarah Jane Howard. However, rejecting the request of a bereaved daughter would have reflected very poorly not only on Caroline Fenton but Shady Acres. Regardless of her feelings about the man, Sarah Jane Howard was a resident of Shady Acres. She deserved to be remembered. Plus, I was providing the food and the drinks, and I was even providing my own priest. How could she say no.

Nana Jo and the girls were there, and they'd enlisted the help of several others to unload everything from my car.

Gaston stopped me and gave me a pouty look. "Storebought chicken wings? Samantha, you have wounded my soul. You know I can provide herb marinated chicken wings with a scallion goat cheese dip that would make your soul sing."

I laughed. "I know you're an excellent chef, but this was rather last minute."

He shook his head. "I forgive you this time, but next time, you call me."

I promised him I would.

The lounge was decorated in MISU colors, with streamers hanging from the ceiling, in preparation for the tailgate party, but we would have to ignore that.

Frank and Benny arrived shortly afterward. This time, Benny looked very clerical with his black shirt and white cleric collar. He had a beautiful embroidered stole, which he wore around his neck.

"Thank you so much for agreeing to do

this, especially last minute." I shook his hand.

Benny smiled, but the smile didn't reach his eyes. "Anything for Frank. I owe him so much."

I felt horrible using my relationship with Frank, but I didn't have much time to dwell on my feelings. People were starting to fill the lounge.

Rosemary Lindley arrived with Isabelle in a wheelchair. The fragile girl looked tired, but her eyes were bright.

"Thank you so much for coming." I looked at Isabelle. "Both of you."

She smiled. "It's a sad occasion, but I'm glad Mom let me come."

Rosemary wheeled her daughter into the lounge.

I glanced at my watch. Detective Pitt had yet to arrive, but I didn't think we could wait any longer.

Ten minutes after the appointed time, I gave Benny a nod to get things started and went into the lounge for the Mass.

I wasn't Catholic, so I hadn't attended very many Masses, but the ones I had attended always impressed me. I remember wondering how the congregation knew how to respond and when. "Peace be with you. And also with you," threw me for a loop the first time I attended Mass. The service was short, but Benny made it very meaningful.

"Are you sure this is going to work?" Nana Jo asked.

"No."

"Well, okay."

"How did you get Velma Levington to agree to stay?"

"I did what you suggested. I told her we might need her help with security. Since she was so skilled in aikido, I asked her to be part of the security team." She chuckled. "Don't worry. Dorothy and I will be nearby."

I nodded. I looked around and was relieved when Detective Pitt arrived with Bob Marcus in tow. That had been the trickiest part of the entire plan, but Detective Pitt came through.

Bob sat near the door. Detective Pitt walked up to me and handed me a large envelope.

Inside the envelope were articles and notes, receipts, and even napkins with information scribbled on them. There was an envelope addressed to Rosemary and a flash drive. I wished I'd had time to check the drive, but instead, I quickly flipped through the notes.

The stage was set.

When Benny finished the Mass, he asked if anyone had anything to say. That was Detective Pitt's cue. He walked to the front of the room and looked around at everyone.

"Hello . . . I'm . . . um . . . I'm . . . my . . . ah . . . name," he stammered and stumbled.

"Dear God, the man's afraid of public speaking," Nana Jo whispered.

The crowd's energy and interest began to waver and the impact of the detective's performance was lost.

"Do something," Nana Jo said.

I sighed. "Detective Pitt has been battling a bit of a cold, and I think he could use some water." I grabbed a bottle of water and walked to the front. I handed the bottle to the detective, who immediately feigned a coughing fit and stepped back to allow me to talk.

"I think Detective Pitt wanted to thank all of you for coming out to honor and remember Max Franck and Sarah Jane Howard." I looked up and saw that Velma Levington, Dorothy, and Nana Jo had moved closer to Bob.

I took a deep breath. "Many of us didn't know Max Franck long. In fact, many of you may not have known Max Franck had been an investigative reporter for many years. He won many prizes over the course of his long career."

Caroline Fenton snorted.

I ignored her outburst. "He was a published author. In fact, he was in the process of writing another book." I held up the envelope Detective Pitt gave me. "He had information that would send a murderer who has gone unpunished for decades to prison." I took a deep breath. "That's why he was killed, to prevent him from revealing the truth."

Detective Pitt stepped forward and whispered in my ear. "What are you doing? This wasn't part of the script. The murderer's going to think . . ."

I nodded. "Yes, exactly."

"But you're making yourself a target."

"It's the only way."

I stepped forward and announced loudly, "Sarah Jane Howard knew who murdered Max Franck, and that's why she was killed. Once the police get a chance to look through this evidence, they'll know what I do." I took a deep breath. "But, we're here to honor Max Franck and Sarah Jane Howard. So, please bow your heads for a moment of silence."

Everyone looked stunned, but they bowed their heads. I waited several seconds and then said, "Amen. Now, please help yourself to refreshments."

I walked toward the back of the room. Frank was beside me by the time I got to the lobby. "Just what do you think you're doing?"

I looked at him. "I need you to trust me."

He stared at me as though I'd lost my mind. "This isn't about trust. This is about your safety."

"I need you to trust me. Please?"

I could see the internal struggle, but, after a few seconds, he let go of my arm and allowed me to walk out alone.

I walked to the back of the building and stood near the door and waited. It didn't take long. I heard a crunch of a foot in the snow.

"You're one gutsy broad." Velma Levington slipped around the corner of the building. She had a large gun leveled at me.

Velma Levington laughed. "How did you know it was me?"

"It was something Sarah Jane Howard said. She noticed everyone and she mentioned that you stayed on the bus, supposedly asleep. She also said she was the first one back on the bus and you were already there. Several people said you were on the bus . . . asleep. No one saw you get off. I found it hard to believe you could have slept

349

through a man getting stabbed in the kidneys."

She frowned. "That's it?"

"Then you said Bob stabbed Max and
Sarah Jane, but the police hadn't released
the cause of death. There's no way you
could have known that, unless you were the
one who stabbed them. You were the only
one who said you saw Bob standing over
Max's body. You were the one who saw Bob
push Irma." I tried to regulate my breathing
so I didn't sound as nervous as I felt.
"Then, when Caroline Fenton fainted, you
said you had medical training from when
you were in the military." I took a deep
breath. "Is that where you learned how to
kill silently with a knife to the kidneys?"

She nodded. "I saw plenty of silent kills in
my time. After a while, you get desensitized
to it."

I saw a slight movement in the distance
but tried not to focus on it and focused on
keeping Velma talking. "How'd you get into
killing for money?"

She laughed. "When I left the military, I
was broke. I had no money. No job. Nothing. The war was supposed to make things
better, but it wasn't long before I realized
nothing had changed." She sneered. "Well,
nothing outside had changed, but I had. I

was different. I wasn't the same bright-eyed, naïve girl who had gone into the military. I'd seen too much." She shrugged. "Done too much. Then, I met a man who asked if I wanted to make a lot of money." She paused. "Give me the envelope."

I clutched it to my chest. "If I give you the envelope, you're going to shoot me."

She nodded. "You're right."

"Why don't I leave the envelope on the ground." I bent down. "I'll step away and you can take it and get away."

She shook her head. "I can't do that. I don't believe in loose ends. That's why I had to kill Sarah Jane. Sooner or later, I knew she would remember something that could lead the police to me. She was a loose end."

"And, Irma?" I whispered.

"She's a dingbat, but I couldn't take a chance that she'd have an epiphany and realize it wasn't Bob who pushed her." She shrugged. "She was another loose end. You'd be another one." She held out her hand. "Give me the envelope."

I shook my head. My throat was too dry to talk.

She leveled her gun. "Have it your way. I'll have to shoot you first and then take the envelope."

351

Nana Jo moved out from the shadows. She had a gun pointed at Velma Levington, and her eyes looked like black ice cubes.

"Josephine, I wouldn't if I were you. I've got this gun pointed straight at your grand-daughter. I'm just as good of a shot as you are and I suspect I've got less of a con-science about killing people than you."

"I wouldn't be so sure about that," Nana Jo growled. "I don't think I'd lose much sleep about taking you out."

Velma Levington laughed. "Maybe, but, either way, your granddaughter will be dead."

There was a noise from behind and, in the split second that Velma Levington's eyes moved to see what was behind her, Nana Jo fired.

Velma Levington's gun flew out of her hand.

Strong arms grabbed me and pushed me behind what felt like a solid wall but was actually, Father Benny.

Nana Jo spun around and drop-kicked Velma Levington and then Irma pounced on Velma's chest and started to pummel her with her fist.

Frank picked up Velma's gun and pointed it at her head.

It took both Ruby Mae and Dorothy to

pull Irma off of Velma, all the while, Frank kept the gun pointed at her head. His confident stance, the way he held the gun, and the steely look in his eyes told me this wasn't the first time he'd been in this position.

Eventually, Detective Pitt came around the corner. It wasn't until Velma was handcuffed and lying on the ground that I breathed.

"You okay?" Frank asked.

I nodded. The words wouldn't come.

He turned Velma's gun over to Detective Pitt and then walked over and grabbed me by the shoulders. "That was the craziest thing you have ever done and if you do anything like that again, I'll . . ." His voice shook. He pulled me to his chest and held me tightly. His body shook, and I felt guilty for the scare I'd given him.

My legs were jelly, so I was grateful for Frank's strength. He led me inside to the lounge.

Most of the residents weren't sure what had happened, but word spread quickly and the room was abuzz.

Detective Pitt took statements and arranged for his prisoner to be picked up.

Rosemary Lindley thanked me. "I still don't understand what happened. Why did she kill my father?"

"While researching his book about the assassination of Robert Kennedy, your father recognized Velma in a photo and discovered she was a contract killer."

She looked surprised. "But I thought that man . . . Sirhan killed Robert Kennedy."

I nodded. "There have been a lot of theories." I smiled. "I wasn't even aware of them until I read your father's book. He found a photo of a woman he recognized. After some digging, he believed the woman was a paid assassin responsible for killing some politicians in Chicago."

She folded her arms across her chest. "It just seems so cold."

"She was cold." I handed her an envelope.

"What's this?" She looked puzzled.

"Detective Pitt said it was okay for you to read this. It was in your father's locker."

Rosemary Lindley looked puzzled but opened the envelope and took out the paper. She started to read, and I saw a wave of emotions cross her face. Plus, surprise at seeing her father's words. That was followed by shock and disbelief. Then tears of joy flooded her eyes. She looked at me. "He was tested." She covered her mouth and cried silently. When she was able to talk, she said, "He found out, not only wasn't he a match for Isabelle, he wasn't my father."

I hadn't expected that and watched her closely to see if I could sort through all of her emotions. "Are you okay?"

She nodded. "Yes. I don't care about that." She took several breaths. "He got tested. I have had so much hatred in my heart when I thought he wouldn't even get tested when he knew it could save Isabelle." She glanced around at her daughter, who was chatting with Frank and Melvin. "That was so . . . cold. But now I know he did care. He got tested. I can accept that he wasn't my biological father. I couldn't accept that he wouldn't at least try." She cried, but there was joy and relief in her tears. She hugged me. "Thank you."

We both cried for several moments. Eventually, she pulled away and wiped her face with the sleeve of her coat. "I better get Isabelle home." She looked at her daughter, who appeared to be having a serious game of chess with Melvin, Irma's new friend.

We said our goodbyes.

"You ready to go home?" Frank whispered.

"I'm not going home. We have a tailgate party."

He stared at me as though he didn't recognize me. "You're joking. After everything you've been through?" He felt my forehead. "Maybe you're sick. You could be suffering from shock."

I shook my head. "I'm not suffering from shock. I'm fine." I struggled to find the right words. I looked around. Nana Jo and Freddie were arguing over the remote control. Irma had recovered from her hysterics earlier and was flirting with Melvin while he played chess. Ruby Mae had her knitting out and was sitting on the sofa, and Dorothy was engrossed in conversation with Benny. "These people have become my family, just as much as Jenna, Tony, the twins, and my mom. When Leon died, I thought my life was going to be so empty without him. He'd been such a big part of me, but now I've got you and all of them." I waved my arm around. "I've got Dawson and so many people in my life. I want to start this new year surrounded by the people I care about."

He pulled me close and I smiled at him. "There's only one thing that could make this day more special."

He raised an eyebrow. "What?"

"If the MISU Tigers win the Appliance Bowl."

He smiled. "Go, Tigers!"

ABOUT THE AUTHOR

V. M. Burns was born and raised in the Midwestern United States. She received a bachelor's degree from Northwestern University, a master's degree from the University of Notre Dame and a Master of Fine Arts degree from Seton Hill University. She is a member of Mystery Writers of America, Dog Writers Association of America, Thriller Writers International and a lifetime member of Sisters in Crime. She is the secretary of her local chapter of Sisters in Crime (The East Tennessee Smoking Guns) and the Education Grants Coordinator for the national Sisters in Crime. She currently resides in the warmer area of the U.S. with her two poodles. Readers can visit her website at http://www.vmburns.com

The employees of Thorndike Press hope you have enjoyed this Large Print book. All our Thorndike, Wheeler, and Kennebec Large Print titles are designed for easy reading, and all our books are made to last. Other Thorndike Press Large Print books are available at your library, through selected bookstores, or directly from us.

For information about titles, please call:
(800) 223-1244

or visit our website at:
gale.com/thorndike

To share your comments, please write:
Publisher
Thorndike Press
10 Water St., Suite 310
Waterville, ME 04901